Colonel Brandon's Diary

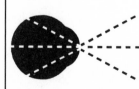

This Large Print Book carries the
Seal of Approval of N.A.V.H.

COLONEL BRANDON'S DIARY

AMANDA GRANGE

THORNDIKE PRESS

A part of Gale, Cengage Learning

Detroit • New York • San Francisco • New Haven, Conn • Waterville, Maine • London

GALE
CENGAGE Learning

Thorndike Press® Large Print Clean Reads.
The text of this Large Print edition is unabridged.
Other aspects of the book may vary from the original edition.
Set in 16 pt. Plantin.
Printed on permanent paper.

LIBRARY OF CONGRESS CATALOGING-IN-PUBLICATION DATA

Grange, Amanda.
  Colonel Brandon's diary / by Amanda Grange.
    p. cm. — (Thorndike Press large print clean reads)
  ISBN-13: 978-1-4104-2152-4 (alk. paper)
  ISBN-10: 1-4104-2152-X (alk. paper)
    1. Guardian and ward—Fiction. 2. England—Social life and customs—18th century—Fiction. 3. Diary fiction. 4. Large type books. I. Austen, Jane, 1775–1817. Sense and sensibility.
  II. Title.
  PR6107.R35C65 2009b
  823'.92—dc22   2009033449

Published in 2009 by arrangement with The Berkley Publishing Group, a member of Penguin Group (USA) Inc.

Printed in the United States of America
1 2 3 4 5 6 7 13 12 11 10 09

COLONEL BRANDON'S DIARY

1778

Tuesday 16 June

I thought the holidays would never arrive, but I am on my way home at last.

'Remember, you are to visit us in August!' said Leyton to me as he boarded the stage.

'I will not forget,' I promised him.

His coach pulled out of the yard and I went into the inn where I ate a second breakfast before it was time for my own coach to leave, and then I was soon on my way to Delaford. As the buildings of Oxford gave way to open countryside, I fell into desultory conversation with my fellow passengers, but it was too hot to talk for long and we were soon silent, watching the fields and rivers and hamlets pass by.

The light began to dwindle. Night fell, and the coach stopped at a respectable inn. I partook of the ordinary and now here I sit, in my chamber, looking forward to the summer.

I dozed through the first part of the journey, but as I neared home, I took more interest in my surroundings. My eyes travelled over the fields adjoining the estate and then I saw a welcome sight. It was Eliza, walking by the river with her straw hat dangling by its ribbons and her brocade skirt held up in her hand.

The coach slowed to turn a corner. I opened the door and, much to the consternation of my fellow passengers, I threw out my pack and then jumped after it, slithering down the grassy verge before reclaiming it at the bottom and calling to her. She turned round and, eyes alight, ran towards me. I caught her up and spun her round, thinking, I cannot remember a time when I did not love Eliza.

'Did you miss me?' I asked her, as at last I put her down, though I kept my arms around her, for I could not bear to let her go.

'And what am I to say to that?' she said with a smile. 'Am I to tell a lie, or am I to tell the truth and make you conceited?'

I laughed, and she slipped her arm round my waist, then we began to follow the river towards the house.

'How was Oxford?' she asked me.

'Much as ever. The lectures were dull and the fellows, save for a few, either dissolute or boring. But never mind, in a few more years I will have qualified for the law, and then we will buy a house somewhere, a snug little cottage —'

'Though you do not need a profession, because we will have my fortune to live on.'

'I will not touch a penny of your fortune,' I said seriously.

'Why not? It will make us comfortable, and more than comfortable. When I come into it, it will make us rich.'

'I want to support you.'

'Then what are we to do with it? It seems a pity to waste it, when it is there for the taking.'

'Save it for our children,' I said.

'Our children? Pray, do you not know it is indelicate to speak of such a thing to an unmarried woman?' she asked me saucily.

'Our children,' I said, unrepentant. 'Once we are married —'

'*If* we are married. You have not asked me yet.'

I dropped my pack and fell to one knee, taking her hand.

'Eliza, will you marry me?'

'When you have nothing to offer me, indeed when you are far too young to think of marriage, being a mere stripling of eighteen?' she teased.

'A stripling, am I?' I asked, rising to my feet.

'A stripling!' she said tauntingly, then she turned and ran. I gave chase and, easily catching her, I lifted her up and put her over my shoulder. She beat on my back with her fists, laughing all the while.

'Put me down!'

'Not until you say you are sorry!'

'For what? For speaking the truth?' she asked.

'For calling me a stripling.'

'Very well, I apologize.'

'That is better.'

I put her down again.

'It was very wrong of me. You are not a stripling, I see that now, you are a sapling,' she said.

'But a sapling you will marry?'

'If you do not know the answer to that already, my dearest James,' she said tenderly, 'you never will.'

She lifted her hand to my face and I kissed it, saying, 'Then as soon as we are of age we will be wed.'

'You will have to ask your father for his permission first,' she said, reluctantly pulling away from me. 'He is my guardian, and he must have his say. Only do not do it yet. I want to have some time to ourselves, with no one knowing; no fuss made; no calls to make and return; just the two of us, secure in our love.'

'Whatever you want, it is yours. You know I have never been able to deny you anything.'

We walked on for some time without speaking, rejoicing in the day, with nothing but the sound of the river and the song of the birds to break the silence. We came to the gate in the wall and entered the grounds, going in through the orchard, where the trees were beginning to swell with fruit. The house lay before us, and as I saw its solid façade I realized how much I loved it. I thought of all the happy years Eliza and I had spent there, and all the happy years to come.

We began to talk again, and I asked her what she had been doing whilst I had been at Oxford.

'What every other young lady does,' she replied. 'I have been practising my music and improving with my watercolours. I painted a very pretty view of the bridge last week, though the proportions were wrong and the colours false; however, it was very pretty. And I started a portrait of Miss

Jenkins.'

'And how is the estimable Miss Jenkins?'

'She is very well, though a little deaf.'

'And how did you manage to evade her this afternoon?'

'I told her I needed some exercise, and as she was sleepy after a heavy lunch, she was content for me to go out alone, as long as I did not stray beyond the grounds.'

'And what else have you been doing?'

'I have been netting a purse and singing and dancing —'

'Ah, yes, so you told me. I believe you said you had a new dancing master. I am very glad of it, for the last time I was at home I noticed that Monsieur Dupont was ruining your feet. I believe he stepped on your toes more often than not. This new man is very ugly, I believe you said, with a face like a gargoyle. Poor fellow.'

'Not a bit of it, he is very handsome; I will go further, and say that he is very handsome indeed. He has dark hair, clear eyes and good teeth. His chin is pronounced and his forehead is noble. Moreover, he has a finely turned calf, broad shoulders and overall the air of a gentleman. His address is good, and his manners pleasing. We are very lucky he condescends to be my master.'

We left the orchard behind us and entered the pleasure gardens, where the roses were in bloom. They filled the air with their perfume, and their dancing heads bobbed on their stalks as the breeze blew them this way and that.

'He does very well for an elderly man, then, for I believe you said he was in his dotage,' I remarked.

'On the contrary, he is very young, not a day over five and twenty,' she returned.

'Nonsense! Dancing masters are never five and twenty. They are always at least sixty. They would not be allowed in the house otherwise, especially if they were handsome — young ladies being prone to unsuitable fancies.'

'I do believe you are jealous!' she said, turning to me with a mischievous gleam in her eye.

'Of Mr Allison?' I snorted. 'I hardly think so.'

'There you are, you see, you even remember his name, a sure sign of jealousy!'

'It is nothing of the kind. It is just because you mentioned it so often in your letters.'

'I mentioned it once!' she contradicted me.

'And once was all I needed, for I have an excellent memory.'

'Your memory is abominable,' she returned.

'Nonsense. I never forget anything.'

'Then what colour is my new ball gown, which I mentioned to you in my letters?'

'It is . . . that is to say . . . I believe, yes, I am sure . . .'

'Well?' she asked.

'I do not immediately recall.'

'No? Not even with your good memory?' she asked satirically.

'Ah, I have it! It is blue,' I said, hazarding a guess.

'And what material is it?'

'Broc . . .' I saw that she was about to say *No* and changed my mind. 'Probably . . . that is to say, it was satin. Yes, I remember now. You distinctly said it was made out of satin.'

'Fie upon you, James. I told you at least three times, it is made of silk.'

I was undaunted.

'Whatever it is made of, I am sure you will look enchanting in it,' I said.

She laughed.

'Well recovered, sir! You should be a courtier, not a lawyer. It is a great skill to be able to turn a pretty compliment, especially when you have just been bested! You should see if they have any openings at St

James's!'

We had almost reached the lawns and she stopped, letting her skirt drop from her hand and settling her straw hat on her head.

'Here, let me help you,' I said, tying her ribbons for her.

'I had better go in through the French windows,' said Eliza, when I had done. 'I am meant to be practising the pianoforte. I promised your father I would heed my music master's instruction and practise for two hours every day, but I could not settle to my music this afternoon, knowing that you would be home.'

'So you came to the field on purpose to catch an early sight of me,' I said with a feeling of satisfaction.

She raised her eyebrows and said lightly, 'How vain men are! I merely thought some exercise would do me good and so I walked through the fields accordingly. The fact that you happened to arrive at that moment was the merest coincidence.'

And with that she left me.

I watched her walk away from me, admiring the line of her back, and I kept watching her until she was out of sight, and then I slung my pack over my shoulder and carried on my way.

I walked round the house, and as I passed

the stables, I saw my brother Harry coming out of them. He was looking dissolute, with his cravat pulled awry, and he was adjusting his breeches. My mood darkened.

'Some things never change,' I said, as I drew level with him. 'Who was it this time? The milkmaid, the scullery maid, or one of the farmers' daughters?'

He leered.

'Molly Dean, as it happens, one of the most beautiful girls hereabouts. You should take the trouble of getting to know her yourself. She'd soon put a spring in your step. A girl like Molly's just what you need on a morning like this one. A roll in the hay with her would wipe that sanctimonious look off your face. It would make a man of you.'

'I do not think I like your idea of being a man.'

'No? University has taught you nothing, then. A pity. I was hoping you would learn to hold your liquor and develop a taste for women, so that we could carouse together, as brothers should, but it seems that you have returned as dull as you went.'

We went into the house together, but we could not think of anything further to say to each other. We parted in the hall, he to go upstairs and I to go in to my father.

I found him in his study, looking through a pile of papers.

'So, you are back,' he said, glancing up once then continuing with his work.

'Yes, indeed, Father, as you see.'

'And what have you been doing since you went away?'

'I have been studying, sir.'

'Studying?' He threw his quill down on the desk, then looked up at me in astonishment; whether feigned or real I could not tell. 'Studying! You take my breath away. I had no idea you would do such a thing. It seems I have raised a scholar! Dear me.'

'Hardly that,' I said uncomfortably, for somehow he always manages to disconcert me.

'No?'

'No, sir, I have simply been trying to repay your kindness in sending me to Oxford by working hard for my degree.'

'A degree?' he asked, as though it were some kind of rare and exotic animal. 'So that is what you hope to gain, is it? It seems an unusual desire for a young man of your background. Pray, tell me, what do you intend to do with it when you have it? Do you mean to set yourself up as a clerk, perhaps? Or maybe you have higher aspirations?'

'I have indeed, sir,' I said, trying hard not to squirm.

'I am glad to hear it. And to what do you aspire? To become a schoolmaster, perhaps, or do you hope to reach the exalted ranks of a tutor?' he asked satirically.

'No, indeed . . .'

'No? Surely you do not have an even higher calling in mind, for what could be a higher calling than looking after another man's brats; brats who will treat you with insolence, at best, and more probably openly revile you?'

'I hope to go into the law.'

'Ah. The law,' he said, leaning back in his chair and steepling his fingers. 'The law,' he repeated, savouring the words as though they were a glass of wine; though what his pronouncement would be on the vintage, I could not guess. 'I congratulate you,' he went on, with a smile that lacked any humour. 'If you work hard, then at the end of ten years you might have enough money to buy yourself a horse.'

'The law has greater rewards than that —' I said, stung to reply.

'But not for an honest man,' he interrupted me, 'and you have always struck me as honest, James. Unless you mean to surprise me?'

'No, sir.'

'I should not have sent you to university this year, it was too soon, but I allowed myself to be swayed by your tutors, who assured me that you had learnt everything they could teach you, and that you were intelligent and likely to thrive. But you were not mature enough. And now you have set your feet on the wrong path and you stand in need of some advice. Abandon all these notions of hard work and degrees and do what I intended you to do when I sent you to Oxford in the first place. Make some friends —'

'I have friends, sir.'

He raised his eyebrows.

'Really? You pick a strange time to mention them. Nevertheless, I am very pleased to hear it. Friends are the basis of life. They can be very useful if treated properly, so tell me about these friends of yours, James, and tell me of what use they can be to you?'

As so often, when talking to my father, I felt as though we were speaking different languages, which shared the same words but not the same meanings.

'I do not understand you, sir.'

He sat forward in his chair and rested his elbows on his desk.

'Dear me. I must have been very remiss in

19

my duties towards you if you do not know what I mean by useful. What connections do they have? What help can they give you? And how many sisters do they have?'

'I never took any account of those things . . .'

'You astonish me. How is it that a young man such as yourself, not deficient in intelligence, an avid student — so he tells me — with no defects of person or manners can fail to take account of such things? Tell me, how do you mean to live once you are out in the world?'

'By going into the law, sir, as I have already told you.'

'And as I have already told you, a man cannot live on what the law provides. Therefore, my advice to you, James, is to return to Oxford in a better frame of mind than the one in which you left. Think of your friends in the light of the help their families can provide. They might have livings at their disposal, or better yet, they might have impressionable daughters with generous dowries who would welcome the attentions of a handsome young man such as yourself. Cultivate those who can be useful to you and disregard the rest.'

'I do not think —'

'No, my boy, I'm well aware of that!' he

said with a dry laugh.

'What I mean is, I prefer my friendships to be with my friends.'

'Ah. I have not just raised a scholar, I have raised an idealist, it seems. Well, my boy, I wish you well of it,' he said, taking up his quill. 'I hope you will be very happy. You will invite me to your lodgings one day ten years hence, I hope, so that I might see the splendours you have won with your labours.'

He said no more, but turned his attention to his books, and after waiting a minute or two to see if he would speak again, I left the room.

I wriggled my shoulders, as if to shake off something unpleasant, a habit acquired through long years of conversations with my father, and then I found myself wondering what he would have said if I had told him of my plan to marry Eliza. Would he have congratulated me on becoming affianced to an heiress? No, probably not. He would have berated me for not finding another one. Nothing would please him more than to marry Eliza to an earl and gain a string of great relations, and I believe he would have laughed at me if I had told him of my intentions.

I returned to my room and found that my

trunk had already arrived. Dawkins had unpacked it and my evening clothes were laid out on my bed.

I had time to write a few letters before changing for dinner and then I went downstairs. Eliza was in the drawing room, her hair bound up with a ribbon that matched the blue of her eyes. Harry was already drunk. As we walked into the dining room, his gait was unsteady. My father merely smiled, as though Harry afforded him great amusement, and I guessed that this was not an unusual state of affairs.

'I will be giving a ball in three weeks' time,' said my father to me as we began our meal. 'It is a long time since we have had such a gathering at Delaford and it is time we entertained our neighbours. They need an opportunity to criticize our house, find fault with our arrangements, disparage the efficacy of our servants and revile our taste. Your studies will allow you time to attend, I hope?'

'Yes, Father. As you know, I am on holiday now.'

'Very true. But an industrious young man such as yourself might wish to work on high days and holidays. Indeed, if you are to advise the neighbouring farmers on their contracts, you must work hard now to make sure that you do not lead them astray in the future.'

Eliza glanced at me and we both hid our laughter behind our napkins, whilst Harry laughed outright.

'What! You mean to become a lawyer!' he said, reaching for the bottle and pouring himself another drink. 'My brother, the attorney!'

'It is a noble calling,' replied my father gravely. 'If your brother applies himself, then he might one day own a gold watch.' He turned to Eliza. 'I hope you are looking forward to the ball, my dear. Now that you are seventeen it is time you went into company. You have your new gown, I know, and a very pretty gown it is, I am sure, but is there anything else you require? You have only to ask and it will be yours.'

'A fan, perhaps,' said Eliza, 'and some new slippers.'

'Then you must go into town and buy anything you wish. You will be opening the dancing with Harry, so you must look your best.'

Eliza looked at Harry and then sighed as he spilt wine down his coat, but he only laughed and poured himself another glass.

I was glad when the meal came to an end. When Eliza withdrew, my father and Harry were silent, and I waited only five minutes before following Eliza. She was singing with great sweetness when I entered the drawing room, and as I sat and listened to her, I thought I would endure a dozen such evenings for the pleasure of hearing her voice.

My father and Harry did not follow for some time, but when they returned, they robbed our time together of its sweetness. Eliza finished her song and then retired. I soon followed. If not for Eliza, I would be off again tomorrow, but her presence keeps me here.

Friday 26 June

I rose with the dawn, awakened by the birds, which sang lustily outside my window. I was soon dressed and went down to the stables, where I lost no time in saddling Ulysses and setting off across the fields. There was an early mist which hugged the ground, turning the green fields white, but it soon burnt off to reveal a glorious day. The sky was a brilliant blue and skylarks soared, and I felt my heart expand with the joy of being at home again. I rode down to the village and then I walked back along the country lanes with the trees making a canopy above me.

I returned to the stable yard with a hearty appetite, and having given Ulysses into the charge of my groom, I went inside. There was no sign of Harry but my father was there, eating his breakfast. He looked up once as I entered the room, but after a few remarks on the poverty of lawyers, he returned to his steak. Soon afterwards he finished his meal and, without another word to me, left the room. I helped myself to ham and eggs from the food laid out on the sideboard and made a hearty meal.

Sitting back at last, I looked out of the window, over the lawns and down to the lake. It was a perfect morning for rowing, and I decided to see if the boat was in good order or if it had been allowed to decay.

I went down to the boathouse and I was pleased to find that the boat was sound. Once I had taken it out and tied it up by the jetty, I returned to the house to ask Eliza if she would care to spend the morning on the water.

As I approached, I heard music coming from the ballroom. When I passed the window, I saw Eliza practising her steps with an elderly gentleman whose hair was white and whose shoulders were bowed. I laughed, and she turned and saw me. I clutched my hand to my chest in a charade of a broken heart, and she had the goodness to laugh, too. I heard her dancing master asking her what she found so amusing, and she was chastened until the lesson came to an end.

I waited for him to leave and then I joined her in the ballroom.

'What are you doing here?' she asked me. 'I thought you were out riding.'

I pulled a tragic face.

'I have come to release you from our engagement. I see now that I was wrong to ask for your hand. Your dancing master is so handsome that I cannot keep you from him. I wish you happy, my dear.'

She looked at me saucily, and stopping only to fetch her bonnet, gloves and parasol, she took my arm and walked out into the garden with me.

'Were you a little bit jealous?' she asked me.

'My dear Eliza, I was so jealous that, if he had been as handsome as you declared, I would have asked my father to dismiss him at once.'

'Good. I am glad you were jealous.'

'And I am jealous of Harry for being able to open the ball with you.'

She frowned.

'I would rather open it with you. But I am only to dance the first two dances with him and then my card is empty.'

'Then you must dance the next two with me.'

She sighed happily.

'Is this not perfect, James?' she asked, looking round her. 'The sun up above and the scent of the roses perfuming the air? How I love the summer. I believe I could never bear to leave here, with everything so dear to me, if it were not for you. We must have a rose garden when we are married.'

'We will have one, even if I have to make it for you myself,' I promised her. 'And we will have everything else your heart desires. My father may laugh, but I am young and ambitious, and I have a reason for succeeding. We will be happy and prosperous, Eliza.'

'I do not doubt it.'

We walked down to the water's edge and I helped her into the boat. She steadied herself as it rocked from side to side and then, having gained her balance, she sat down, arranged her skirt and opened her parasol, which framed her face as beautifully as a picture.

I climbed into the boat, untied it and picked up the oars. Having settled them into the rowlocks I pulled on the right oar and sent the boat out onto the lake. The water lilies were in bloom, their leaves as large as saucers and their white flowers opening like stars to reveal the gold at their heart, whilst around them the water reflected the bright blue sky.

Eliza removed her glove and let her hand trail in the water. I watched the quicksilver liquid flow over her slender white fingers, mesmerized.

'How perfect this is,' she said. 'To be here, with you.' She murmured softly, *'Rejoice, waters of the Lydian lake, and laugh out loud all the laughter you have at your command. Your master is home.'*

She smiled at me, and I was so much in danger of drowning in her smile that I reprimanded her, and said, 'Your Catullus is faulty,' hoping to break the mood, but it was no good; the mood was not to be broken.

'My Catullus might be faulty, but not my heart,' she said softly.

I could fight it no longer. The splashing of the water against the oars, the soft kiss of the breeze, and the sight of Eliza there before me, drew me into the moment and held me there as though silken tendrils had wrapped themselves around my heart.

'If I could write the beauty of your eyes,

And in fresh numbers number all your
   graces,
The age to come would say, "This poet
   lies;
Such heavenly touches ne'er touch'd
   earthly faces." '

As I spoke, I felt that Shakespeare must
have written those lines for Eliza.

She lay back, allowing the sun to slip
beneath her parasol and drift across her
face, painting her skin with golden rays, and
I marvelled at her beauty, and the wonder
of her loving me.

'If I could trap a moment in time, then I
would trap this moment and hold it for all
eternity, with the sun on my skin and the
water cool on my hand and the skylarks
singing and you here with me,' she said.
'When I am old and grey I will come back
here in my memory and we will be young
again, in the first throes of love.'

'When you are old and grey I will bring
you back here and we will row on the lake,
just as we are doing today,' I said.

We fell silent, needing no words, and we
did not go in until the clouds began to
thicken, and the first fat drops of rain began
to fall.

I tied up the boat and gave Eliza my hand,

and we ran back to the house, reaching it as the rain began in earnest.

'I have a fitting with my dressmaker this afternoon,' she said.

'Then I will not see you until dinner time.'

'No.'

We could not bring ourselves to part and we lingered there a while, but when the clock on the stable chimed, we knew we had to go our separate ways so that we could meet again this evening.

I passed the afternoon on horseback, riding hard, and then went in to change for dinner, arriving early in the drawing room in my impatience to see her again.

She came in at last, in a yellow dress that set off her hair.

'Was your fitting successful?' I asked her, going forward.

'Yes. I need make only one more visit to the dressmakers and my dress will be ready.'

'Good, good,' said my father, who had entered the room in time to hear her. 'You need something special to wear, for the ball will be one to remember. James, you must wear something special, too. In the light of your future plans, perhaps you will honour us by appearing in a periwig.'

'I am glad I thought of going into the law, since it has afforded you so much amusement,' I said, having grown used to his ways again.

'My dear boy, pray do not do it on my account. Your brother affords me quite as much amusement as a man has a right to expect from his children,' he said, glancing at Harry, who looked the epitome of a dissolute rake. 'Indeed, I have been very fortunate in that respect.'

Harry ignored him, but poured himself another drink and carried it through to the dining room.

When we were all seated and the soup had been served, I said, 'I am glad you are holding a ball, sir.' For he spends too much time alone, and I am sure that that is the cause of his strange humours.

'At this present time I must make the effort, indeed I must,' said my father, tasting the soup and adopting a resigned expression, for, in truth, it was insipid. 'It is not every day that my son and heir contracts an eligible alliance.'

I almost dropped my spoon in my astonishment.

'An eligible alliance?' I asked, looking at Harry and then back to my father.

'Yes, your brother is engaged,' remarked my father calmly, between mouthfuls of soup.

'But I have heard nothing of this!' I said.

'And will not hear anything of it, officially, until the ball,' said my father. 'That is when it is to be announced. The ball will add an element of grandeur to the announcement, and will lend it due weight and importance. Ladies like such things.'

Eliza and I exchanged startled glances, for to hear of my brother's engagement in such a manner seemed strange indeed.

'And who is the lucky lady?' asked Eliza.

Harry lifted his glass to her and smirked. 'You.'

'Me?' she asked in bewilderment, then laughed.

'I am glad to see it affords you so much joy,' said my father, dabbing his lips fastidiously as he finished his soup.

'But who is she really?' asked Eliza. 'Is she anyone we know?'

'My dear, I know that Harry is not always the most honest young man in the world, but on this occasion he speaks nothing but the truth. His bride is, indeed, to be you.'

'But . . . this is a joke!' said Eliza, but she did not sound sure.

I was not sure, either, and now the glances we exchanged were perturbed.

'A joke! How you young people express your good humour these days! In my young day, we would have said, *This is delightful.* But times move on and language, just like fashion, is always changing. Yes, my dear, it is *a joke.'*

'You are teasing me, sir,' she said, looking at me anxiously and then looking back at my father.

'Is this another of youth's sayings?' he asked. 'I am sadly behind the times, I fear, and I do not always understand them.'

'Pray, do not jest with me, sir,' she said. 'Put me out of my misery and tell me it is not true.'

'Your misery? My dear Eliza, not a moment ago you were in raptures about it,' he said incredulously; but, as so often happens with my father, I did not know if his manner was real or feigned.

'I assure you, sir, I was not,' said Eliza. 'I thought you were teasing me.'

'For what purpose?' he enquired curiously.

'I do not know.'

'Nor do I. I cannot see how claiming you are to marry my son and heir can be construed as teasing, but since you seem to be in some doubt then I will say it plainly. As your guardian, I have found you a suitable husband. The engagement will be announced at the ball and the marriage will take place at the end of the summer.'

33

'No!' said Eliza, rising in her seat and throwing her napkin down on the table.

'No?' asked my father in surprise.

'No, sir, I am sorry, but I cannot marry Harry.'

'Well, well, that sounds very definite.'

'I do not love him.'

'And what, pray, does that have to do with anything?'

'It has everything to do with it,' she cried passionately.

'Marriages are contracted for the good of the parties involved, not for some romantic notions. You are of a marriageable age and it is my duty as your guardian to find you a husband. Your fortune entitles you to an eldest son, one from an old and respectable family with a fine estate, who can provide you with comfort, ease and security, and that is what you will have.'

'It is not enough for me. I will not marry without love!' she declared vehemently.

'Dear me, you have been reading too much poetry. You have confused it with reality. There is no such thing as love.'

'That is where you are wrong, sir. There is; I have found it. I am in love with James.'

'James?' asked my father, surprised. 'The future attorney? My dear, it is you who surely jest. What kind of life can he give you, a mere boy of eighteen with no influential friends or relations to help him, and no prospects? Unless he marries an heiress he will have next to nothing, and if he marries a young lady with thirty thousand pounds then he can hardly be expected to marry you as well.'

'*I* am an heiress,' she said defiantly.

'Ah, I see,' he said, turning to me. He raised his glass. 'I must congratulate you, James. It seems I have underestimated you. I believed all your nonsense about studying hard and gaining a degree, but I see now that your interest in the law was nothing but a screen. You have not been cultivating useful friendships at university, for you needed none. You have been courting an heiress closer to home.'

'I do not want Eliza's fortune,' I declared, having had enough of his humours and, being so nearly touched, becoming angry. 'Indeed, I will not touch a penny of it.'

'I should hope not, for it will belong to your brother, and although he is an idle fellow in many respects, I imagine he would make a fuss if you tried to steal his money.'

'You cannot marry Eliza to Harry, sir. Look at him!' I said, for Harry was slumped across the table. 'Let me marry Eliza. Give me your permission, give us your blessing, and you will not regret it, I promise you.'

'There can be no question of it. I would be remiss in my duties if I allowed my ward to marry a younger son.'

'But a younger son who loves her!'

'Love again! And this time from a young man, who ought to know better, instead of a naïve young girl. It must be education that has done this to you. Indeed, education appears to have ruined both my sons; it is the curse of literature. My eldest son seems to think he is Tom Jones, for he is busy seducing every wench in the countryside, whilst my youngest thinks he is Romeo! Worse still,' he said, turning to Eliza, 'he has convinced you that you are Juliet, my dear.'

'It is nothing of the sort,' I said. 'We are not children who do not know the ways of the world. We are quite old enough to understand the realities of life, sir, I do assure you. But we have known for some time that we are in love with each other, and we planned to marry anyway.'

'Do you not think, if your intentions towards Eliza had been honourable, you should have asked her guardian's permission to pay your addresses to her?' he asked.

'I . . .' I drew myself up. 'You are right, sir. I should have done so. I ask you now.

May I have your permission to address your ward?'

'Certainly not. You are far too young, and you have nothing to offer her. Furthermore, she is already engaged.'

'To a man she does not love. You are abusing your position. You are marrying her to Harry for her money.'

'It is good of you to give me the benefit of your experience and to advise me on my responsibilities as a guardian, but you must allow me to do as I think fit instead of following the guidance of an eighteen-year-old boy.'

'Harry can have my money,' said Eliza. 'I do not want it. I will marry James without it.'

'My dear, I cannot allow it. It seems sensible to you now, at seventeen, but you would never forgive me at twenty-seven, and rightly so. You will gain stability and security from your marriage, as well as standing in the neighbourhood, and your future will be assured. Harry, in return, will gain the means to pay off the family debts and restore the estate. It is an estimable match in every way.'

'I cannot stand by and —' I began, but he cut me off.

'What have they been teaching you at

Oxford? Sedition and revolt, it would seem, when they should have been teaching you to respect your elders. However, amusing as this conversation might be, I regret I must now put an end to it. Eliza, you will wed Harry, and, James, you will find your own heiress to marry.'

He pushed his chair back from the table.

'And if I do not want to be Harry's wife?' asked Eliza defiantly.

He stood up.

'We none of us have what we want in this world. If we did, I would have dutiful children who would do as I bid them with a smile; instead of which I have a drunkard for an heir, a fool for a younger son and a disobedient girl for a ward. But we all have our disappointments in life, and I see no reason why you should not have yours as well as anyone else.'

He would discuss it no more in the dining room, and once we retired to the drawing room, he took up his newspaper so that we could not discuss it then, either.

Harry snored in a corner. Eliza played the piano listlessly and soon, declaring she was tired, retired for the night.

'I will not marry him,' she said to me in an undertone as she passed me on her way out of the room.

'Never fear, it will not come to that,' I said.

And it will not. I will not let her marry my brother.

Saturday 27 June

I slept badly, and when I found Eliza walking in the garden at dawn, I knew that she had slept badly, too.

'James!' she said, turning towards me with an anguished face. 'What are we to do? I cannot believe that twenty-four hours can make so much difference. Yesterday we were so happy — and now . . .'

'Never fear,' I said, taking her hands consolingly. 'I will speak to my father again. Now that he has had time to think about it, he must see that it is impossible and he will relent.'

She sighed from the bottom of her heart.

'That is a vain hope, you know it as well as I do. He has already decided, and nothing you or I can say will change his mind. Even if he relents as far as your brother is concerned, he will never allow me to marry you.'

'Courage!' I said, taking her arm and walking on with her. 'We will be together, no matter what, Eliza. That I promise you.'

'But how can you promise it? If he refuses to see reason, then we are lost.'

'No. If all else fails, then we will elope.'

'Elope?' She turned to me with hope in her eyes. 'Oh, yes, James, that is what we must do. We can go to Scotland and be married there.'

'But first I must speak to my father again,' I said. 'I must give him a chance to change his mind. An elopement must be our last resort, for it will ruin your reputation —'

'What do I care for my reputation if I can be with you?'

'And we will have very little to live on. I have some money from my mother which should enable us to manage —'

'Until I come into my inheritance.'

'Until I find some employment. I have told you before —'

'The situation is different now. You must see that! Without the support of your family, we will need more money, and I have money. We must use it, James.' She set her chin stubbornly. 'I will not marry you otherwise.'

'We will talk about this later.'

'No,' she said, determined. 'We will talk about it now.'

'Very well,' I conceded. 'We will use your fortune *if we need it.*'

'And that is as much as I can hope for, I suppose, though it seems nonsensical to do without it when our lives would be so much more comfortable with it.'

'You forget, it will not be yours for some years yet. Even if I agree to use it, we will have to manage on our own for some time. We will have to live simply, and we will not have money for the elegancies of life, but we will be together.'

'As long as your father gives in. Go and speak to him now, James, do not delay. See if you can persuade him. Let us know our fate.'

'There is no point in speaking to him before he has had his breakfast, for he will not listen to me favourably on an empty stomach. But once he has eaten, I hope to find him in a mellower frame of mind, and then, perhaps, he will see that we are determined not to be parted.'

We continued on our way, making plans for the future, until at last I felt it was late enough to speak to my father. I went indoors and found him in his study. He looked up when I entered but then looked down again and carried on with his letter.

'I hope you have not come to speak to me again about your brother's engagement.'

'No. I have come to speak to you about Eliza's engagement.'

'They are one and the same.'

'You cannot mean to force her into a marriage that is distasteful to her,' I said. 'She deserves more from you than that.'

'She will soon accustom herself to it, as will you, no matter how much you both think otherwise at the moment. Young people always think it is the end of the world if they cannot choose their own spouse, but they quickly realize that the elegancies and comforts of life are worth more than so-called love, for elegancies and comforts are solid and longer lasting. If the young couple are fortunate, and have sensible elders to protect them, they realize this fact before they rush into a precipitate marriage. If they are unlucky, they realize it afterwards, when they are left with nothing but penury and bitterness to comfort them for their folly.'

I remonstrated with him, but he would not listen, and at last I had to retreat, defeated.

Eliza saw by my face that my news was not good, and when I had told her what he said, she replied, 'Then we have to elope.'

I did not like it, but I could not see any way of avoiding it.

'You are right, my love, there is no alternative.'

'We can leave tonight.'

'Yes, tonight. Have your maid pack your

things whilst we are at dinner. We will leave at midnight, when my father and Harry have retired. I will have a carriage meet us at the end of the lane, so that the horses do not disturb the household, and then we will be away.'

She took my hands and I felt them tremble.

'Frightened?' I asked her.

'No. Excited at the thought of our new life together. Where will we go once we are married, do you think?'

'We will go to Oxford. We can take lodgings and set up house there. You will like Oxford, it is an interesting place, and there are some remarkable people. Besides, I have a friend whose father is a lawyer there and I think he might find a place for me.'

She took my arm and squeezed it as we walked towards the stables.

'I am looking forward to it already!' she said. 'This has been a good thing, after all, James, for it has brought all the waiting to an end. Now we can be together, as we were meant to be.'

We continued to talk of our future until we reached the stables, then she left me and I went into town to make the necessary arrangements.

Once my business was done, I returned

home and told my valet to pack my things as I was going away. I wrote a letter to my father and put it in my pocket, ready to place on his desk just before midnight.

I dressed for dinner and was about to go downstairs when the door opened, and to my surprise, my father entered the room. His presence there was so unusual that my heart misgave me, and as soon as he began to speak, I knew that we were undone.

'I have some advice for you, James,' he said, in his dry manner. 'Always believe the worst of people, my boy, and then they will never disappoint you. I have thought the best of people, and I have been sadly deceived, for I have discovered that my ward has been planning to elope to Scotland behind my back, and that my son has been her partner in this treachery; and this, when he has plans to become a lawyer.'

'I can assure you, sir —'

'You can assure me of nothing, my boy, so pray do not add falsehood to your many faults. Eliza's maid is loyal to me, or, at least, loyal to the reward she hopes I will give her, and she has told me everything I need to know. You will go to your great-aunt Isabella, and you will not be welcome in this house until your brother is safely married to Eliza.'

I drew myself up.

'Then, sir, I shall never be welcome here again, for Eliza will never marry my brother.'

'Dear me, how vainglorious young people are! I hesitate to shatter your illusions, but Eliza's future has nothing to do with you. She will see reason and she will do her duty, like every other young girl before her.'

'She does not love him, and you cannot force her to marry him,' I said coldly. 'Would it not be better to accept that she is in love with me and allow our marriage?'

'We have already spoken of this at length and we will speak of it no more. You will leave for your aunt's house at once. The carriage is at the door.'

'I am sorry to disappoint you, sir, but I will not go without Eliza.'

He grew irascible.

'That sounds very definite, but I assure you, you are mistaken, for if you refuse to leave, then the footmen will escort you to the coach.'

I looked beyond him and saw that two of the footmen were standing in the passage behind him. I could tell that they did not like it, for their faces were grim, but I knew that they would do their duty or lose their positions, so to spare them, and myself, the indignity of a forcible ejection, I said, 'You have me at a disadvantage, I see. Very well. I will do as you say.'

I knew there was no more I could do for the moment, so I picked up my portmanteau and he stood aside to allow me to leave the room. I went along the corridor, followed by my father and the footmen, but as I did so, I was already planning to return for Eliza. I would do it when my father was away from home, making his annual visit to London to attend to business matters. I was only sorry that I would not have a chance to speak to her before I left and tell her of my new plan.

As I reached the top of the stairs, however, I heard the sound of footsteps and I saw Eliza running towards me from her chamber in the east wing. Harry, unusually alert, was following her, and he caught up with her at the top of the stairs, putting his arms round her to restrain her. He grinned at me as he did it, and I lunged towards him, ready to knock him down. But the two footmen closed in behind me and held my arms.

'I will never marry him!' cried Eliza, struggling to free herself. 'Never. They cannot make me. Nothing will ever make me abandon you. I love you, James. Only you.'

'We will be together, I promise you,' I said. She became calm and my brother let her go. My last sight of her was of her standing upright, with a defiant gleam in her eye, at the top of the stairs.

I went out to the carriage.

Instead of setting out for Gretna Green, as I had hoped, I found myself setting out for my great-aunt's house. But I knew that all was not lost. It was a delay, and not a disaster.

Tuesday 30 June

The journey was long and uncomfortable, for my father had ordered the old coach, and it rumbled along at a funereal pace, stopping only to change the horses on its way to Langley Castle. I fell asleep at last, rocked by the motion, and arrived with aches and pains in my neck and legs but otherwise refreshed.

The house was as grim as I remembered it. Grey turrets were outlined against the gloomy sky, and I felt my spirits drop as I went inside.

There was an air of decay in the hall, with its suits of armour and weapons from bygone eras displayed as though they were treasures. They had not been cleaned for a very long time. The metal was dull. The portraits of dour ancestors frowned down on me, as if condemning me for being young and in love.

Horsby, looking even more ancient than the last time I saw him ten years ago, walked unsteadily in front of me with a disapproving air and showed me into the drawing room.

It was as cheerless as the hall, with its heavy, old-fashioned furniture and its tapestries on the walls. But there was one unexpected gleam of colour, for a young woman was sitting on a faded sofa, and as she rose in a rustle of silk, I saw that she was my sister.

'Catherine, what are you doing here?' I asked her.

She looked at me as though I were a disobedient seven-year-old.

'George and I are visiting Aunt Isabella. I do not need to ask what you are doing here. A letter arrived from my father several hours ago, delivered by messenger; and if you needed any proof of how angry he is, you have it in the fact that he went to the expense of using a messenger instead of relying on the post. Really, James, I cannot think how you came to be so foolish! Attempting to elope with Eliza. What nonsense!'

'I happen to love her,' I said, with dignity.

'That would be ridiculous enough coming

from a schoolgirl, but coming from a man it is unforgivable. I am not surprised that our father sent you away. Fortunately, I know just the young woman to make you forget about Eliza. Her name is Miss Heath. She is utterly charming. Her hair and eyes are just like Eliza's. In fact, she is so like her that you will scarcely notice the difference.'

'I believe that I can tell the difference between the woman I love and a complete stranger,' I remarked.

She stared at me.

'Really, James, you are always so odd, I do not know what to make of you. I am offering you an unexceptionable young woman for a wife and do you thank me? No. You simply continue to talk of Eliza. You must put her out of your mind. She is not for you. Miss Heath, however, is an amiable and rich young woman, and would welcome an offer from you, as long as you can keep your oddities hidden for a week or two.'

'If Miss Heath is amiable and rich, I can hardly believe she will welcome a proposal from a younger son.'

I sat down gloomily, thinking that I would rather have endured one of Great-Aunt Isabella's lectures than my sister's misguided attempts to find me a wife.

She hesitated.

'There is that about her ancestry . . . to be sure, it is very little . . . but her father made his money in trade. There, now you have it! So you see, she cannot attach a man from one of the best families. But you need not fear that her family will embarrass you, for her father had the good sense to die last year, thereby increasing his daughter's chances of making a respectable match; and although his wife is still with us, you will not have to see her above once or twice a year.'

'You are too kind.'

She stared.

'There you go again with your incomprehensible remarks,' she said. 'You were dropped on your head, so your nurse said, when you were an infant, and that must account for it, I suppose. But make an effort, James. Miss Heath is worth pursuing, and if you make up your mind to it, she could be your wife by the end of the summer. And now,' she went on, looking at me from head to foot, 'you had better make yourself presentable, for Aunt Isabella will be wanting to see you before the hour is out.'

Horsby showed me to my room, and I washed and put on fresh linen before going downstairs again to wait upon Aunt Isabella.

She was by this time sitting in the drawing room, with Aunt Phoebe on one side of her and Aunt Cicely on the other. She raised her lorgnette and looked at me disapprovingly.

'Well, young man, and what have you to say for yourself?' she asked me.

'How do you do, Aunt,' I replied.

'Do not *how do you do, Aunt* me,' she returned. 'You are a fool, it seems, like the rest of your sex.' She consulted the letter in her lap. 'You tried to run off with Eliza, your father tells me.' She looked back at me. 'I have no sympathy for him. If he had remained single, as I advised him to do all those years ago, instead of marrying your mother, he would not be in this predicament now. I told him how it would be. I told him she would run through his fortune before the year was out, and so it was. You, at least, had the sense to fall in love with a fortune. Did you speak?'

'No, Aunt.'

'And a good thing, too, for you can have nothing sensible to say. And so, your father sends you to me. And what am I to do with you, pray?'

'Nothing, Aunt. I am ready to leave at once.'

'So you can make mischief? I am seventy-eight years old, James. I have lived long

51

enough in the world to know you will not accept the situation. Your father knows it, too, which is why he has charged me to keep you here until Harry and Eliza are married.'

'And do you mean to do his bidding?'

'You will keep a civil tongue in your head. I have no interest in doing your father's bidding, but every interest in preventing you from making a mistake that will ruin your life. You will forget Eliza immediately and marry another heiress. It is too soon; you are too young; but it appears to be the only way to prevent your doing something foolish. Your sister has found a wife for you already, I gather, a Miss Heath. You will meet her tomorrow at my ball. You will flatter her and ask her to marry you, and Eliza will be forgotten. Is that understood?'

'Yes, Aunt,' I said, for I certainly understood her.

'Very well, you may go.'

As I left her, I thought, on reflection, that it was no bad thing that I would have to remain at Aunt Isabella's for a time. Eliza would be safe at home, and as she would never consent to marrying my brother, I would have time to secure a position in a lawyer's office and take lodgings, arranging both by letter. Then, with everything planned, it would be time to elope with

Eliza, and we would have a life already waiting for us when we returned from Scotland.

Wednesday 1 July
After a good night's sleep, I felt refreshed, and before breakfast, I wrote to Leyton, asking him to mention my name to his father with a view to finding me employment. I finished by requesting him to look for some respectable lodgings for us. *Nothing too expensive, but the sort of place that would suit Eliza,* I wrote to him.

I was half-afraid my aunt would read it after I had sent it to be posted, but the house was in a state of turmoil as last minute arrangements were being made for the ball, and the letter left the house with its seal unbroken.

I did my best to avoid the bustle as footmen carried chairs into the ballroom and set them against the walls for those guests who preferred not to dance, or arranged card-tables in the sitting room, or placed vases of flowers on console tables. Maids ran about with dusters and the housekeeper followed them, inspecting everything they had done and calling them back to finish any work they left half-finished.

I escaped into the library, where peace reigned, broken only by the ticking of the longcase clock. Dust motes swirled in the air, revealed by sudden beams of sunlight that danced in through the window and then dimmed as though crushed by the pervading gloom.

I thought of Eliza and wondered what she was doing. Having her dancing lessons and music lessons as usual, I supposed; listening to my father's lectures; and counting the days until we were together again.

I had no enthusiasm for the ball but I knew it could not be avoided, so, dressed in my knee-breeches and ruffled shirt, I went downstairs as the guests began to arrive.

I headed towards the card room, meaning to spend the evening there, but my sister waylaid me. To my dismay, she had a vulgar-looking woman, accompanied by her daughter, in tow.

'James, I want you to meet Mrs Heath and her charming daughter, Miss Heath,' said my sister.

Mrs Heath was dressed in a gown more suited to court than a country ball. Her panniered gown was covered in swags and flounces, her hair was powdered and her cheeks were highly rouged. She walked with the air of a woman who thought she was in the height of fashion, but in this she was deluding herself, and my aunt's friends pulled their skirts out of her way as she walked past.

Miss Heath was dressed with more restraint. Her hair was unpowdered and her face was unrouged, but she had her mother's expression.

'Charmed, I'm sure,' said Mrs Heath. She turned to her daughter. 'What d'you think of him, then, Sally? An 'andsome one, ain't 'e? Look at 'is calves!'

I saw my sister shudder, and I believe only the sight of Miss Heath's exquisitely matched pearls encouraged her to continue with the introduction.

I bowed politely but coldly.

'Well, go on then, Mr Brandy, ain't you going to ask 'er to dance?' said Mrs Heath jovially.

I wished I was not a gentleman, for then I would have been able to walk away, but as it was, I offered Miss Heath my arm.

As I led her onto the floor, she looked around her, saying, 'Coo, ain't it grand?'

I wondered if my sister knew what kind of paragon she had picked for me to marry, or whether Miss Heath's blue eyes, corn-coloured hair and thirty thousand pounds had blinded her to her protégée's faults.

'Miss Heath,' I said. 'I believe my sister has given you to understand . . . that is, I want you to know that I am not in a position to marry. I am already in love, with a lady my family does not approve of — or, rather, they do not approve of her for me. If they have misled you in any way, then I apologize.'

'Oh, thank goodness,' she said, in completely different tones. 'I am in love, too, with our curate. I am sorry if I embarrassed you, but I wanted to repulse you so that you would not offer for me. Mama wants me to marry into the gentry, you see, and so I have to humour her, but I would never be happy with rarefied people, living in a house like this. A country parsonage is where I belong, with people I know and love.'

'Then we may enjoy our dance together,' I said with relief.

'We may indeed! And if you would care to dance with me again, and to take me into supper, we may be comfortable then as well. Our relations will be satisfied, for they will see us together, and so they will not plague us and tell us we are disobedient. I confess, it will be a relief, for I am tired of being paraded in front of the gentry like a prize mare and then berated for not being grateful.'

The orchestra began to play and we

danced, talking, when we passed each other, of our loves, I of Eliza, and she of Mr Abelard.

Catherine smiled on me for paying attention to Miss Heath, and even my aunt managed something that passed for a smile when she saw me at supper, whilst Mrs Heath watched at us benignly and declared that I was *a right 'un.*

I danced with Miss Heath again after supper and we talked of our loves again, and the evening passed agreeably.

Thursday 2 July
The ball did not end until the early hours, and it was almost midday when Fildew pulled back my curtains this morning. I thought myself back at home to begin with, and leapt out of bed, eager to see Eliza. Then I remembered, and I dressed more slowly before going down to breakfast.

'I told you how it would be,' said my sister as I sat down beside her. She, too, had only just risen. She had finished her plate of rolls and was drinking a cup of chocolate. 'Did I not predict this very thing? I knew you would forget Eliza. And who can blame you? Miss Heath is a charming young woman. There is everything in her favour. She has beauty and wealth, and, best of all, her mother approves of the match. But you still have work to do, and you must not rest until she is your fiancée. You need to propose to her whilst she is in the country, for after she finishes her visit in the neighbourhood she will be returning to town. She will no doubt be surrounded by suitors there, so you must ask her to be your wife in the next five weeks. You will marry quickly, in an autumn wedding, and then you will have finished your wedding tour in time for Christmas. You will be safely established in town by the new year, and George, and I can visit you for the Season.'

I listened in silence, glad that Miss Heath and I had come to an understanding, for I could not have borne my sister's words otherwise, nor her determination to order my life.

Catherine took my silence to mean that I agreed with her, and continued to tell me what to do as I ate.

As soon as I had finished, I excused myself and went down to the stables, where I chose a suitable mount and I went out riding, relieved to be away from my relations and from the house.

As I wore off the worst of my frustrations, I found myself thinking of Leyton and hoping that he had received my letter, so that he could act for me whilst I was incapable of acting for myself. From there it was a short step for my thoughts to stray to Eliza, and to picture her in our new home.

I wished she was with me, for it was just the sort of morning she loved: fine, with hazy cloud and a light breeze to temper the glare of the sun.

When I returned to the house, my aunt summoned me to her sitting room. She was an impressive sight, with her hair powdered and arranged in a towering style and her brocade dress taking up most of the sofa.

'Your sister tells me that you are making good progress with Miss Heath,' she said. 'She will no doubt be overawed by your style of living but that is all to the good as she will be eager to please. Your sister has an idea of visiting you for the Season, but if you have any sense, you will not allow your wife to use her London house once you are married, except out of season. A woman with a London house is prey to all sorts of temptations that do not exist in the country-side, and she is apt to forget her place. Well, boy?'

'I was not aware that you needed an answer,' I said.

'Do not be impertinent. What do you have to say?'

'Yes, Aunt,' I replied.

It satisfied her, and she went on.

'I have invited the Heaths to dine with us tomorrow. It will give Miss Heath an opportunity to become more intimately acquainted with the family, and it will give her a chance to exhibit. Her mother has spent a great deal on her education and she will wish her daughter, at the least, to play the pianoforte and to sing.'

'I look forward to hearing her.'

'As well you might. Miss Heath, so her mother tells me, is a proficient. I should not be surprised if she also plays the harp. You will compliment her on her taste, and you will say that it is a most superior performance. You will also compliment her mother on providing her with the very best masters.'

I thought of Eliza's music masters, and of her light touch, and of her sweet voice, and I smiled.

'Why are you smirking?' my aunt demanded.

'I — nothing,' I said.

'You will not smirk tomorrow, or our guests will think you have a toothache. If you wish to smile, you will lift the corners of your mouth, like so.'

She demonstrated with a grimace, and I nodded my head.

She eyed me as though I was a poor specimen, and then, with a wave of her hand, she dismissed me. I left her sitting room to amuse myself by fishing and then by playing billiards with George.

Friday 3 July
I looked for a letter from Leyton this morning, but the only letters on the silver salver were for my aunt. I was not surprised, for although I had hoped for a letter, I knew I could not really expect anything so soon. I could not expect Leyton to leave his own business and attend to mine straight away, and so I hoped for a letter in a few days' time.

I escaped the house with George and we rode into town. He had some business to attend to and so we parted, he to go to his lawyer's office and I to go to the local inn. Once there, I was tempted to write a letter to Eliza, but I knew it would be hopeless because my father would not let her see it, so I contained myself, thinking that, God willing, it would not be long before we were together again.

When I returned to the house, I found that the table had already been laid for dinner. The party was to be a small one, just ourselves, Mrs and Miss Heath, the Bormans and the Maidstones. I was thankful for it as I had no mind for company.

'Do you like Miss Heath?' asked George idly as we went into the billiard room.

'She is very agreeable,' I replied vaguely.

'Agreeable before marriage is not the same as agreeable afterwards,' he said. 'Believe me, I know. Stand out against them, my boy, if you do not wish to marry; and I am sure you do not wish it. Let them blow and bluster, and then go back to Oxford and forget all about it.'

I was glad of his support, and we passed the time with a game or two before we changed for dinner.

The Heaths arrived promptly, a fact which would have annoyed my aunt had she not been so desirous of my marrying Miss Heath.

Miss Heath was looking very pretty, and if I had not been in love with Eliza, I believe I might have been in some danger, for I knew her to be agreeable and intelligent as well, but as my feelings were already attached, I could approach her without risk. We fell into conversation, and were smiled upon by those around us.

Dinner was announced, and Mrs Heath entertained us by comparing my aunt's plate to her own. She then launched into a description of her wealth.

'Folks say Miss Stallybrooks is an heiress, but she's no more than twenty thousand pounds. My Sally'll 'ave thirty thousand pounds when she marries. What d'you say to that?' she asked, looking at each of us triumphantly.

Miss Heath murmured, 'Mama,' reproachfully, but did no more, being well used to her mother's ways.

My aunt ignored her, whilst my sister murmured, 'Delightful.' Mrs Borman hid a smile and Mrs Maidstone looked shocked.

'*And* an 'ouse in town,' added Mrs Heath, for good measure. 'Nothing but the best for our girl, that's what 'er pa and me decided. Got to look after 'em, eh, Lady Graves?' she asked of my aunt.

'Lady Greaves,' corrected her daughter.

'Children!' said Mrs Heath indulgently. 'What would we do without 'em? D'you 'ave any children, Mrs Poorman?' she asked Mrs Borman, who murmured that she had two, a girl and a boy.

'Grown up by now, I'll be bound,' she said.

'Henry is seven and Katherine is five,' replied Mrs Borman repressively.

'Lawks, I took you for forty!' said Mrs Heath. 'And you, Mrs Mandibles? D'you 'ave any little 'uns to bless your 'earth?'

Mrs Maidstone dabbed her mouth fastidiously with her napkin and revealed that she had five, the eldest being fourteen and the youngest seven.

'A fine family,' said Mrs Heath. 'Me and Arthur wanted a fine family, but —'

Fearing a description of Mrs Heath's troubles, my sister cut in with, 'Do you play, Miss Heath?'

'A little,' said Miss Heath.

'A little! Lawks! The best player in the country is my Sally,' said Mrs Heath. 'All the masters said so. "Ain't my Sally the best little thing you've ever 'eard?" I used to ask them, and they all agreed, every one!'

'Mama,' said Miss Heath, shaking her head.

'You must perform for us after dinner,' said my aunt.

'There you are, Sally. Singing for a Lady!' said Mrs Heath, much pleased.

The ladies soon withdrew, and the gentlemen lingered over the port.

We talked of the political situation, but at last we could delay no longer and we joined the ladies. Miss Heath was sitting at the pianoforte when we entered the drawing room, and she was soon persuaded to play. She had a fine voice and it was a pleasure to listen to her as she entertained us.

'What d'you think of that?' asked Mrs Heath triumphantly, as Miss Heath came to the end of her song.

'A fine performance,' said my sister. 'Do you not agree, James?'

'Very fine,' I said with a smile at Miss Heath.

'There you are, Mrs Mandrake,' said Mrs Heath. 'Pay for the best masters, and one day your little 'uns could be playing like that.'

Mrs Maidstone did not deign to reply.

The party then broke into groups, some playing cards, some gossiping, and some turning over the pages of a fashion journal. The evening passed agreeably enough, but I was glad when it was over, all the same, for I would swap a dozen such evenings if I could spend one moment with Eliza.

Saturday 18 July

At last! I heard from Leyton today. He would have replied sooner, but he was away from home when my letter arrived. He promised to speak to his father and he assured me that he would search for some suitable lodgings.

My father will soon be going to London and I must have everything ready, for then I can rescue Eliza and take her to her new life. I am looking forward to it. It will be difficult, at first, for we will not have a proper establishment when we are married, but we are young and strong, and as long as we are together, then nothing else matters.

I hope that Leyton will be able to find some lodgings with a garden, for I do not want Eliza to be separated from her precious roses. But, good fellow that he is, I am sure he will find something that will suit.

Monday 27 July

My aunt summoned me to her sitting room this morning. She was dressed in her usual style, in heavy brocade and with an elaborate wig that extended her height by eight inches. When I entered the room, she was seated at her desk, and she held a letter in her hand.

'You wanted to see me, Aunt?'

She raised her lorgnette and looked at me through it for a full minute before speaking. Then she lowered it and said, 'Your father has written to me and desires me to tell you that you may return home whenever you wish.'

I was astonished, and then I thought, Of course! He has seen that he will never have his way, and he has relented.

I could not hide my joy, for now there was

no need for me to approach the house in stealth. I could go home and marry Eliza in church, for if my father had seen that she would never marry anyone else, then he must surely give his permission for her to marry me.

I did not deceive myself. I knew that her fortune was the temptation for him, and that, seeing she would not marry my brother, he had decided she had better marry me, for in that way her fortune would enrich the Brandons. But I did not care about the reason, just so long as Eliza could be mine.

I wondered when he would allow us to marry. Would he make us wait until I was of age? Or would he be so eager to secure her fortune that he would let us marry at once? The latter, I hoped, for once Eliza was mine, he could not change his mind.

'You are pleased?' asked my aunt.

'I am. I thought he meant to stick to his word and forbid me the house until Eliza had married Harry. But now, everything will be different.'

'Your father has many faults, but going back on his word is not one of them,' said my aunt. 'He has *stuck to his word,* as you put it. Eliza was married yesterday.'

I could not take it in. I was bemused.

'I do not understand you,' I managed to say at last.

'It is simple enough. Eliza and Harry are now married, and as they have embarked on their wedding tour, your father feels it is safe for you to return to the house.'

'But this is impossible,' I said, wondering what game my father was playing.

'I cannot see why you are so surprised,' she remarked, looking at me as though I were a half-wit. 'You knew they were to marry.'

'But Eliza would not marry my brother. She does not love him. She does not like him. She has given me her word that she will not consent to the match.'

'A word like that means nothing. No young woman can give her word to a young man without her guardian's approval. Come, come, now, you must have known how it would be; that, with time, her own conscience and common sense would show her that she was in the wrong. It would have been nonsensical for her to refuse a good marriage on nothing more than a whim.'

'A whim, you call it? Love is a vast deal more than a whim,' I said, still not knowing whether to believe it or not.

'Whatever the case, she is now married; and you, I might remind you, are as good as engaged to Miss Heath.'

I gave an exclamation of disgust.

'I mean nothing to Miss Heath and she means nothing to me.'

My aunt raised her thin eyebrows and looked at me again through her lorgnette.

'You cannot mean to say you have been making love to her all this time without any serious intentions? Such conduct is unbecoming for a gentleman.'

'She knows my intentions, and I know hers,' I remarked.

'And you know hers?' demanded my aunt sharply. 'Pray, what do you mean by that?'

I regretted my hasty words, for I was not willing to give her away.

'Nothing,' I said.

But my aunt was not so easily satisfied.

'I will not be trifled with. You have declared that you know Miss Heath's intentions, and you will be so good as to tell me what you mean.'

'I mean nothing, Aunt.'

'You have been a considerable disappointment to your family all your life, James. I suggest you make amends for it by being frank with me now.'

'I have nothing further to say to you. Since my father has given me leave to return home, that is what I intend to do. I will leave at once.'

'You will leave when I say you may go.'

'No, Aunt, I will leave now,' I said.

And without waiting for further argument, I left the room.

I packed my things myself, not wishing to involve any of my aunt's servants in case they incurred my aunt's wrath, and ran down the stairs.

'Where are you going in such a hurry?' asked my sister, coming out of the drawing room.

'Home.'

'But you have been forbidden —'

'My father has changed his mind.'

'But what am I to say to Miss Heath?'

'Pray tell her that I wish her happy,' I said.

She attempted to argue further, but I ran on through the hall and out the front door, arriving in the stables where I had a horse saddled and, accompanied by a groom, rode to the stage. There I dismounted, and telling the groom to lead my mount back to the stables, I waited for the coach.

How different were my feelings from the last time I had taken a stagecoach. Then, I had been full of happiness, for I had been going to see Eliza. Now, I was full of apprehension, for I did not know what I would find at home.

Tuesday 28 July

I travelled overnight and arrived at Delaford before dawn, when the birds were just beginning to wake and the air was full of promise. But what did it promise for me? Good or ill?

Good, surely. Eliza could not have married Harry. She would never have agreed to it, and my father could not have forced her to the altar if she had refused. He did not have so much influence in the neighbourhood that he could compel Mr Liddle to perform the ceremony when the bride was unwilling, and Eliza did not lack the courage to tell him that she was being coerced.

Then, too, there were the neighbours. My father did not court their company, but he had too much family pride to turn them against him by committing such a monstrous act.

But why, then, did my aunt say that Eliza had married? To persuade me that the case was hopeless, and so encourage me to offer for Miss Heath? Perhaps. But why, then, was I allowed to go home, where I would discover the truth for myself?

Unless my father had sent her to London and had lured me home so that, when I found her missing, I would believe the evidence of my own eyes, as I would not

71

necessarily believe his assertions, and believe that all was lost.

It seemed only too likely.

With a lighter heart I shouldered my bag and completed the last part of my journey on foot.

The early morning mist was covering the lake, like a quilt covering a sleeper who had not yet awoken. There was a hush in the air, a sense of expectancy, and I lingered there, unwilling to go on, for I knew that the morning would either bring me the fulfilment of my dreams or else dash my hopes for ever.

The birds began to sing more lustily and the mist began to rise from the lake. Morning was coming in earnest and I could delay no longer.

I went in to the house through a side door and I went upstairs, calling for Eliza, softly at first and then more rousingly, until I had reached the door of her room. Throwing decorum aside, I went in and found it empty. Her hair brush was not on the dressing table. There was an air of abandonment everywhere.

This only tells me that she has left the house, I reminded myself.

I went downstairs, and then, deciding there was only one way to know for sure, I began to walk, then run, to the village and to the church. The venerable building, with its Norman spire, was serene in the early morning light. The low sun was casting long shadows from the tombstones in the grave-yard, and from the body of the church itself.

I approached from the east, with the sun on my back, and went in. I felt the cold as soon as I stepped through the door, and I shivered.

I looked around me for the register and saw it on the lectern. I went over to it and opened it with trembling hands. And there was recorded the marriage of Eliza Williams and Henry Brandon, concluded three days before.

I reeled. It could not be.

But it was.

I went outside and sank down amongst the gravestones, feeling I belonged there, amongst the dead.

How had it happened? How had she been induced to marry?

I let out a wail, and my cry was heard.

Mrs Upland, an elderly widow, came to my side and looked at me pityingly. She put a hand on my shoulder.

'You are the Brandon boy?' she asked me.

I turned my face to hers.

'Ah,' she said, recognizing me, for she had

often seen me out walking or riding with Eliza.

I sat up, ashamed of my tears.

'You are mourning Miss Williams?'

'You know what happened?' I asked, wiping my eyes on my sleeve. Then I remembered that she had a granddaughter who had just started as a maid at the house. 'How did they persuade her to marry my brother? There must have been some trickery involved.'

'There was no trickery, but there was great unkindness,' she said.

I began to grow angry. What had my father done to her?

I listened as she told me that Eliza had been confined to her room. She had not been allowed any society, and her virtual imprisonment had been the talk of the neighbourhood.

I was angry with myself. Why had I not returned sooner? Why had I not guessed what they would do? With no one to turn to, she had been ground down, until at last, in a moment of weakness, she had given her consent to the union, and had then been married by special licence before she could take it back.

I thanked Mrs Upland for her kind words and left her to lay her flowers on her husband's grave, for though he had died ten years earlier, she still placed fresh flowers there every day.

Without any idea of what I was going to do, I started walking towards the house. I grew more and more angry as I went on. I entered through the French windows and went straight into my father's study. He was there, sitting at his desk, his quill in his hand as he examined a pile of papers.

He looked up when I entered the room, and then continued with his work.

'So, you are home.'

'Yes, sir, I am home, and I demand an answer from you. What did you mean by it, blighting the happiness of a young woman, your own ward, for ever? When I think of the inducements, nay the cruelties, you used to get her to consent to the match —'

'How very dramatic you are,' he said drily, without favouring me with so much as a look. 'You speak as though I locked her in a dungeon and fed her on bread and water.'

'You locked her in her room —'

'Which is a comfortable apartment, decorated to her own taste, complete with a sitting room, filled with needlework, paints and other amusements to help her to pass the time.'

'You deprived her of society —'

'She had her companion.'

'— and frightened her into the match.'

'Not a bit of it. She saw the folly of clinging to you when she knew I would never consent to the match, and she grew to like your brother. He presented himself to her in a sober condition and sat with her on many occasions in her sitting room, taking her gifts, and telling her of the happy future that awaited her as his wife.'

'She would never have married him if she had not been ground down. You cannot deny it, for if she had changed her mind freely, then there would have been no need for a hurried wedding, nor any need to forbid me the house until she was married.'

'Whatever the case, she is married now, and in London, which means that there is no purpose to your rantings. Accept it. It is done.'

'Never.'

'Now that she has gone, you may stay here for as long as you wish,' he said, as though I had not spoken.

'Remain here, where every corner reminds me of her?' I asked in disbelief. 'Where I have to see you every day, and be reminded of the heinous thing you have done?'

'Then return to Oxford, and go on with your studies,' he said, whilst giving nine tenths of his attention to his papers, and only one tenth to me. 'Let me know when you achieve your ambitions. Perhaps I will employ you as my clerk.'

To say more was useless. I left the study, passing my hand over my eyes as I reached the hall, and then, turning my back on Delaford, I walked to the stage post and at last boarded the stage for Oxford.

As it travelled away from the neighbourhood, I felt myself travelling away from all my happiness in life, into a future that was cold and dark.

Wednesday 29 July

My thoughts were in turmoil this morning, for I knew I could not resume my studies without the backing of my father, and I was determined never to touch his money, or anything of his. Besides, the idea of becoming a lawyer was suddenly abhorrent to me, for its purpose had been to support Eliza and without that purpose there was no point to it.

I was in the midst of this turmoil when the stagecoach stopped at the Black Swan. Feeling tired, for I had not eaten since yesterday, I left the stage and went inside. I ordered a plate of mutton and sat in a corner, not wanting company, but as luck would have it, company found me anyway, and company of a sort to do me good.

'Brandon? Brandon, is that you? It is!'

I looked up to see Geoffrey Parker and his uncle.

'You look as though you need some company,' he said.

My mood began to lift at the sight of his friendly face, for we had been friends at Oxford, and when he asked me how my family was, and how Eliza was, saying, 'Is she as pretty as ever? No, don't tell me, she is prettier!' I broke down and told him everything.

'And now I must find something to do with myself, or go mad,' I finished.

'You should join the army,' said his uncle.

It turned out he had some influence and he promised to help me if I had a mind to enlist.

'I have a little money from my mother,' I said. 'How much would it cost me to buy a commission?'

He gave me all the particulars and I saw that it could be done.

'You will have activity, employment and company,' he said, 'all good things for a man in your condition.'

I began to see a future for myself; not the future I had wanted, but one in which I could at least be respectable and respected.

It was little enough, but it was better than the alternative, to spend my days sunk in despair, lost in the past, a past to which I could never return.

And so I thanked him, and asked him to use his influence, and now, who knows what the future holds?

Tuesday 6 October

'It was a bad business, a very bad business,' said Leyton, shaking his head, as we met again for the first time in months, in Oxford, an Oxford changed for me for ever, for it was no longer the scene of youthful hopes, but the scene of a fool's paradise.

I told him what had happened to me.

'I wondered why you had changed your mind about the lodgings,' he said, 'but when your letter arrived two months ago, I was too busy to wonder very much, and I am only sorry the reason was such a sad one. I can understand why you did not feel you could continue at Oxford, but whatever induced you to buy a commission?'

I could not help thinking that if things had been otherwise, our conversation would not have been about my plan of going into the army, it would have been about the lodgings he had found for Eliza and me, and our future in Oxford.

'I had to do something,' I said. 'I thought the bustle of a new career would distract my thoughts, but I still think about her constantly. I cannot stay in England, and I plan to purchase an exchange.'

'Where will you go?'

'The Indies. Once I am far away, I must hope to forget her, as I must hope she forgets me.'

He looked at me doubtfully.

'I *must* hope she forgets me,' I said. 'How else can there be any happiness for her? If she remembers what we were to each other and compares it with what she has now . . . But if Harry treats her well, if she has friends and fine clothes and parties, with plenty of distractions, I am persuaded she can be happy in her new life.'

He looked at me pityingly, for he knew I believed it as little as he did.

But Eliza was married. She was beyond my reach. If I went to her, I would dishonour her, and so I must go far away.

'Give it some time before you purchase your exchange,' he said. 'You will grow more accustomed to the situation with time, and you will find a hundred miles as efficacious a distance as a thousand.'

'I do not trust myself with only a hundred

miles between us. I must have half the globe, or else what is to prevent me from going to her and ruining her? For to live without her is agony. I must have occupation, and change, and distance from Eliza.'

He looked at me sympathetically then turned the subject, trying to take my mind from my troubles by his lively conversation. I was grateful to him, but it did no good. I could not tear my thoughts from Eliza.

1779

Wednesday 24 March

And so I find myself on a ship bound for the Indies, and at last I have found my sea legs and I can manage to keep my food inside me. The vessel is an East Indiaman, and as fine a ship as ever sailed the seas, or so her captain tells me. He is a talkative fellow, prosperous and well-made, and instils confidence into those around him.

'This is my fourth run,' he told me as we stood together on the deck. 'Yes, I've done very well out of the East India Company. I've had three good runs and amassed a fortune. How much do you think I have made?'

I guessed at five thousand pounds, and he laughed. Then I guessed at ten thousand, and he laughed again.

'Double it and then some,' he said. 'Almost thirty thousand pounds! What with free transport for freight giving a man a chance to make something out of his own bit of cargo, and the salary, it's a good life, being a captain. A man would have to be a fool to make less than four thousand a trip, and I'm no fool! On my last trip I made twelve! But this will be my last voyage. I could make more money by staying, there's always work for experienced captains, but I'm tired of making it. I want to spend it. When my ship retires, so do I. It's a hard passage, and it takes its toll on men and ships alike.'

He told me of his plans to buy a small estate and find a wife, and I wished him well, but being in no mood to hear him talk about the woman he would like to marry, I soon left him and joined my comrades; a varied group, but I liked Green and Wareham, and I thought I would soon be able to call them friends.

The talk was all of Warren Hastings. Being eager to learn as much as I could about the strange new world that was opening up around me, I listened avidly as they spoke of bribery and corruption, and of Hastings's governorship, and of the difficulties that lay ahead of me. As I imagined the exotic locations awaiting me, England seemed a long way away.

Friday 30 July

The Indies are strange beyond my expectations. The heat is like a furnace. I rise early and work as much as I can before the sun explodes over the horizon. By the afternoon it is too hot to do anything at all, and the evenings are little better.

The men who have been here some time say that I will get used to it, but I wonder if I ever will.

The colours are as fierce as the heat, and the food is fiery, burning my mouth and throat. I ate my first Indian dish today, and I had not taken two mouthfuls when I grabbed at my throat and felt the tears running down my cheeks. The others laughed, and poured me more wine, but drinking it only made my mouth burn the more and the sweat ran down my face in rivers.

I tried to remember the soft summers of England to cool me, but I could not bring them to mind, for it seemed impossible that I had ever been cold.

I ate no more of the strange dish, but I must accustom myself to the food ere long, or else die of starvation.

Monday 9 August

I have seen my first elephant!

I remember hearing about such beasts

long ago, but I thought the stories were exaggerated. Having seen one, I think that, if anything, the stories were too tame.

It was the oddest thing I have ever come across. It dwarfed a horse as a horse dwarfs a dog, and it was covered in a thick leathery hide that hung in folds from its legs like a pair of ill-fitting breeches. It had a short tail at the back, and at the front it had a head of such monstrous appearance that it seemed impossible such a thing could exist. Large ears, eyes too small, and huge tusks were the least of it, for in between them was the strangest thing of all: a nose, but what a nose! It had the length and appearance of a snake, and it swayed from side to side as the creature walked, snuffling along the ground like a blind thing looking for food. Then, finding something, the trunk lifted like a misshapen hand and dropped the morsel into the creature's mouth.

I stood still to watch it. As I did so, it found another use for its appendage and, lifting it up like a ceremonial trumpet, it let out a great bellow.

'It sounds like a cow with a cold,' said Green.

'Though a good deal louder,' said Wareham.

'Quite a sight, is it not?' said Green, as

the creature walked past.

'I have never seen such a monstrous thing in my life. Those tusks, that nose —'

'Almost as large as Ullswater's proboscis!' said Wareham, to much laughter.

Ullswater took the raillery in good part, saying, 'The elephant has the advantage of me, for I have not learnt how to forage with mine.'

'Yet,' said Wareham.

Ullswater laughed with the rest of us, but added, 'You may laugh, but when rations are short and I turn up delicacies, then I will be the one doing the laughing!'

Thursday 2 September

I am becoming used to my new country, with its elephants and bullocks, its spicy food and its scents of jasmine and musk. I am becoming adept at giving orders and having them carried out. I can fire a musket, and I believe the men respect me; those who are still on their feet, for the life is cruel and many of those who arrive from England do not survive. Sickness, the climate, accident and injury carry off more than half of them.

Friday 10 September

Wareham wanted to buy a necklace for his sister and he invited me to go to the bazaar with him. We were soon wandering between the stalls, surrounded by the din of money-changers arguing with their customers, the sight of bright fabrics and the smell of pungent spices. The goldsmiths and jewellers were busy, and Wareham stopped to buy his sister a gold chain. I watched the jugglers as he completed his purchase and then we returned to camp, where I found a letter waiting for me.

I felt a chill as the air of England seemed to blow over me, for the handwriting was my sister's. Knowing that whatever news the letter contained would already be a few months old, I opened it and scanned the pages quickly, learning that my father was dead.

I folded the letter and stared in front of me, unseeing. If only Eliza had been strong for another few months, my father's death would have removed the barrier between us. We could have been married. Only a few months! The shock of it turned me to ice.

'Not bad news I hope?' asked Wareham.

I roused myself.

'My father is dead.'

'I am sorry,' he said.

I thought of my father as he had been when my mother was alive, and I remembered him smiling. And then I thought of him as I had last seen him, showing no remorse at the fact that he had forced Eliza to marry my brother, and I crumpled the letter in my hands.

Now he was dead and buried, and my brother was the new head of the family, and the owner of the estate.

And suddenly everything I had worked so hard to run away from caught up with me and I could no longer deny my memories of England. I recalled it in every detail: the soft landscape, overshadowed by mist; the variety of greens, from the verdant emerald of the lawns to the lime-green of the ferns and the dark sage of moss and late summer leaves; the clear water, running through streams and basking in lakes; the sun rising, mild and clement, in the morning. And Eliza would be there now, cutting roses in the garden and wandering across the meadows, her hat swinging by a ribbon from her hand. I prayed my brother treated her well, and that she was happy. With kindness and diversion I hoped she would be, if not happy, at least not unhappy, and it gave me some comfort to think of her at Delaford, where she was meant to be.

I went outside and was immediately scorched by the sun, so different from the mild friend of England. The buzz of the mosquitoes irritated my ears, and I slapped at my neck in anger as they bit into me. The exotic colours dazzled my eyes, and I thought how far we had come in such a short time, Eliza and I, for if not for her marriage I would still be in Oxford, with its mellow stone and its rustling river, and she would be there with me.

Monday 13 September

I woke early and set to work. The sergeant soon came to me and, after the usual preamble, said, 'Johnson is dead, sir.'

I rubbed my eyes and said, 'Very good,' and thought, Another man lost to the climate.

I dismissed the sergeant and then threw down my pen and went out of the tent, watching him drill the men and hearing the familiar commands: wheel, turn, march, counter march, advance, retire.

Their numbers were depleted, for there were the usual absences due to illness, caused by the heat or tainted food or disease, and to deaths. I thanked God I had acclimatized, and that I no longer felt the agonies produced by the exotic spices and rotten meat.

My eyes wandered to the bullocks walking past, carrying loaded panniers, and I wondered if we would have enough of them to pull the guns and ammunition wagons when we broke camp.

Carstairs joined me, evidently thinking the same thing, for he said, 'Do you think we should buy a couple of elephants to pull the heavy guns?'

'They are expensive,' I said. 'Can we afford them?'

'The purchase price, yes, but the maintenance?' He shook his head. 'Perhaps not. At least with bullocks, they can graze off the land. It is a pity, though. A couple of elephants would make easy work of it.' His eyes wandered to the men, who were forming a square. 'They seem to be shaping up well.'

'Not well enough. They are not ready for battle. Their formation is sloppy, and they do not react quickly enough to commands.'

'They will improve.'

'I hope so, or they, too, will soon be dead.'

He looked at me curiously, for I used not to be so grim, but I cannot rid myself of the thought that, if only Eliza had had more strength, we could be married now, she and I, and we could be happy.

Tuesday 21 September
Another letter from Catherine arrived this

morning, already many months old, giving me news of my father's funeral, and telling me of Eliza.

We are staying at Delaford with Harry and Eliza. Harry is worse than ever. I lectured him on the evils of drink but he took no notice of me. He was already drunk when we sat down to dinner and he could barely stand by the time Eliza and I withdrew. Eliza was pale and seemed unwell. Her spirits must have been sadly affected by my father's death, for she spoke barely two words to me all evening, and I cannot think what else she has to make her un-happy.

I hope it is only the melancholy occasion and my sister's presence that caused her low spirits, but I fear it is her marriage. If she still regrets it, what torment for her.

What torment for us both.

Friday 24 September
I am finding it impossible to control my thoughts. They are not here with me, but at home, with Eliza. Is she happy? Is she well? Is she thinking of me?

I turn a thousand possibilities over in my mind. If I had not left home, if I had returned sooner, if . . . if . . . if. . . .

I must gain control of my thoughts soon or I fear for my sanity. My only solace is work, and I am determined to think of nothing else, for how else will I survive?

1781

Thursday 24 May

A letter from Catherine this morning, the
first in two years, for not since my father's
death has she written to me. I opened it
with nerveless fingers, wondering what news
it would contain, and wondering if it would
mention Eliza. For all my efforts to forget
her, I cannot banish her from my mind, and
when there is a lull in my duties, I find
myself thinking of her.

I read Catherine's news of her family with
little interest, scanning the page until Eliza's
name caught my eye.

. . . and so Harry has divorced her.

Divorced? I sat back in my seat, rocked.
I steeled myself to read on.

It is not to be wondered at. Harry drank, it
is true, and gambled, and had numerous

93

mistresses, but Eliza should have borne it. I always knew that she was unsatisfactory. There was something ridiculously romantic about her, for which I blame you, James, for you encouraged her. It is true that Harry should not have invited his mistresses into their London home, but if Eliza had only been sensible and withdrawn to the estate, instead of going into a decline and then falling prey to the first man who showed her a little kindness, she would be a married woman still. I have no patience with her. She should have valued herself, and her good name, more. Of course, Harry was obliged to divorce her, and I would not be surprised if he marries again. He has run through Eliza's fortune, and you know how Harry has always needed money. If he finds an heiress who will have him, I feel sure he will take another wife.

I put my head in my hands. All that hope and beauty coming to nothing. She was divorced, disgraced, cast off, and by my brother, a fiend who should never have been allowed to marry her. I felt ill, even worse than I had felt when hearing of her marriage. At least then I had been able to hope she would not be too unhappy. But now I could hope for nothing.

I read on, feeling worse and worse with every word, for she had been abandoned by her first seducer. Without an adequate allowance, for my brother had been mean and vengeful and had not given her an income that was either adequate to her fortune or sufficient for her comfortable maintenance, she had sunk still further, finding another protector and sinking yet again.

I folded the letter at last and willed myself to turn to stone, for if I remained a creature of flesh and blood, I feared the pain would kill me.

1782

Monday 9 December

How strange it feels to be in England again after almost four years away. I had forgotten how low the sky was, and how grey, and how it leached the colour from everything, leaving the world a dreary place.

As I stepped ashore, I fastened the buttons of my greatcoat and hunched my shoulders against the rain. My countrymen hurried past with their colourless faces, dreary and sad, and I felt a stab of homesickness for the Indies, for sunburnt skin and bright colours and the heat of the sun, but then I shook it away. It was not England that had called me home again, it was Eliza.

I thanked God that I was at last able to take some leave so that I could do what I had longed to do ever since I had learnt of her sorrows. Return to England and find her. Care for her. Comfort her. And, perhaps, make her happy.

Wednesday 11 December

I set out early this morning, walking to the inn where I would catch the stage for home.

Home! Delaford is no longer my home. It ceased to be my home the day I was cast out, the day my father irrevocably set Eliza and me on a path to misery.

The coach arrived, and amidst the general bustle, I climbed aboard. The gaiety of the other passengers could not touch me. I was lost in my memories, and in my distaste for what was to come, for having learnt that my sister no longer knew of Eliza's where-abouts, I knew that, in order to find her, I had to see my brother.

Thursday 12 December

As the coach approached Delaford, to my surprise I was thrown back in time to the day I returned from Oxford as a young man, full of hope and optimism. I remembered it clearly, and not only remembered it, felt it, with the same sensations assailing me.

When the carriage came to the bend where, all those years ago, I had seen Eliza walking through the fields, and when I remembered my elation as I had leapt from the carriage and rolled down the hill to meet her; when I recalled the love that had coursed through me as I had picked her up and swung her round, then I was nearly unmanned.

How could it have happened? How could such love and happiness have led to such misery and despair?

My hands clenched themselves into balls, and I began to wish I had not come.

The coach rolled on, past the scene of such happiness, and continued along the road. Before long it was pulling into the inn yard. There were the usual cries of the ostlers as they changed the horses. The door was opened and the steps pulled up. I waited whilst a well-dressed woman and her daughter climbed out and then I followed them, looking about me.

The inn was very much the same, with its half timbering and its freshly painted sign, and the yard, though larger, was still clean and well run. I had no difficulty in hiring a horse to take me on, and I was gratified that Bill Sanders, who still worked at the inn, remembered me.

'If it isn't Master James!' he said, his face creasing in deep lines — his only appearance of age — as I asked him for a horse. 'You're looking well. Been in the Indies, have you?' he asked.

'Yes, I have.'

'Thought so by the colour of your skin.

Shouldn't like it myself, but they do say it's an interesting place.'

We exchanged news, and he assured me that he would tell his wife he had seen me, for she would be pleased to know I was keeping well, and then I mounted the horse — 'the best the stable has to offer, Master James, a real beauty, with a soft mouth and a sweet temperament, but spirited with it' — and was away.

The day was cold but bright, with a weak sun shining from a slate-blue sky, and every moment brought with it a new memory as I travelled the familiar road, each one more painful than the last.

I turned into the drive at last and halted for a moment, too overcome with emotion to go on, though whether the emotion was anger, fear or sorrow I could not say. And then I continued up the drive, with the parkland stretching away on either side of me; that same parkland where Eliza and I had played as children, chasing kites, throwing a ball, running, laughing. Always laughing.

I saw the house rising up before me with feelings so painful I could hardly bear them. There was her window, with the vine beneath it; there the terrace where she had walked.

I came to a halt in the turning circle and dismounted. No groom ran forward, as he would have done in my father's time. With deep misgivings I climbed the steps to the house. The tall windows flanking the doors were dirty. I rang the bell, which clanged with a cracked note. And then the door was opened by a servant I did not know.

He asked my name and then he stood aside to let me in, and I entered the house. As I stepped over the threshold, I saw the same signs of neglect that I had seen outside. There were no flowers in the vases. The mirrors were dull and the console tables were filmed with dust.

I was shown into the drawing room, and I was overcome once again with memories as I saw the familiar wallpaper and the Aubusson carpet. I stood a moment looking round, and then my eyes came to rest on my brother. He was heavier than the last time I had seen him, with the signs of dissipation already on him. His skin was an unhealthy colour and his eyes were dull. His clothes had an unkempt look, and as he rose to his feet, he almost fell back again. I smelt his breath and knew that he was already drunk. He righted himself, smirking as he said, 'Well, well. James. The prodigal son returns. Our father is dead —'

'I know.'

'Then what are you doing here?' he asked.

'You know why I have come.'

'To ask after that harlot who was once my wife, I suppose,' he said.

I took a step towards him and he laughed, then poured himself a drink. He waved the decanter towards me in invitation.

'Not at ten o'clock in the morning, I thank you, no,' I said scathingly.

'You are as self-righteous as ever,' he said mockingly. 'I see the Indies have done you no good. It seems that not even foreign climes could make a man of you. So, what do you want to know?'

He sat down, lolling in his seat; I doubt if he could have sat upright.

I had intended only to ask him where she was, but in the familiar surroundings where the memories of Eliza were all around me, from the vases that she had filled with flowers, to the carpet on which she had danced, all my feelings rose up inside me and my anger poured out of me in a torrent.

'Why did you marry her? You were never in love with her. Why did you ruin her life? Why did you take her from me?'

'Because she was rich. Why else?' he said. 'The estate was encumbered and we needed her money. But you know all this.'

'But why Eliza?' I demanded. 'Why not some other heiress? Some woman who would have sold herself happily in order to gain a respectable name and an old estate? Someone old enough to have given up on all idea of love, or someone too practical to look for it in the first place? Why Eliza, who would be crushed by such a marriage, her health and happiness destroyed?'

'Why go to all the trouble of courting a stranger when Eliza was right here?'

'Did you have no feelings for her? No tenderness? No pity? You had known her all her life. Did you have nothing inside you that said, "No, I will not do this. Not to Eliza"?'

He looked at me as though I was speaking a language that was unknown to him and then said, 'No. Not at all.'

'How could you! How could you do it?'

He took a drink.

'How you do rant on! Anyone would think I forced her to marry me at gunpoint. She knew what I was, and yet she married me anyway. She deserved what she got.'

'If you were not my brother, I would call you out,' I said, shaking with rage.

'If you were not my brother, I would throw you out,' he returned.

'You are welcome to try.'

He reached out his hand to the bell.

'Ah, I see,' I said scathingly. 'You mean you would have someone else throw me out.'

'Of course. That is why I have servants. To do the things I cannot, or will not, do myself.'

I mastered my emotion, for it was doing nothing but hurting me and amusing him.

'Then tell me this, and I will go,' I said. 'Where is she now?'

He shrugged.

'I have no idea.'

'But you must have. You must write to her from time to time —' He laughed in derision. 'At the very least you must have an address to which you send her allowance.'

'I did, to begin with, but no longer. She made her allowance over to someone else several months ago.'

'What do you mean?'

'She sold it, or gave it away.'

I was horrified.

'And you allowed this?' I demanded.

'It was her money. She had a perfect right to give it to anyone she pleased,' he said calmly.

'But why should she do such a thing? She must have been coerced.'

'If she was coerced, it was by necessity. She was always extravagant. I have no doubt that she lived above her income and then, when her debtors pressed her, she had to have money quickly and so she sold her allowance.'

'She will not have received a tenth of its value, and without an allowance, how is she to live?' I asked.

'I have no idea,' he said carelessly, getting up to pour himself another drink.

'And you do not care,' I said. 'Have you no compassion in you at all? She was your wife, Harry. Your *wife!*'

'And she betrayed me,' he said, with the first hint of emotion I had heard in his voice. He had no sympathy for her, but he had plenty for himself.

'Because of your cruelty,' I said.

'Cruelty! I gave her everything,' he snapped.

'Everything? You gave her love, friendship, affection?'

He laughed at me.

'I gave her something better than that. I gave her a town house and plenty of clothes.'

'Eliza could not live without love,' I said.

'Love? Is that what you call it?' he asked derisively. 'Her seducers gave it another name.'

I could bear it no longer.

'You have no idea where she is?' I asked him.

'None at all.'

'Then give me the last address you have for her, and I will conduct my own enquiries.'

'I cannot remember it.'

I was not going to leave without finding what I had come for, and so, angry and impatient, I picked him up by his coat and said, 'Then you had better think harder.'

He knew it right enough, and, seeing I was serious, he gave it to me, and then I took my leave of him. I stayed only long enough to speak to the servants and call on the tenants who remembered me, and then I set out for town.

Monday 16 December

The rain continues. London is awash with it. The pavements are dirty and the roads are muddy. I was almost knocked down by a brewer's cart as I went out this morning, and I only narrowly avoided a rearing horse. I returned to my club where, to my surprise and great joy, I saw Leyton, sitting by the window and looking the same as he had done last time I saw him, apart from a new moustache.

'Whatever induced you to grow the thing?'

I asked him with a smile as, having clapped each other on the back and asked after each other's health, we sat down together, prepared to while away the morning by reacquainting ourselves.

'It is the fashion,' he said.

'Nonsense! I have not seen a single man with a moustache since I set foot in England.'

He looked sheepish, and said, 'If you must know, Brandon, I am married.'

'Ah! I see. And your new wife likes moustaches?' I said.

'It is for her I grew it. I find it a confounded nuisance, to be honest. It itches. But she likes it, and so it stays.'

I was happy for him, and I said so. He smiled and said that he had been fortunate, more fortunate than he deserved.

As we talked, I could not help thinking that, if life had been kinder, Leyton and I would be two lawyers together, plump and prosperous, and both married to women we loved. Instead of which, I was a soldier, hard and lean, and looked older than my years, whilst he looked younger. His face was soft, and there was still a look of innocence in his eye. The world had dealt kindly with him, and it showed.

'You must come to dinner,' he said, when

we had talked ourselves to a standstill. 'Caroline is eager to meet you, and I believe we may gather together sufficient friends to make your evening enjoyable.'

'It will be enjoyable even without additional company,' I said. 'It is good to see you again.'

Our talk then moved on to my family and Eliza. Leyton hesitated as he asked after her at first, but his ready sympathy was engaged when he heard of her fate, and he was able to recommend a man who could help me to find her if I should not be able to find her myself.

'I have used him before in one or two cases where information was essential. He is good at finding people,' he said.

I thanked him and we parted, he to return to Caroline and I to begin my search for Eliza. I went to the address my brother had given me, that of Eliza's first seducer, Sir William Rentram, but he was out. I declined to state my business, but said that I would call again on Tuesday.

Tuesday 17 December
I went to Sir William Rentram's today and found him at home. He was in his dressing gown when I arrived, though it was close on midday, and he had a sore head, but he

agreed to speak to me. He could tell me nothing of her, however, for he had not seen her since they parted. He claimed that he had treated her well and that she had been happy with him for as long as their liaison had lasted. Whether it was true or not I had no way of telling, nor did I care. I only cared about finding her, and to that end I asked him what had become of her when they parted.

'She left me for another man when my interest began to fade,' he said.

'And his name?' I asked.

He shook his head.

'I have no idea. A foreigner, I think. A Frenchman. You know what Frenchmen are like. They have a way with women. He set out to win her, and as far as I know, he succeeded.'

'But you do not know his name?'

He thought, but then shook his head again.

'No, I cannot recall.' He looked at me speculatively and said, 'What business is it of yours, if you do not object to my asking?'

'I am . . . a family friend,' I said. 'I am concerned about her. I want to make sure that she is well, and to assist her if she stands in need of it.'

He looked at me thoughtfully for some

minutes and then said, 'I think his name was Claude, Claude Rotterdam or some such thing. Not Rotterdam, but something like it. He used to live in Berkeley Square, in a rented house, I believe.'

I thanked him for the information and made enquiries at every house in Berkeley Square, but only one was for hire, and that had had an English tenant for over a year. I asked after the Frenchman in a number of clubs but I could find no one who could give me any information about such a man and I returned to my club in low spirits.

Saturday 21 December

It was a relief to dine with Leyton tonight and forget my troubles for a while. He had assembled a small party, but they were all interesting people: Mr and Mrs Carlton, an entertaining couple who were known to Leyton through his business; Sir John Middleton, who had just come into property in Devonshire, a few miles north of Exeter; the Doncasters, who were cousins of Leyton, with their two daughters; and the Prossers, with their daughters.

Leyton's wife was a pretty, lively woman, and the two of them seemed very happy together. The mood was cheerful and the conversation good-natured, ranging from family affairs — Sir John's cousin had married a widower and had had two daughters; the Prossers' oldest son had just had his first child and Mrs Carlton's sister was engaged — to the state of the East India Company.

After dinner, Miss Doncaster played the harp and her sister sang. It was a convivial evening.

At the end of it, Leyton's wife gave me several hints as to the desirability of the Misses Prosser, but Leyton turned the conversation aside, for he knows I can think of no one but Eliza.

1783

Wednesday 8 January

After several promising leads, my enquiries have led nowhere, and I am still no closer to finding Eliza. I thought that when I found the new owner of her allowance, I would find some useful information, but the allowance had already changed hands several times since she parted with it, and he had no knowledge of her.

I decided, this morning, to call upon Sanders, the man Leyton recommended to me, as I could not think of anything else to do. He seemed a reliable man with a good deal of experience in finding people, and we agreed on a fee. Now it remains to be seen if he earns it.

Friday 14 February

Alas, there has been no progress. Sanders has done all he can, and so we have parted by mutual consent.

Thursday 20 February

I dined with Leyton again this evening. He, Sir John Middleton and I are becoming fast friends. It is a relief for me to have some cheerful company, for without it I would be sunk in a continual gloom. I have resisted Sir John's good-natured efforts to find me a wife, and this evening I felt I owed him some explanation for my reluctance to marry. I hinted at an unhappy love affair and he, good fellow that he was, promised me that he would not tease me about any more young ladies.

Thursday 26 June

I ran across Parker at my club today, and we took great pleasure in discussing our lives, for we had not seen each other for years.

'I saw one of your old servants the other day,' he said. 'Dawkins. A handsome fellow, and what a size! I was always in awe of him.'

He pursed his lips and shook his head.

'He is not ill?' I asked.

'No, not that. The fact of the matter is, Brandon, he has fallen on hard times. He left your father's employ soon after you left and secured the position of butler to the Yarboroughs. He married a respectable woman who was the Yarboroughs' housekeeper, but she became ill and he gave up his position to look after her. His savings dwindled, and after her death, he was left with large debts. I am afraid to say I came across him in a sponging-house.'

I was horrified.

'Which one?' I asked.

He told me, and I resolved to go and see him as soon as I could and assist him if possible.

Friday 27 June

I went to visit Dawkins this morning. The sponging-house was a run-down building in a poor part of town, and walking through the other inmates as I searched for him was something of an ordeal. Although some were well-dressed and waiting only for friends and relatives to bring them the necessary funds to release them, others were hopeless.

I saw Dawkins at last and told him how sorry I was to find him in such circumstances. After some natural shame in being found in such a position, he was pleased to see me, and he was glad that I remembered him. I offered to pay his debts, but he was too proud to let me do so. I promised him I would try to find him a position, and I left him much happier than I had found him.

I walked back through the sponging-house, trying not to look at the wretched women and children who had been detained there, but I stumbled over the uneven floor, and as I righted myself, I caught a glimpse of the bluest eyes I had ever seen. I started, and my heart began to hammer in my chest, for I thought they were Eliza's eyes. But then I took in the woman's wasted face and bloodless lips, her emaciated frame and her scanty hair, so different from Eliza's thick tresses, and I knew that I was mistaken.

And yet her eyes, her eyes . . .

And then they turned towards me and they locked on to my own and they looked into my soul and I let out a cry, for it was Eliza, my Eliza. But in what a place! And in what a state!

And then she was in my arms and I was cradling her against my chest and she was smiling up at me and we were lost to all else, for she was my Eliza and we were together again.

'It is a dream,' she said, her eyes never leaving mine as she clutched at me with weak hands. 'But oh! What a pleasant dream.'

'No dream,' I said, rocking her in my arms as I tried not to weep. 'It is real. I am here, Eliza. At long last I have found you.'

'You came for me. I knew you would,' she said with a sigh, leaning her weight against me.

She was so fragile that I scarcely dared embrace her and I gentled my touch. Her wasted body told me what was wrong with her even before she coughed, holding her handkerchief to her mouth and taking it away covered in blood.

'You see I have consumption,' she said. 'I will not live long. But I am glad I saw you again before I died.'

'Eliza! Oh, Eliza!' I cried, burying my face in her hair. 'But I must get you out of here,' I said, recalled to the present, and the noisome place in which I had found her. Lifting her into my arms I stood up, preparing to carry her out, when she spoke.

'My debts —'

'I will pay them. I will get the money somehow, no matter how heavy they are.'

'No, James, it is no good,' she said gently. 'You must put me down. I cannot go with you, even if you pay my debts. I am not on my own. I have a daughter.'

A daughter. The words stopped me at once. A daughter. A child who should have been mine.

She turned her head and I followed the direction of her gaze, seeing a small child sleeping on a dirty pallet. She was about three years old, with Eliza's features and fair hair.

'Take care of her for me when I am gone,' she said.

'I will take care of both of you,' I promised her. I put her down nevertheless. 'Wait here a moment, there is someone I want to fetch. Dawkins, do you remember him?'

She smiled as she recalled the past.

'Yes.'

'He has fallen on hard times. I promised him I would try and find him a position, and it seems that I have just found him one. I will hire him to be your manservant. I will fetch him at once and he can help me take you to my lodgings, you and your daughter both. You will be safe there until I can secure something better for you.'

'You are very good to me,' she said.

'I love you, Eliza,' I said.

'Still?' she asked, searching my eyes.

'Yes, still.'

She gave a sigh of contentment.

'I should have been stronger,' she said. 'I should have held out against them, for I have loved only you.'

I set her down gently and went to fetch Dawkins. He was astonished when I told him that he had been in the same sponging-house as Eliza, for he thought he should have recognized her, but when he saw her so changed, he understood. I took Eliza in my arms and Dawkins carried the little girl, together with Eliza's few belongings, and having paid her debts, I hired a hackney cab and took her back to my rooms.

She was exhausted by the time we arrived, and I left her sleeping. Dawkins stayed with her whilst I engaged a nurse to take care of her as well as a maid to look after her. Then I returned to my rooms.

She was still sleeping. I sat and watched her, tracing in the lines of her ravaged face the lines of the Eliza I had known. They were one and the same, and having reconciled the past with the present, I took her hand and held it as she slept.

Monday 30 June

I have decided to let Eliza stay in my rooms as she is too ill to be moved, and I have rented a fresh set of rooms for myself. I sat beside her all day and all night, and her suffering cut me to the heart. But for her sake I did not show it. I let her talk, pouring out all her griefs: her cruel treatment at my brother's hands as he exposed her time after time to humiliating meetings with his mistresses; her feelings of hopelessness; her gratitude to her first seducer for a kind word; her flight from my brother's house; her despair when her seducer left her because she had a child; her gratitude, again, for a kind word from another man, and her life with him; her destitution when again she was abandoned; her desperation; her selling of her jewellery, then her fine clothing, then last of all her allowance; and her descent still further when she had nothing left to sell.

'And then you found me,' she said.

'I should never have gone away,' I said, my heart wrung as I looked at her. 'I thought it would make it easier for you, for both of us, but my absence left you friendless. Had I been in England, this could never have happened.'

'Let us not dwell on the past, unless it be happy, and much of it was. All of it was, until we were separated. Do you remember the morning on the lake?'

'How could I forget?'

'I think of it often. I always have. Whenever life was too painful to bear I would go there in my dreams, and be with you again. You recited poetry,' she said, smiling. 'I liked to remember it, when I was cringing from the curses of other men. It warmed me to remember that once I had been loved, and loved by such a man as you.'

'You are loved still, Eliza,' I said, my voice breaking.

'I know.'

She lifted her hand to my face, but before she could touch me, she was seized with a violent fit of coughing. I held her until it passed and she lay back, exhausted.

'I think I will sleep now,' she said.

She passed into slumber, and I was grateful for it. She was beyond pain in sleep, and a smile touched her lips, showing me her dreams were happy.

Wednesday 23 July

Eliza's daughter and I are coming to know each other. The little girl, named Eliza after her mama, is intelligent and, now that she is clean, very pretty. She loves her mama, and it brings me great joy to see them together. Eliza is never happier than when her daughter is beside her, unless it is when I recite poetry to her, for we are both transported back to a sunlit world where sorrow never entered, and where we thought we would live for ever.

Thursday 14 August

Eliza was very weak today. I took her hand as she lay in bed and said:

'If I could write the beauty of your eyes,
And in fresh numbers number all your
  graces,
The age to come would say, "This poet
  lies;
Such heavenly touches ne'er touched
  earthly faces." '

'Alas, I am not so beautiful now,' she said.
'You are to me.'

She closed her eyes, a smile upon her lips,
and I was glad to have brought her some
pleasure, for I could tell that she was sinking fast. I sat back so that my tears would
not fall on her face and I thanked God for
every precious moment she was spared to
me.

Friday 15 August
Eliza is dead. She died in my arms.
  Oh God! Eliza.

Saturday 16 August
The funeral was a quiet affair. Leyton, good
friend that he is, stood by me as I buried
her.

'Come back with me,' he said, when it was
over. 'You should not be on your own at
such a time.'

I thanked him from the bottom of my

heart, but said, 'I must get back. I have her daughter to think of now. Poor child! She has suffered a terrible loss.'

'You both have.'

'Then we will comfort each other.'

'And what will you do then?'

'I would like to keep her with me always, but I have to return to the army, for without my pay I cannot live. I mean to find a good school for her so that she can be happy.'

'I will ask Caroline if she knows of anywhere that might suit,' he said.

I thanked him and then we parted, he to go back to his wife and family, and I to go back to Eliza's daughter.

Monday 8 September

Leyton has been as good as his word, and with Caroline's help, I have found a school to take little Eliza. It is run by honest and loving people, and I am persuaded that she will be happy there.

I have recommended Dawkins to Caroline's brother, and now I must return to the Indies and rise as far as I can in my profession, for a colonel's salary will enable me to look after myself and my charge far better than a captain's pay.

1792

Thursday 14 June

As I came off duty this morning, Green sauntered up to me and said, 'Come with me if you want some sport.'

'What is going on?' I asked.

'Wait and see.'

I followed him along the dusty road, with the sun hot on my back and the scent of musk in my nostrils, until we came to a turning. He led me along a little-used path until we came to a place far away from the camp. The noise hit us first, a whispering like the sea far off, and then growing louder as we drew nearer until we could distinguish cries and then words.

'Three pounds on Cattering.'

'Five pounds on the bullock!'

We entered a crowd of men who were busy placing bets, with money changing hands at a great rate. The objects of their betting were standing at one end of a dirt track. Cattering was harnessing himself to a heavily laden cart, whilst next to him was a bullock similarly harnessed. The carts and their loads were the same, and Green said to me, 'Who's your money on, Brandon?'

I looked at the bullock and then Cattering. The bullock was stronger, I had no doubt, but I had never met a more determined man than Cattering and I knew his will to win would be stronger than the bullock's.

'My money's on Cattering,' I said, placing my bet.

Green wavered, but then said, 'The cart is too heavy for a man, even a man like Cattering. He will never move it.'

He placed his bet on the bullock.

There was some more fevered betting and then the race was on. The bullock made a good start, pulling the cart away whilst Cattering strained to start his cart moving. His muscles flexed and his sinews strained. Great veins stood out in his neck. And then the cart began to move, slowly at first, but picking up speed as he leant forward, driving his legs into the ground and pushing himself forward by main strength and sheer force of will.

He began to gain on the bullock, which had stopped to munch a blade of grass. Its driver drove it forward, but the bullock seemed to take a delight in dallying.

Cattering pulled ahead, cheered on by his friends. He had almost reached the finish line when the bullock suddenly decided it would like to move and it put on a turn of speed that drove the men into a frenzy of cheering and catcalls.

Bullock and man were neck and neck. Cattering stuck out his head, pushed with his legs, heaved with his shoulders and surged across the finish line, leaving the bullock to take second place.

'Well done, man!'

The words echoed from dozens of lips as Cattering's friends — of whom, at that moment, he had a great many — clapped him on the back. Cattering could not reply, for he was done in. Sweat ran freely down his back and face, and he drew in his breath in deep, heaving gasps. But by and by he began to recover, and by the time Green and I left, he was being carried aloft and hailed as a Titan.

'I was going to put in an order for two more bullocks to pull the guns, but I think I will use Cattering instead!' I said.

Green laughed.

'He would cost you too much. Bullocks can find their own grazing. Cattering needs solid meat.'

We walked back to our quarters, and when we arrived, I found a letter waiting for me. Green bid me adieu and I went inside, taking my letter with me. It was from Eliza. I opened it with pleasure, and saw at once that her writing was maturing, for the rounded babyish characters had given way to the more stylish hand of a young lady of twelve years old.

She told me all her news, that she was happy at school, that she and her friend Susan had been singled out by the dancing master as examples for the other girls to follow, and that her sampler had been judged the neatest in the class.

She enclosed a self-portrait for me, done in water colours. *It is the wrong way round,* she explained, *as I took it from a looking-glass, but it is otherwise very like.*

I hoped not, for the eyes were of different sizes and the mouth was distinctly crooked, but I treasured it none the less. It showed her with dark hair, which, if the colouring was to be believed, meant that she had lost her babyish fair hair and was now unlike her mother, perhaps resembling her father. I could not understand his abandoning her, for a more cheerful and charming girl it would be hard to imagine; romantic, too, like her mother, for she had discovered Shakespeare's sonnets, and told me that I must read them, for she was sure that I would like them.

I folded her letter and put it with her others, a treasured pile in my desk, then turned my attention back to my work.

It has been my solace this last nine years, and climbing the ranks to colonel has given my thoughts a positive direction, but I find lately that I am dissatisfied with it and wanting something more. But what more can there be for a man who is above thirty, and whose heart is in the grave?

Monday 9 July

I looked over the new troops this morning and was pleased to see that they looked strong and likely to survive, for the climate kills off so many men I sometimes wonder there are any left to fight.

I opened my letters when I came off duty, and I had a jolt when I saw that one of them was addressed in Catherine's handwriting. I opened her letter with some misgiving, and I discovered that Harry had been killed. He had been riding home — drunk, I supposed, though she did not say so — and he had taken a fall from his horse.

I looked at the date on the letter. It had

taken four months to reach me. Harry would be long buried, and without a son to succeed him, the Delaford estate was mine.

I sat staring in front of me, not seeing my soldier's quarters but seeing the green fields of Delaford, with the river running through them, and the walled gardens and the dove-cots and the tall windows reflecting the sunlight. I thought of the drawing room and the sound of Eliza's harp, and the ballroom and Eliza's hand in mine, and the dining room and Eliza laughing at me across the table.

I thought of my father turning me out and forbidding me the house, and Harry lolling on the sofa, saying he neither knew nor cared what had become of Eliza, and my desolation on my last visit. And I wondered, Can I go back there, or will my memories haunt me?

I folded the letter and said nothing of it to anyone, not even to Green, for I wanted to be sure of my feelings before I shared them. If I claimed my inheritance I could leave the army and offer a home to Eliza. I could give her the life of which her mother had been deprived, and in time I could see her marry a good and honourable man, some-one who would love her and would not care about the circumstances of her birth.

I thought of my Eliza, and how happy she would have been to think of her daughter at Delaford. I remembered her saying to me, in the rose garden, how much she loved the house, and I knew then that I would go home.

Tuesday 10 July

I spoke to my commanding officer, telling him that I would be leaving the army. He expressed his surprise and dismay, but, on learning that I had come into property, he congratulated me and wished me well for the future.

My fellow soldiers rejoiced at my good fortune. Only Green was downcast, but once I had invited him to stay with me the next time he was home on leave, he became more cheerful and sincerely wished me well.

And so I am to leave the Indies, which have been my home for more than a decade, and return to England. I do not know whether I am happy or apprehensive, but, whatever my feelings, I am now irrevocably set upon that path, and a few more months will find me at home.

Wednesday 5 December

This morning I visited Eliza's grave, something I have never dared to do since the terrible day I buried her. I told her of my good fortune and I promised her that I would make her daughter happy. The wind sighed, and I thought that she had heard me.

Thursday 6 December
I dined with Leyton. He is now the proud father of four children, and he was delighted to learn of my inheritance.

'This is splendid news, Brandon,' he said, as we sat over our port. 'It is about time you settled down.'

'I can afford to, now.'

'Have you been back to Delaford yet?'

'No. I have some business to attend to in London first —'

'Buying a carriage, I hope.'

I smiled. 'Yes, I mean to set myself up well. And then I want to visit Eliza.'

It was a relief to talk about her, for he is one of the few people who knows of her heritage. To the world at large she is my ward, although I am aware some people impute a closer connection, believing her to be my child, but to Leyton she is Eliza's daughter.

'It will do her good to have a settled home. Will you take her to live with you?'

'Not yet. She likes her teachers, and she has made many friends at school. I mean to have her with me in the holidays, but I am persuaded she will be happier in familiar surroundings with familiar people for the time being.'

'You must buy her a pony.'

'I intend to, and to teach her to ride.'

'And a pianoforte. Abigail has one with a sweet tone. You must come to dinner tomorrow, and I will encourage her to play for you.'

'I am relieved you have two daughters, Leyton, for at least I have someone to ask about Eliza's welfare. Otherwise I would be lost.'

'We are all lost!' he said. 'Women are incomprehensible creatures, even at so tender an age, and having two daughters has not made them any more comprehensible to me. They can be inconsolable over a ribbon that is the wrong shade of blue, but let some real tragedy befall them and they bear it like a man, indeed far better than many men I have known. But I will do my best to help.'

Wednesday 12 December

I visited Eliza at school today. She was lively and cheerful, telling me all about her studies, her masters and her friends. I told her I had inherited a house, and that I had left the army. She was excited to learn that she would be able to visit me in the holidays, and I have promised her that she can invite a friend to stay.

1793

Thursday 10 January

I was apprehensive about coming back to Delaford, but my fears were misplaced, for Delaford as my estate is very different from a Delaford ruled over by my father or brother. I have found a good manager and appointed a new housekeeper and together we are setting about restoring Delaford to its rightful condition. The house is already looking brighter, for with a new staff of maids to help her, Mrs Trent has seen to its cleaning. The main rooms are now well polished, with not a trace of dust to be found anywhere. They need new decorations, however, and I thought how Eliza would have loved to choose them!

The stables are improving. I have a hunter and a road horse for myself, and I have found a suitable pony for Eliza. It is gentle, and yet it has some spirit. She should really have learnt years ago but it is not too late, and I mean to make a horsewoman of her.

Monday 21 January
I dined with Leyton at his home and I was pleased to renew my acquaintance with Sir John Middleton.

'I cannot believe you have not met my wife, Mary, yet. You must come and stay with us at Barton, then you and she can get to know each other,' he said, in his usual warm and friendly manner.

He would not take no for an answer.

'You can meet my sons, too. Upon my soul, they are the finest boys you have ever seen. Mary and her mother agree with me. Ay, I know what you are thinking, it is a family's partiality, but you are wrong. I will prove it to you when you come and stay with us. You will be able to see for yourself.'

Leyton laughed and said that he must lay claim to the finest boys I had seen, and the two fathers argued it out, deciding in the end that there were four fine boys in the world and their names were Leyton and Middleton. I said that I would lay claim to the finest girl, and then paused, for I had not meant to mention Eliza. But the words could not be recalled, and I told Sir John about my ward, and he said she sounded a very fine girl, at which Leyton suggested we join the other fine girls, and we finished our port and rejoined the ladies in the drawing room.

Tuesday 29 January
I arrived at Barton this afternoon and was warmly greeted by Sir John and his wife. Mary was as elegant and beautiful as John claimed, and she seemed to be good natured. Her mother, Mrs Jennings, was with her, and her younger sister, Charlotte. They were all besotted with the children, who looked much like other children to me. I did not say so, however, but said they were fine, handsome boys.

'You'll be wanting a fine handsome boy of your own before long, Colonel,' said Mrs Jennings.

Her remark took me by surprise, but I soon learnt that although her conversation was vulgar, her heart was good. I was surprised to find that she was the mother to such a refined creature as Lady Middleton but I liked her none the less. True, I was disconcerted when she remarked, several times, that a fine man such as myself must have plenty of girls dangling after him, but fortunately she was too much interested in her grandchildren to talk about me for long, and returned to cooing over them.

As the ladies continued to play with the boys, Sir John took me outside and showed me over the estate. He has the same problems as I have with Delaford, and we talked over the solutions we had found, sharing ideas and experience, so that it was a very useful afternoon.

In the evening, Charlotte, who was about seventeen years old, entertained us by playing on the pianoforte, and although her performance was full of a great many stops and starts, and a great many wrong notes, her mother was delighted with her, and assured her she would break a lot of hearts when she was not very much older. Charlotte giggled, and Mary pretended that she had not heard them.

'Do you intend to live at Delaford, or do you intend to live in London?' Mary asked me politely as we sat in the drawing room.

'At Delaford,' I said. 'It is not ready for visitors yet, but I hope that, before very long, you will join me there.'

'Thank you, we would like that,' said Mary.

'Oh, yes!' said Mrs Jennings. 'We always like to see a fine place, don't we, Charlotte? Are there any young men in the neighbourhood, Colonel? A nice young baronet with ten thousand a year? Or a knight, perhaps?

For I would not mind parting with my Charlotte if a personable young man was to offer for her.'

'Oh, Mama!' said Charlotte.

'I do not think Charlotte is old enough to be worrying about such things yet,' said Mary.

'Lawks! Mary. Fine young men don't grow on trees. We have to start looking about us, don't we, Charlotte? Otherwise you'll be running off with the dancing master. Ay, miss, you may well look sly, but I've seen him, and a better calf I never saw, and I know what the sight of a fine calf does to a young girl.'

'Mama, you will put me to the blush!'

'A nice young man with a few hundred acres, that's all I want for my girl, just like I found for her sister.'

Sir John bore this remark good-naturedly, but Mary was less pleased. She proposed whist, and whilst she sat out, Sir John, I, Mrs Jennings and Charlotte made up a four. The play was poor, for Mrs Jennings and her daughter could not keep their minds on the cards, but at least I was not asked more than four or five times when I intended to marry.

Monday 11 March

Delaford is thriving. The threadbare carpets have been replaced, the worn furniture has been taken to the attics, and fresh flowers fill every room. The broken fences have been mended, the lake has been cleaned, and the barns have been rebuilt. I am pleased that, at last, I can repay the hospitality of Leyton and Sir John, and I have invited them, with their families, to visit me in a month's time.

Tuesday 26 March

I decided not to alert Eliza's school to my proposed visit, so that I could see it in its natural state, and I was pleased to see how healthy the children looked as I arrived, and how well they were treated by their teachers.

Miss Grayshott welcomed me cordially and agreed to me taking Eliza out of school for two weeks.

'It will be a treat for her. We were all delighted to hear you had come into property. Eliza is excited about her pony. She has talked of nothing else since you wrote to her about it.'

At this moment Eliza, who had been summoned to the headmistress's sitting room, made her appearance. She was looking well and happy, and she greeted me with a warm smile. We made our goodbyes, and then we were off. I was glad that Leyton had warned me to hire a maid for Eliza, for I would not have thought of it myself, and I would have been dismayed when we stopped for the night, for only then would I have realized my omission.

Wednesday 27 March
Eliza's excitement as we reached Delaford was everything that I could have wished for, and after running round the house, looking at the room where Mama had sat or slept or eaten her dinner, she at last collapsed in exhaustion. She soon revived, however, and a hot meal replenished her energy, so that she was ready to go out and look at the grounds afterwards.

As we went down to the lake, she disconcerted me by asking, 'Are you my father?'

'No,' I said.

'Oh. Only Melissa Stainbridge said that you were.'

'Melissa Stainbridge is a very pert young lady and she is wrong,' I replied.

'But you were in love with Mama?' Eliza asked.

'Yes,' I agreed, though I wondered how she knew.

'I remember very little of her, only that she was sad and that she coughed a lot. And then you came and took us out of the cold house and took us to your apartments and Mama said to me that we would be safe, and we would have food to eat because you would look after us. She said that you had been going to marry her but your father prevented it, and then you decided to run away together but her maid betrayed you, but she always knew you would find her, one day.'

I was surprised that she remembered so much, for she had been very young at the time, but the circumstances had been unusual and it was evident that they had made a deep impression on her.

'That is true,' I said. 'However, it is not polite to talk of such things. It is all right between the two of us, but it is better not to speak of it in public.'

'Oh.' She thought for a moment and then said, 'Why not?'

I did not know how to answer her, and I realized that, in the years ahead, she would have a great many questions that I could not answer. Although school was catering for many of her needs, it was not able to cater for them all, and I thought that she would need a companion before very long, some kindly, motherly woman who would explain to her the ways of the world and teach her how to go on. If she had been a boy, I could have done it myself, but I was all at sea with young ladies.

'That is just the way it is,' I said.

'Oh.'

She fell silent, but soon she was running down to the lake and enjoying herself again, an odd mixture of little girl and young lady as she hovered between the two worlds.

We walked until she was tired and then returned to the house, where she joined me for dinner before retiring.

I liked the sound of her footsteps going upstairs and knowing that she was in the house, and I thought again of her mother, and how she would be pleased to know that her daughter was at Delaford.

Thursday 28 March

Eliza has been introduced to her pony and after a little apprehension she was ready to feed it a carrot. She sprang back when she felt the animal's lips touching her hand, but soon stepped forward again and laughed.

'It tickles,' she said.

'She's too old to be learning,' said Jacobs, who I am sure must be a hundred, for I remember him sitting me on my first pony, and he appeared to be at least seventy then.

But she proved him wrong, mounting with courage and soon gaining confidence as she walked around the stable yard.

'Ah, just like her mother, a natural horsewoman,' said Jacobs, shamelessly changing tack as he saw that she had the makings of a fine horsewoman. 'I always said she'd take to it. It's in the blood.'

Wednesday 10 April
I returned Eliza to her school today and I was pleased to see that she was greeted cheerfully by the other girls. I am lucky that she is so happy.

Friday 12 April
The Middletons arrived this afternoon, together with Mrs Jennings. She is a strange mixture of a good heart, a long tongue and an ear for gossip. She soon learnt from one of the maids that a little girl had been staying with me.

'A pretty little thing by all accounts,' she said.

'That was my ward,' I told her.

'Your ward, eh, Colonel? My, but you're a sly one. Well, well, we'll say no more about it.'

She was not as good as her word, however,

for she continued to talk about wards, secret children and the wrong side of the blanket for the rest of the evening. Her daughter ignored her, being too well-bred to understand what her mother was making plain. Sir John, as always, pretended not to hear. It is a gift he has cultivated, and one which, I am sure, is necessary, when he spends much time with his good-hearted mother-in-law.

Saturday 13 April

I took a great delight in showing my guests around Delaford. Leyton was much impressed and said I had done well for myself. He said he would like to buy some small place in the country, and we talked about suitable properties in the neighbourhood, although he felt it would probably be too far from town. Sir John was impressed with the improvements I had made to the estate.

This evening, I invited some of my neighbours to dine, for I knew that Sir John liked company, and we had a convivial evening.

'Lord, Colonel, how you did set all the maidens in a flutter!' said Mrs Jennings, as the last of my guests left the house. 'You'll have to choose one of them, so better make it sooner rather than later, before you break too many hearts!'

I borrowed Sir John's habit and, after smiling politely, did not hear her.

Friday 19 April

Charlotte Jennings joined us for dinner this evening, as she was on her way to visit a friend and had to pass through the neighbourhood.

Mrs Jennings, who had gone to meet her from the stage, lost no time in saying that Charlotte had acquired a collection of beaux on her journey.

Charlotte, growing more and more like her mother, replied, 'Oh, Mama, you make me laugh! As if Mr Walstone had eyes for me, and me still in the schoolroom.'

'Not for much longer, eh, miss?' asked Sir John. 'What is it, another month or two and then you'll be free of the schoolroom, and coming out, if I do not miss my guess.'

'And married soon after, I'll warrant,' said Mrs Jennings. 'My girls are beauties, though I say so myself. Just look at Mary.'

Mary contrived to busy herself with the tea things.

'And now there's Charlotte blossoming before my very eyes. I shall have trouble fighting all the men off. Your little ward will not be in the schoolroom much longer, either, Colonel. They grow up so quickly.

One minute they're crawling round on all fours, the next minute they're getting married! I declare it only seems a week ago since Mary was in her cradle.'

She ran on in similar vein, and as she did so, I thought that, although it was some years away, I would need some advice on finding a good woman to live with Eliza. I did not disturb Mrs Jennings, but I asked Leyton's wife when I had her alone for a time, and she gave me some sensible guidance, for which I was very grateful. She also said that I could call on her for assistance at any time, and I am persuaded I will take her at her word when the time comes.

1796

Tuesday 5 January

I laughed at Mrs Jennings three years ago for saying that children grow up very quickly, but Eliza is growing up before my eyes. She has gone to Bath with a school friend, Susan Southey, whose father, a man I know to be respectable, is visiting the town in order to take the waters. I am persuaded that she will enjoy herself, for bonnets seem to form the chief part of her conversation and there are plenty of bonnets in Bath!

I have decided to buy her a new horse. She will need something better than her pony when she joins me for Easter.

Tuesday 19 January

I had a letter from Eliza this morning, telling me all her news.

I have never seen so many shops, *she wrote.* Susan needs a new bonnet and her maid is taking us to the milliners this afternoon, then we are going to the circulating library. There are some very fine books on history to be found there.

I smiled at the notion of her carrying home a pile of books on history. If she shared her mother's tastes, she would be carrying home a pile of books on poetry, or the latest romances!

Thursday 4 February
Eliza has disappeared! Oh God, where is she?

Southey's letter reached me this morning, and couched in roundabout terms, he told me that Eliza had vanished. I was immediately alarmed and I set off for Bath at once.

Southey, looking very frail, could tell me nothing except that Eliza and Susan had gone out walking on Tuesday and that they had become separated.

'Susan did all she could to find her friend but at last she had to return home alone,' he said. 'She hoped to find Eliza waiting for her, but alas! that was not the case. We kept expecting her at any minute, but when it grew dark and there was still no sign of her, I felt I ought to write to you.'

'And did you not send the servants out to look for her?' I enquired.

'I am a sick man, I cannot think of everything,' he said peevishly. 'If I had known what sort of girl Eliza was, I would not have invited her to keep Susan company.'

I fought hard to master my temper, for he was ill, confined to his chair. I saw that he could tell me no more and so I said, 'Might I speak to Susan?'

'She can tell you nothing. Poor Susan is as much in the dark as I am.'

But I was determined, and Susan was brought into the room. I questioned her closely, and grew cold at what I heard, for it became clear that, because of her father's ill health, the girls had been free to go out without an adequate chaperon. Susan's maid was meant to go with them, but it soon became clear that she had a sweetheart, and that she was in the habit of allowing the girls to range over the town and make what acquaintance they chose whilst she conducted her own dalliance.

'That was very wrong of her,' said Mr Southey.

I pressed Susan, but she declared that she knew no more: that she and Eliza had gone out for a walk, that her maid had stopped to speak to her sweetheart, that Eliza and Susan had walked on together, that they had been separated in a crowd, and that Susan had had to return home alone.

As she spoke, I was convinced that she was lying. There was an air of obstinate and ill-judged secrecy about her. She kept giving me sly looks, to see if I believed her, and I was convinced that, at the very least, she knew more than she was saying. But question her as I might, she would not admit to knowing what had happened.

I left the house at last, disgusted with Susan, and set about conducting my own enquiries, but I could find no trace of Eliza.

I returned, at last, to the inn, where I wrote to Sanders, telling him that I needed his help, and then I set myself to thinking.

Either Eliza was ill, or she had been abducted, or she had run away with some-one. The more I thought about it, the more I thought that the last of these was the most likely, for only a love affair could have caused Susan to remain silent.

But why had Eliza run away? If she had met a man, a good man, I would not have stood in her way, even though she was only sixteen. My spirits sank. She had not met a good man. A good man would not have run off with her. She had met a scoundrel. And now she was at his mercy.

I thought hard. Where would he have taken her? But my spirits sank again, for he could have taken her anywhere.

Then I realized that he must have had some sort of conveyance. I asked again at the inn, and then at all the stables in Bath, but I discovered nothing.

Then he must have had his own carriage, which meant that he was a man of means. And he had taken her, for what purpose? To set up as his mistress? Surely Eliza would never have consented to such a thing. But with no mother to guide her . . . and then I grew cold, for I thought of another possibility: Eliza, knowing that her mother and I had planned to elope, would have been an easy target for a plausible villain. If he had said that he loved her and if he had promised to take her to Gretna Green . . .

But perhaps he had. Perhaps I was worrying precipitately. Perhaps a letter would arrive in the next few days explaining everything.

I clung to the hope, the better to sleep, for I needed sleep in order to be able to search again, refreshed, on the morrow.

Friday 12 February
It is more than a week now since Eliza dis-

appeared and still no news. Surely she would have written to me if she was married? But she might be enjoying herself and her new life too much to think of me. She might write in another week.

I must hope so, for I have been able to discover nothing and Sanders has had no better luck. I mean to keep searching, and I have told him he must do the same.

Saturday 12 March
It is over a month now since Eliza disappeared and there is still no news. I dread to think what might have happened to her. If she was alive, surely she would have written to me? She would want my congratulations if she was married, or my help if she was not. Surely I should have heard something?

Friday 26 August
I met Sanders in London, and my hopes were dashed again as he told me he had no news. In seven months I have discovered no trace of her.

I retired at last to my club, where I met Sir John Middleton. He greeted me cheerfully, for I had not told him about Eliza.

'You must come to visit us next month, Brandon,' he said. 'We have not seen you at

Barton for months.'

I was glad to talk to him, for his good cheer lifted me out of my own gloomy thoughts, and I accepted his invitation with gratitude.

'Good, good. We will make you very welcome, and we will be able to offer you some new company. A relative of mine, Mrs Dashwood, who has recently been widowed, has come to live at Barton Cottage with her daughters. The cottage is only small, but it is capable of improvement, and if the ladies like it, I will alter it according to their taste.'

'You do not have to introduce me to new company in order to induce me to visit,' I said. 'I am very happy with the company I always find at Barton.'

'But you will not object to finding some new faces when they are there,' he said jovially. 'Four ladies! A mother and three daughters, and lucky for me that it is so, for a mother and three sons would have not been to my taste. The sons might have been sportsmen, and if so, I would have been obliged to offer them my game. And if they were not sportsmen, it would almost have been worse, for I would have found precious little to talk to them about. But it is different with ladies. Ladies never take a man's game! I saw them once, many years ago, pretty little things, and I believe they are held to be very handsome now that they are grown.'

'I am sure they are,' I said as we went into the dining room.

'It is about time you married, Brandon. Yes, I know you have had your share of unhappiness, but that is in the past. You need to look to the future. You are still young. A wife is just what you need.'

'I have no intention of marrying,' I said to him shortly, and then I was sorry for my bad manners, for he only wanted to help.

'Well, you know best,' he said.

We talked of other things as we ate: of his family and the political situation, of the price of corn and new ideas in farming; and then we parted, he to go back to Barton and I to return to my rooms.

And now my thoughts are once again with Eliza. That she has run off with someone I am sure. As long as she is happy, that is all I ask. But why does she not write to me?

Monday 5 September
I arrived at Barton Court today and I was glad to be among friends.

After admiring the family and greeting Mary, I walked down to Barton Cottage with Sir John. He was eager to show it to me, and to point out what he had thought of doing for the Dashwoods' comfort.

The day was fine and the walk was a good distance, not so close that the inhabitants of each house would be forced into constant company, but not so far that walking between the two residences was difficult.

We came to the cottage at last, and I was surprised at its appearance, for it looked more like a house than a cottage. It was regular in shape and the roof was tiled, whilst there was a small green court in the front with a wicket-gate leading into it. There was not a trace of thatch or honeysuckle anywhere.

'Well, what do you think?' he asked as we stopped at the gate.

I cast my eyes over it and saw that it was in a good state of repair. The roof was sound and the paint on the door and windows was new.

'From the outside, it looks well enough,' I said.

'Come and see it inside.'

We went in. A narrow passage led directly through the house into the garden behind. On each side of the entrance was a sitting room, about sixteen feet square, and beyond them were the offices and the stairs. Four bedrooms and two garrets formed the rest of the house. It had not been built many years and was very convenient in its arrangement.

'The situation is good,' said Sir John.

He looked out of the window at the high hills which rose immediately behind and at no great distance on each side. Some of them were open downs, the others were cultivated and woody. I went to join him at the window and saw the village of Barton nestling against one of the hills.

'The prospect in the front is even more extensive,' he said, moving to a different window. It commanded the whole of the valley, and reached into the country beyond. 'Well, what do you think. Will they like it?'

'I am sure they will,' I said, thinking that they were fortunate to have found such a home, and such a good neighbour and relative as Sir John.

'Ay, it will do.'

We walked back to the house and found that the children were downstairs with their nurse. John was well grown for six, whilst William was not far behind him, and Anna-Maria was growing into a pretty girl. Mary indulged them and Sir John played with them until they began to grow fractious, whereupon their nurse took them upstairs again.

'I tell you, Brandon, you should be setting up your nursery,' he said to me.

'I hope they play,' said Mary, ignoring him. 'I am very musical, and if the Misses Dashwood choose to entertain us, I shall not say them nay.'

Tuesday 6 September

'I think I will just go down to the cottage and see if the Dashwoods have arrived,' said Sir John as he pushed his chair back from the breakfast table this morning.

'You will do no such thing,' said Mary. 'It is far too early for them to have arrived, and even if they have, the last thing Mrs Dashwood will want is a visitor. She will have enough to do without a stranger to take care of.'

'A stranger?' he asked, astonished.

'A stranger, for that is what you must be to begin with. She will want to set her house in order before she receives guests.'

Sir John hummed and hawed but at last he gave way and said that he supposed he could wait until tomorrow to see them, but that Mary must take the blame if they felt themselves slighted.

I suggested we go for a ride, and he was happy to fall in with the suggestion, for he likes to be doing something.

'What do you make of John Dashwood?' he asked me, as we rode out to the hills. 'Mrs Dashwood's stepson, you know, and half brother to the girls. Inherited the family home when his father died but made no provision for his father's second wife and left her to the mercy of a distant relative. Seems bad to me.'

It seemed bad to me, too, but I said only, 'We know nothing of the circumstances.'

'Ay, you are right, though what could prevent a son doing right by his father's wife I do not know. Family is family, and a man should take care of his own. Though lucky for me he did not, eh, Brandon? It will do us good to have some new faces to look at.'

Wednesday 7 September

Sir John lost no time in looking at his new faces. As soon as he had finished breakfast, he said, 'No one can object to my calling on my cousins this morning, I am sure. I am determined to walk down to the cottage and greet them. The girls will not remember me, for they were very small when last I visited them, but Mrs Dashwood will know me. I am looking forward to seeing them all again. Will you come with me, Mary?'

'Certainly not. I do not believe Mrs Dashwood will be ready for such a call. But pray tell her I will call on her as soon as it is convenient for her to receive me,' said Mary.

He left, intent on making the new arrivals welcome, and I went out with the dogs, returning to find that Sir John was in the drawing room, regaling Mary with an account of his visit.

'Charming people,' he said, 'and what handsome girls! The youngest is only thirteen, but the other two are older and are both out. What manners! And what pretty faces! Oh, it will do us good to have them about the place. We will find them husbands, eh, Mary? And then we will have a wedding or two to look forward to. I have promised to send them my newspaper every day, and to convey their letters to the post for them.'

'Did Mrs Dashwood say when she would be receiving?' asked Mary, ignoring most of his speech.

'She was touched by your message, my love, and said she would be happy to welcome you at any time.'

'Then I will go tomorrow,' said Mary. 'I do not wish to be backward in showing them any courtesy, for they have suffered a grievous loss. I wish to make them welcome here. I think I might take the children with me. They cannot help but be cheered by the sight of my two splendid boys and my beautiful little girl.'

Thursday 8 September
Sir John and Mary visited the cottage today. In the end they took little John with them and left the two younger children behind. The visit went well, and they have invited the Dashwoods to dine with us tomorrow.

Friday 9 September
Sir John spent the morning visiting the neighbouring families in the hope of procuring some addition to our society this evening, but it was a moonlit night and everyone was already engaged.

'I never thought I would consider it unlucky to be giving a dinner on a moonlit night, but so it is, for if it were dark, then there would be plenty of families sitting at home.'

'And therefore not willing to visit us,' said Mary.

'What? Not willing to come such a short step, and with the offer of a carriage being sent for them if necessary? But at least your mother is coming,' he said. 'She will be here before the Dashwoods arrive —'

'As long as she has a tolerable journey,' Mary put in.

'And will cheer the young ladies. She will

be able to tease them about their beaux!' he said with a laugh. 'Young ladies always like to be teased about their beaux.'

I thought of Mrs Jennings, with her jokes and laughter and vulgar humour, and I wondered what the Dashwoods would make of her.

The post arriving at that moment, I saw that I had a letter from Sanders. I excused myself and retired to my room where I opened it eagerly, but Sanders had no news. I put my disappointment aside as best I could, but I was in no mood for company, and when the Dashwoods arrived, I was silent and grave.

My silence was not noticed, however, for Sir John and Mrs Jennings were boisterous enough, with Sir John asking his cousins how they liked the cottage and Mrs Jennings teasing the Misses Dashwood about the beaux they had left behind.

Miss Marianne was asked to sing after dinner, and the music roused me from my melancholy thoughts. I turned to look at her, and as I watched her, I was struck by how difficult the last few months must have been for her. She had lost her father; after which she had had to leave her home, travelling across the country to live in a small cottage, when she was used to a mansion house. She had found herself in a strange place with strange people, far from her friends, far from everything, save her family, that she knew and loved. And I was aware of all this because it was all going into her music. Her feelings of loss and heartbreak were pouring out of her through her voice and her fingers.

I could not take my eyes away from her. The emotion on her face was now light and now shade, now sadness and now regret; and the room faded and I saw nothing but Marianne until the song had finished.

I came to myself, to find that the others were chattering, and I thought, How can they chatter when such music is being played?

I walked over to the piano, and as Miss Marianne was about to leave the piano stool, I said, 'Will you play this?'

'Gladly,' she said.

I opened the music and she settled herself again, resting her hands over the keys, and then began to play. I stood by the piano, the better to listen to her, and I turned her music for her when she needed it.

There was a pause when the song finished, and I was ashamed to find that there was no applause, for the song had certainly deserved it. Then Mary, remembering her duties as hostess, said how delightful it had been and asked Miss Marianne to play 'The Willow.' Miss Marianne and I exchanged surprised glances, for she had just played that very song.

I pulled another piece of music forward and asked her if she would not sing that one instead.

When she had finished, the others did not even look up from their conversations, and I said, 'A very pretty song.'

'Pretty?' she asked me, turning towards me and arching her eyebrows.

'You do not find it so?' I asked her.

'No, I do not,' she said, and as she continued her voice became passionate: 'Haunting, yes; lyrical and wistful; but *pretty,* no.'

I was surprised, for she was very forthright for someone so young, and my eyes followed her as she returned to sit beside her sister.

'Well, Colonel, and what do you think of Miss Marianne?' asked Mrs Jennings when the Dashwoods had gone. 'You seemed mightily taken with her.'

'She is charming,' I said.

'Charming? Ay, that she is, and pretty, too. Just the match for a man such as yourself, a fine bachelor with a good bit of property.'

'I scarcely know the lady,' I returned. 'Besides, she is too young for me.'

161

'Tush! What's a few years in a marriage? Nothing at all. A rich man like you, Colonel, should be married, and who better than Miss Marianne? You could listen to her play the pianoforte every night! Ay, I saw you attending to her, and what more proof of love could there be than that?'

'I like music,' I said.

'But not as much as you like Miss Marianne, eh, Colonel?' she said.

I could do nothing to curb her, for with her own two daughters married, she has nothing better to do than to try and arrange a marriage for everyone else.

Monday 12 September

We dined with the Dashwoods at the cottage, and I took Miss Marianne in to dinner. I wondered if I would be disappointed in her, if the extraordinary qualities I had found in her music and the forthright opinions it had called forth, would not be found elsewhere; but to my pleasure I found her to be just as interesting when we were discussing other subjects.

She was generous in her praise of her sister, amiable in her attentions to her mother, and interesting in general conversation, displaying a lively mind and a quick intelligence, as well as a great degree of sensibility.

She spoke of the home she had left behind, the woods and gardens, the walks and the view, and as she talked about it, I saw it all before me, with its fine prospects and its sheltered groves.

'It must have been difficult for you to leave it, but you find your new home some consolation, I hope?' I asked her.

'What can console me for the loss of such a home, where every tree was known to me?' she asked. 'But we can certainly never thank Sir John enough for his kindness. My sister-in-law's behaviour made it impossible for us to remain at Norland, and we had to live somewhere. If Sir John had not offered us a home, I do not know what we would have done, for we could find nothing in the neighbourhood of Norland to suit us. It must have been difficult for us to live there in any case, for we would have had Norland before us always, and yet we would not have been able to call it home.'

As she spoke, I was reminded of Eliza, for Eliza, too, had dearly loved her home.

My thoughts went from Eliza to her daughter, and as the ladies withdrew, I fell silent. I knew I should rouse myself, that it was unbecoming of me to be so morose, that I should help Sir John to entertain his guests, but I could not shake off the gloom that had taken hold of me and I spoke no more.

Tuesday 13 September

I was hoping to take Miss Marianne in to dinner at the Park, but instead I found myself escorting her sister, a sensible young woman with a fund of interesting conversation. I think I entertained her, even though my attention kept drifting to Miss Marianne.

'You will be having visitors of your own before long, now that you have arranged the cottage to your own satisfaction,' said Sir John to Mrs Dashwood. 'You must be wanting to see your friends.'

'Yes, indeed. We are hoping that one of our friends, Mr Edward Ferrars, will soon honour us with a visit. He has an open invitation,' she said.

'Ferrars? Ferrars? Can't say I know the name.'

'He is the brother of our sister-in-law,' said Miss Marianne. 'He is a fine young man, full of sense and goodness, and loved by us all.'

'Does he hunt?' asked Sir John.

Miss Marianne could give him no particulars, and Sir John remarked that he hoped that Ferrars did not enjoy the sport, for then he would be very glad to see him.

Miss Marianne was again prevailed upon to play, but Sir John talked all the way through her performance; Mary upbraided him, saying, 'My dear John, how can you talk when we are being so entertained? I do not understand how anyone can be distracted from music.' However, she herself was distracted a minute later by her children, saying, 'No, William, do not plague your brother. I am sure he does not want his hair pulled. No, my love, he does not.' Four-year-old William argued, thinking it a huge joke, whilst Mrs Jennings declared, 'There's nothing I like better than a good tune,' and kept the beat, out of time, with her fan.

Miss Marianne persevered against this lack of attention for as long as she could and then left the pianoforte, out of spirits. I was about to go over to her and compliment her on her taste when Sir John distracted us all by saying that we must get up a picnic whilst the weather held.

Miss Marianne's spirits were at once restored.

'Oh, yes, Sir John, that would be delightful,' she said. 'I am sure there are some notable beauty spots hereabouts, and

I would relish the opportunity of seeing them. There is so much of Devonshire I have to discover, and I would like to begin. Mama?'

'It is very kind of you, Sir John,' said Mrs Dashwood with a smile. 'We would like it very much.'

'Good, good, then that's settled. We'll get up quite a party, with the Careys, the Raistricks, the Kellys and one or two other families, and have a high time of it.'

A date was set for Saturday.

Saturday 17 September

A fine day for our picnic. We met in front of the house and set out at about ten o'clock. I rode beside Sir John's carriage and as I did so I could not help admiring Miss Marianne. Her face was truly lovely, with a brown skin, tanned by the summer sun, and a brilliant complexion. Her features were regular, her smile was sweet and attractive, and her eyes were dark. It was not their colour which attracted me, however, but the life in them, for they contained a spirit and an eagerness which reminded me of my true self, the self that saw the pleasure in life, the self that I had lost when I lost Eliza.

'You have a comfortable carriage,' said Mrs Dashwood, as Sir John and I rode along by its side. She was sitting facing forwards, with her parasol held over her head.

'Ay, and one I wish you would borrow so that you could mix more in the neighbourhood. It is always at your disposal, and there are any number of families who would be pleased to see you. They are gentlefolk, all, and I am persuaded they will make up to you for the friends you have left behind. You must ask for the carriage any time you want it.'

'Thank you, you are very good, but we must not presume too much on your hospitality,' she said, politely but firmly, and I realized that she did not want to be too far beholden to Sir John; she was a woman who liked her independence. 'Besides, there are plenty of families in walking distance of the cottage.'

'And I believe we have met them all, save the family who lives in the house along the valley,' said Miss Marianne. 'Do you know the one I mean? The ancient mansion house about a mile and a half from the cottage. Margaret and I are planning to visit it the next time we walk in that direction. Do you know who lives there?'

Her sister, Margaret, who, at thirteen, had been too young to join us for dinner, was excited to be joining us for the picnic. She added her own eager enquiry as to the inhabitant of the house.

'Oh, yes, we want to know the name of the house and to find out who lives there,' she said.

'That would be Allenham,' said Sir John. 'Mrs Smith lives there.'

'Mrs Smith? Does she have any children?' asked Miss Marianne.

'No, she is elderly. She keeps to her house; she is too infirm to mix with the world.'

'Then I believe we now know all our neighbours, or all those who are well enough to go into company,' said Miss Dashwood.

We reached the picnic spot in little more than an hour. The carriages rolled to a halt and we assembled on a flat stretch of grass about halfway up the hill.

'Can we not go to the top?' asked Miss Marianne.

'It is too steep for the carriages, but we can walk, if you have a mind,' said Sir John.

Some of the older people chose to remain where they were but the rest of us began to climb the hill. Margaret ran ahead, frolicking from one side to the other and climbing the boulders that lay scattered about, until at last we reached the summit.

'Was this not worth the climb?' asked Miss

Marianne, as she gazed rapturously at the view, looking across the rolling downs to a glimmer of blue on the horizon, the sea. She began to murmur:

'This sceptred isle,
This earth of majesty, this seat of Mars,
This other Eden, demi-paradise,
This fortress built by Nature for herself,
Against infection, and the hand of war
This happy breed of men, this little world,
This precious stone, set in the silver sea,
Which serves it in the office of a wall,
Or as a moat defensive to a house,
Against the envy of less happier lands,
This blessed plot, this earth, this realm,
    this England.

'And it is still England, though I am so far from home,' she concluded in a low voice.

There were murmurs of approval and I became aware of my surroundings once more, for I had been carried away by her poetry. There had been a strength and a vigour about her voice that had made the words, still echoing in my ears, seem fresh and new.

We strolled around the summit until the wind rose and began to blow cold, then the others set off down the hill. Miss Marianne lingered, however, turning to face in the direction of Norland whilst the wind threatened to rip the hat from her head.

'Blow, blow, thou winter wind,
Thou art not so unkind
As man's ingratitude.'

Her words were heartfelt, and I knew where her thoughts were tending. I wanted to speak to her and to bring her some heart's ease, if I could, for I could tell that her feelings were both strong and painful.

'It hurt you when your brother failed to provide for you,' I said.

It was all she needed, and her thoughts came pouring out of her.

'He promised our father on his deathbed that he would look after us, and yet he did nothing to help us. He and his wife arrived as soon as the funeral was over, without even giving Mama any notice of their arrival. I can still remember the look on her face when the carriage rolled up to the house and she realized that they had come to haunt us in our grief. They established themselves in the house and behaved as though it belonged to them, as though we were nothing but guests, and unwelcome guests at that. Poor Mama! How she suffered. I was angry, but Elinor said that I must hide my feelings, that Fanny and John had done nothing wrong, that it was their house from the moment my father died, and that they had a right to move in as soon as they pleased. But courtesy, common courtesy, should have prevented them from taking over with such speed and reducing my mother to the state of being a visitor in her own home!' she broke out. 'Poor Mama was so hurt by Fanny's insensitivity that she would have quit the house at once, but my sister Elinor — my *sensible* sister — counselled against it.'

'Perhaps she did not want a breach with your brother?' I suggested.

'You are right, but what price did she pay? Putting on a false face, and expecting me to put on a false face also. For my own part I was ready to leave the house at once, to save Mama from such cruelty, even though it would have hurt me terribly to leave without saying goodbye to all the places that I loved: the stream where it met the river, *dimpling all the way,* the corner of the walled garden, *best garden of the world.* And yet I would have left them all at once if Mama had asked me to.'

She spoke with passion, and I was struck by her words, because I saw that her interest in poetry was not that of the dreamer; no, for she wanted to pull the poetry into the real world rather than turning the real world into a poem.

I found myself growing more and more intrigued by her, for I had never come across that blend of sensibility and strength in a woman before.

'You think me very impolite, I dare say, for speaking my mind,' she continued, looking at me defiantly. 'I have erred against every commonplace notion of decorum, I am well aware of it. I should have said that my brother John is a fine man and that his wife Fanny is a beautiful and accomplished woman. I should have spoken of their dear little boy and said how much he had grown. I am sorry to disappoint you, Colonel, but I disdain such spiritless deceit.'

And then, before I had time to reply, she called to her sister, 'Come, Margaret, let us run down the hill!'

And the two of them were off, fleet of foot, racing towards the picnic spot with the wind in their faces and their gossamer dresses blowing around their ankles.

But as I watched her go, I thought that she had wronged me when she had said that I wanted her to speak of commonplaces, for that is something I abhor. Indeed, one of the things that I liked about being in the army was that the men spoke their minds, and that, therefore, I quickly gained a knowledge of character that has stood me in good stead ever since.

But women . . . I wish I understood them half so well.

For the most part they are so well bred that it is impossible to find out if they have any thoughts and feelings at all, let alone to find out what those thoughts and feelings might be.

Not so with Miss Marianne, who is as open and as honest as the day; squally in temperament, now stormy, now shining; and who interests me more than any woman I have met since Eliza.

I followed her to the picnic site. About halfway down I came across Miss Carey, who was doing something with the lace of her shoe. As I approached, she rose and said, 'My lace has broken, Colonel, would you offer me your arm.'

'Willingly,' I said.

But as I gave it to her, I was struck with the difference between her and Miss Marianne, for I suspected that her broken lace was a ruse. It would have been disdained by Miss Marianne, for if she had wanted to walk down the hill with me, she would no doubt have said so and scandalized the entire party!

We reached the picnic spot. It was sheltered from the wind, and a milder air prevailed.

Mrs Jennings gave us a knowing look as we joined her on one of the rugs, and when the picnic was over, she called me a sly one and said that Miss Marianne had better look sharp lest Miss Carey should steal her beau.

Miss Marianne, overhearing her, glanced at me, and all of a sudden I saw the disadvantages of total honesty, for, by her look, it was clear that she did not know whether to reprimand Mrs Jennings for her impertinence or laugh at her for her absurdity.

Alas for my pride! The disparity in age might not trouble Mrs Jennings, but it was obvious that it troubled Miss Marianne; indeed, that it rendered the idea of a connexion between us ridiculous in her eyes.

Perhaps, when she has grown up a little, she will not see it as such a disadvantage, for despite my protestations I find myself increasingly attracted to her. She has a vitality that has aroused my interest in life again.

Sunday 18 September
'Well, Colonel, have you decided which one it is to be?' asked Mrs Jennings good-

naturedly this morning as we returned from church. 'Miss Marianne or Miss Carey?'

'I have no intention of marrying,' I said, to silence her.

'Intention? Intention? Of course you have no intention, no man ever does. Mr Palmer had no intention of marrying my Charlotte until I put it to him. "Wouldn't you like a pretty little thing like that for a wife?" I asked him, and he had to admit that he would.'

'Ah, yes, Sir John told me Charlotte was married. I congratulate you.'

'Never a better man was there than Mr Palmer, unless it is Sir John,' she said with satisfaction.

I was glad to have diverted her and, the children entering the room at the moment, I was left in peace.

Tuesday 20 September

I declined to accompany Sir John on his walk this morning, for I had some letters to write, but when he returned he had something to tell.

'I called in at the cottage on my way home,' he said.

'And how are the Misses Dashwood?' asked Mrs Jennings, with a knowing glance at me. 'Was Miss Marianne at the pianoforte, practising for the Colonel? I tease her about it often and often. "What! Are you setting your cap at him? And a good thing, too, for he is worth winning!" Ah, yes, Colonel, you are in luck there!'

'Not a bit of it,' said Sir John. 'You have missed your chance, Brandon. Miss Marianne has another beau now.'

He told us that she had been out for a walk with her younger sister when it had come on to rain. Running down the hill to get home, she had fallen and sprained her ankle, and a passing gentleman had rendered her his assistance by carrying her home.

'What a pity it didn't happen yesterday. You were out in the rain then, Colonel. I distinctly remember you coming in from your ride with your hair all soaking wet. If you had only gone out this morning instead of writing letters, it could have been you carrying her home!' said Mrs Jennings to me. 'But you were too slow!' She turned to Sir John. 'What is his name? I must know who to tease her about the next time she dines here, for if there is one thing a young lady loves, it is being teased about her beaux!'

I thought that she had entirely misjudged Miss Marianne, and said so, but she only laughed and said, 'Tush! Colonel, and what do you know about it? But never fear, we will find you another wife. Oh, yes, one will come along, I have no doubt of it, one even handsomer than Miss Marianne. A man of your fortune was not meant to be single.'

'You will never guess who it was,' said Sir John, eager to impart his news.

Mrs Jennings abandoned her teasing of me and looked at him impatiently.

'Well?' she said.

'Willoughby!' he declared, with the air of one who surprises the room.

'Willoughby!' she said with delight. And then said, 'I do not recognize the name. No, I do not know him, I am sure.'

'Perhaps not, but I do, and he is a very good fellow, I assure you. He is down here every year. A very decent shot, and there is not a bolder rider in England.'

'Well, then!' said Mrs Jennings. 'A fine catch, by the sound of it.'

'He is at that. A pleasant, good-humoured gentleman, with the nicest little black bitch of a pointer I ever saw, though the ladies could not tell me if she was out with him today.'

'Never mind about his pointer. Tell me more about him,' said Mrs Jennings. 'Is he young, old, handsome, rich?'

'Young and handsome, certainly, and a fine dancer into the bargain. I remember last Christmas, at a little hop at the Park, he danced from eight o'clock till four, without once sitting down.'

'That is something in his favour, for I'll wager Miss Marianne likes to dance. And does he have a house here?'

'As to that, no,' Sir John admitted.

'Then what is he doing here?'

'He is staying with Mrs Smith.'

'Mrs Smith? The lady at Allenham Court?' asked Mary.

'He is some kind of relation, her heir by all accounts,' said Sir John.

'Her heir,' said Mrs Jennings, impressed. 'So he will inherit Allenham?'

'He will indeed, and a tidy sum besides. And that is not all,' said Sir John. 'He has a pretty little estate of his own in Somersetshire.'

'Then he is very well worth catching,' said Mrs Jennings. 'I would like to see her well settled. You will have to look sharp, Colonel, else you will lose her!'

'I put in a good word for Brandon, never fear,' said Sir John, looking at me. 'Told her you would be jealous if she did not take care. I teased her about setting her cap at you. "That is an expression which I particularly dislike," she said!'

He laughed uproariously and I imagined Miss Marianne's pained expression at his coarseness.

Mrs Jennings joined him, slapping her knees as she rocked back and forth.

Gradually they sobered.

'I promised to ride over to Allenham and see Willoughby tomorrow, and invite him to dinner on Friday,' said Sir John.

'You had better look lively, then, Colonel, if you want her. You had better speak on Thursday!' Mrs Jennings said.

I took no notice of her, but I could not help feeling an interest in Willoughby, all the same.

Friday 23 September

We were a small party at dinner, just ourselves, the Dashwoods and Willoughby.

He was as young and handsome as Sir John had said, but although he was charming, lively and amusing, being fond of singing and dancing, and an expert in flirtation besides, I thought little of him for I had met his kind before. I knew that he would also be shallow and selfish, caring nothing for anyone's feelings but his own. A not uncommon type: adept at making friends but not at keeping them, easily distracted and unreliable.

Miss Marianne was, however, attracted to him, for he was, at first glance, very desirable. They spent the evening talking together with great animation. She had neither shyness nor reserve and she spoke about her thoughts and feelings with such rapturous delight that it was small wonder that he agreed with her on everything, or, if he disagreed, he did so only for the pleasure of letting her talk him round. Who would not have agreed with so much beauty?

She had only to mention a book and it was a favourite of his; or to say, rapturously, that Mozart was divine, in order to have him say that Mozart was the only composer who deserved the title of genius; or to speak slightingly of second marriages to find out that he, too, thought that second attachments were impossible.

I could not agree with her on the latter, and I was surprised to find that my feelings on the subject had changed, because, for a long time, I thought the same. But I am beginning to think that second attachments, happy second attachments, might be possible: Miss Marianne is the child of a second marriage, and her mother has nothing but good to say of her experiences.

Saturday 24 September

I cannot decide if I am grateful to Willoughby for making Miss Marianne happy or if I am jealous of him; though to be jealous of him seems absurd, when he is so much younger than I am, and when there is nothing of substance about him, and when, indeed, I am not courting Miss Marianne. He sings, he dances, he charms — because he can do nothing else. As I watched him talking to her this evening, I found myself wondering if, when the first flush of excitement has passed, he will be enough for Miss Marianne, for she is intelligent and she feels things deeply, whereas he is all surface, with nothing underneath.

Monday 26 September

Miss Marianne again spent the evening talking to Willoughby, to the exclusion of everyone else. I found myself in conversation with her sister, and before long we were talking about my experiences in the Indies.

'I have always wanted to travel,' she said, 'but I have not had the opportunity to do so. Was it very different there?'

'It could scarcely be more different,' I said, and I proceeded to tell her all about the heat and the mosquitoes, a little about the political situation and a great deal about the bazaars, with their fine silks and jewellery.

'And are the animals as strange as I have heard?'

Encouraged by her interest, I told her about elephants and tigers, and she listened with attention, asking sensible questions.

As we spoke, I thought of the difference between the two sisters. Miss Dashwood was quiet and conventional, with a great fund of common sense, whilst Miss Marianne was open and lively, with a spirit that had reawakened my own. I had forgotten how good it felt to be fully alive, to be stimulated by the world around me instead of being half-dead to it. I glanced again at Miss Marianne and I thought, It is Marianne who has brought me back to life.

After dinner, Mrs Jennings said, 'I hear you are a good dancer, Mr Willoughby.'

'As to that, I cannot say, but I certainly enjoy dancing.'

'As do I,' said Miss Marianne.

'Then we must have a ball. Sir John! What do you say? We must give the young people an opportunity to dance.'

'A splendid notion,' said he, eager, as always, for company and amusement.

'Oh, yes, an excellent idea!' said Miss Marianne.

'We will have it next week. Nothing grand, just fifteen or twenty couples, but mind, Willoughby, I have told the ladies how you danced until the early hours the last time I saw you, and you must not let me down.'

'I believe I can safely undertake to do the same, if Miss Marianne will honour me by partnering me,' he said.

She readily agreed, and Mrs Jennings said, 'You must claim a dance, too, Colonel, and you had better do it now, before there are no dances left.'

I asked Miss Marianne for a dance and she gave it to me, and then I asked her sister, too, whilst Miss Marianne returned to her conversation with Willoughby.

But next week when I dance with her I will have her to myself, and I find I am looking forward to it.

Wednesday 28 September

'A fine time we are going to have of it, Brandon. We shall be twenty couples,' said Sir John this evening, rubbing his hands in glee as he waited for the first of his guests to arrive.

'There is nothing better than a ball,' said Mrs Jennings. 'You mark my words, Colonel, there'll be plenty of young ladies for you here. Willoughby can't take them all!'

The guests began to arrive. The Dashwoods were first, and I could not help my eyes going to Miss Marianne, for her vitality lit up the room. She turned her head this way and that, and I knew she was looking for Willoughby.

The music began and I led Miss Dashwood onto the floor. When our dance was over, I danced with Miss Carey and then it was time for me to claim Miss Marianne. She was silent and I did not start a conversation, for I was content to watch her. She took delight in the music and her step was graceful and elegant.

After dancing with me she partnered Willoughby again. She had already danced with him twice, and I saw her sister looking anxious because if anyone noticed that she was dancing with him for a third time, it would arouse comment.

'No one else will notice,' I said to Miss Dashwood reassuringly.

'But you did,' she remarked.

'Ah, yes,' I admitted, for I could not deny it. 'But that is because . . .' She looked at me curiously and I said quickly, 'I happened to notice.'

Only when I had spoken did I realize how lame the conclusion had been.

I saw a thoughtfulness spring into her eye,

and I thought, I must be more careful. I must not give her the impression that I am interested in her sister.

But as I thought it, I realized that I *was* interested in Miss Marianne, and not just as a friend and neighbour of Sir John's. I was interested in her as a young woman.

Thursday 20 October
Our round of pleasure continues. Today we had a party on the water. Marianne and Willoughby contrived to be alone together in their boat, and everyone had grown so used to seeing them together that their behaviour did not occasion comment. I found myself wondering how long it would take her to see that he was all charm and nothing else.

'This is what I like,' said Sir John, claiming my attention as we returned to the shore. 'To be out in the open with friends. We must do it again next week, as long as the weather holds.'

'Oh, yes,' said Marianne eagerly. 'I am sure it will. Did you ever see such an autumn?'

She looked around her ecstatically, taking in the blue sky, and against it the russets, browns and golds that shone in the sunshine as the trees put forth their autumn colours.

And indeed it was a lovely sight, for the scene was reflected in the water, doubling its beauty and making it glow.

'Never,' said Willoughby.

'Full many a glorious morning have I seen
Flatter the mountain tops with sovereign
    eye
Kissing with golden face the meadows
    green
Gilding pale streams with heavenly
    alchemy.

'But never a morning as glorious as this one.'

'La! Listen to them!' cried Mrs Jennings.

'It is Shakespeare,' said Miss Marianne.

'Ay, I dare say it is,' replied Mrs Jennings, 'and very pretty it is, too, with all its flatterings and kissings. I never knew a beau for so much poetry!'

I turned my attention to him and I wondered if I had been mistaken in him. Had I allowed my wishes to colour my judgement? Had I seen in him a shallow wastrel because that was what I wanted to see? Sir John, Mrs Jennings, the Dashwoods, all saw a charming, lively young man who was a good match for Miss Marianne.

Doubts assailed me. But they were soon

dispelled. He would grow cold, I was sure of it. His kind could not settle for long, nor even remain with one set of people, because, having used up their scanty store of conversation, they had to move on in order to have something to say to someone else.

Friday 21 October
Another ball.

As I was sitting out beside Miss Dashwood, Mrs Jennings came over to us and told us that Mrs Carey was about to marry again, having been a widow for five years. Then she left us to go and share the news with Miss Marianne.

'Though what she will make of it I cannot imagine,' I said to Miss Dashwood as Mrs Jennings hurried away. 'I remember her saying that she does not believe in second attachments.'

'Her opinions are all romantic,' she agreed. 'But they must inevitably change, becoming settled on the reasonable basis of common sense and observation before long.'

I could not help my thoughts returning to Eliza at the words, for she had been forced to abandon her romantic opinions on her marriage. But alas! Common sense and observation had led her on to a dangerous path, for seeing other people embark on affairs, she had done so herself, to disastrous effect.

Without realizing it, I spoke my thoughts aloud, saying nothing of Eliza, but remarking that when the romantic refinements of a young mind were forced to change too rapidly, they were frequently succeeded by opinions which were all too common and too dangerous.

She looked at me strangely, and feeling some explanation was necessary, I said, 'I speak from experience. I once knew a lady who in temper and mind greatly resembled your sister, who thought and judged like her, but who from an enforced change — from a series of unfortunate circumstances . . .'

I stopped, for I could not say more without telling her the whole, and indeed, I had already said too much, for I saw from her expression of sympathy that she had guessed something of my past.

Not wanting to betray myself any further, I asked her if she was ready to dance again, and learning that she was, I led her out on to the floor, where I was silent and grave, lost in my thoughts, only rousing myself when the dance was over, and even then, only so far as necessary in order to retire to the card room.

Saturday 22 October

I now know why Miss Dashwood offered me such ready sympathy yesterday, for it seems that she has troubles of her own. As we sat talking this evening, it appeared that she had left someone behind at Norland. It came out when Mrs Jennings, teasing Margaret, said, 'You must tell us the name of the young man who was Elinor's particular favourite at home.'

Margaret, too young to dissemble, turned to her sister and said, 'I must not tell, may I, Elinor?'

This of course made everybody laugh, and Miss Dashwood tried to laugh, too, but I could tell it cost her an effort. I was about to distract Mrs Jennings when Marianne turned red and, in an effort to defend her sister, turned to Margaret and said, 'Remember that whatever your conjectures may be, you have no right to repeat them.'

'I never had any conjectures about it,' replied Miss Margaret; 'it was you who told me of it yourself.'

Sir John and Mrs Jennings laughed heartily, and Margaret was eagerly pressed to say something more.

'Oh! pray, Miss Margaret, let us know all about it,' said Mrs Jennings. 'What is the gentleman's name?'

'I must not tell, ma'am. But I know very well what it is, and I know where he is, too.'

'Yes, yes, we can guess where he is; at his own house at Norland to be sure. He is the curate of the parish I dare say.'

'No, *that* he is not. He is of no profession at all.'

'Margaret,' said Miss Marianne, with great warmth, 'you know that all this is an invention of your own, and that there is no such person in existence.'

'Well, then, he is lately dead, Marianne, for I am sure there was such a man once, and his name begins with an F,' said Margaret tartly.

I was about to speak when Mary, who disliked the vulgarity of such raillery, said that it rained very hard. I immediately joined in with a comment on the weather, so that the conversation could not return to its painful subject; painful for Miss Dashwood if no one else. I wondered about her young man, and I hoped her love would prosper. And then I thought how beautiful Miss Marianne had looked when she had sprung to her sister's defence.

Miss Marianne subsided, going over to the card-table, where she made a four with Willoughby, Sir John and Mrs Jennings. Willoughby cheated himself to help her, and

I found myself thinking that, although for the time being she found such chivalry charming, there would come a time when it would not be enough to hold her attention.

Monday 24 October
Sir John, always in need of diversion, asked me today if we could get up a party to go and see my brother-in-law's place at Whitwell.

'If you wish it, yes,' I said.

'Capital! This is a treat,' he said to Mrs Dashwood. 'Brandon's brother-in-law is abroad and allows no one to see the house when he is out of the country as a general rule, but he allows Brandon to take friends there.'

'The grounds are very beautiful,' said Mary.

'Indeed they are, and I am a good judge, ma'am, for I have taken parties there twice every summer these past ten years. There's a lake for sailing — you will enjoy that, eh, Miss Marianne?' he asked, turning towards her, and I saw her smile. 'We will take some cold provisions and ride in open carriages so you ladies can enjoy the view, as long as the weather is fine.'

'I am doubtful of that,' said Mrs Dashwood, 'since it has rained every day for the last fortnight.'

'All the more reason for it to stop tomorrow,' said Sir John. 'There cannot be any more rain up there!'

Mrs Jennings laughed heartily.

'I am sure it will be fine,' said Miss Marianne, much taken with the idea. 'An outing to a great house is, above all things, the one I would enjoy the most.'

'And I,' said Willoughby.

'How good are the roads?' asked Mrs Dashwood.

'Very good indeed. It will not take us above an hour and a half to get there, or two, if we admire the views along the way.'

'I will bring my curricle,' said Willoughby. He turned to Miss Marianne. 'I hope you will do me the honour of travelling with me?'

'Oh, yes!' she said.

'You will come in my carriage, I hope,' said Sir John to Mrs Dashwood.

'I am not sure I will be able to join you, for I fear I have a cold coming on,' she said.

I noticed that she looked pale, and that she held her shawl closely about herself.

Miss Marianne looked dismayed and Miss Dashwood looked concerned.

'You should stay at home, Mama,' she said. 'An outing in this cold weather will do you no good.'

'I am probably making a fuss about nothing,' she said. 'I am sure I will be better by morning.'

'You must take care of yourself. No need to fear for the young ladies, they will be safe with us,' said Sir John.

'Indeed, I think you had better not go, Mama,' said Miss Dashwood.

'I will see how I feel tomorrow. But I would not spoil your pleasure, my dears. You will like to see the house, and then you will be able to tell me all about it when you return. Sir John will see that you come to no harm.'

'No, indeed, ma'am.'

It was settled, then, that we should all assemble at the Park at ten o'clock, where we would have breakfast together before setting out.

Tuesday 25 October

The night was wild, with heavy rain, but it stopped by eight o'clock, and by ten o'clock, when we were all gathered together, the morning was favourable. The clouds were dispersing across the sky, and the sun frequently appeared.

'You see, I told you it would be fine,' said Miss Marianne, as we sat down to breakfast.

We were just about to eat when the letters were brought in. I took mine without any real interest, for I was looking forward to the outing, but as soon as I saw the hand-writing on the second letter, all thoughts of the outing were driven from my mind, for it was from Eliza! I stood up and immediately left the room, for I knew that I would be unable to disguise my feelings when I read it.

I retired to my chamber where I opened it and scanned it quickly, seeing that it had been written in great agitation.

I have no right to appeal to you, I thought it would be settled by now, I thought we would be married, he said we had only to wait until she died, it could not be more than a few weeks, and then we would be happy. He said she had had a turn for the worse, he said he had to leave but that he would come back for me. He left no ad-dress, I asked for none, thinking he would only be gone a short while, but it is months — months! — and my time is near. Help me, please! Oh! I do not deserve it, but I don't know what to do.

I felt a rush of relief as I read it, for she was alive! But it was mingled with anger at her seducer — for I could no longer doubt what had happened — and sorrow that she had been used so ill, and compassion for her distress. And over it all I felt guilt that I had not looked after her better.

I made my plans quickly. Her address was on the letter. I packed and returned to the dining room.

'No bad news, Colonel, I hope,' said Mrs Jennings, as soon as I entered the room.

'None at all, ma'am, I thank you,' I said, for I was resolved to protect Eliza's reputation as far as I was able. 'It was merely a letter of business.'

'But how came the hand to discompose you so much, if it was only a letter of business?' she asked eagerly. 'Come, come, this won't do, Colonel; so let us hear the truth of it.'

'My dear madam,' said her daughter, 'recollect what you are saying.'

'Perhaps it is to tell you that your cousin is married?' said Mrs Jennings, without attending to her daughter's reproof.

'No, indeed, it is not.'

'Well, then, I know who it is from, Colonel. And I hope she is well.'

'Whom do you mean, ma'am?' I asked, colouring a little.

'Oh! you know who I mean.'

I ignored her remark and said briskly to Mary, 'I am particularly sorry that I should receive this letter today, for it is on business which requires my immediate attendance in town.'

'In town!' cried Mrs Jennings. 'What can you have to do in town at this time of year?'

'My own loss is great in being obliged to leave so agreeable a party; but I am the more concerned, as I fear my presence is necessary to gain your admittance at Whitwell,' I said.

I saw their disappointed faces, but it could not be helped.

'But if you write a note to the house-keeper, will it not be sufficient?' said Miss Marianne.

I did not like to disappoint her, but I said, 'I am afraid not.'

'We must go,' said Sir John good-humouredly. 'It shall not be put off when we are so near it. You cannot go to town till tomorrow, Brandon, that is all.'

'I wish it could be so easily settled. But it is not in my power to delay my journey for one day!'

'If you would but let us know what your business is,' said Mrs Jennings, 'we might see whether it could be put off or not.'

'You would not be six hours later,' said

196

Willoughby, 'if you were to defer your journey till our return.'

'I cannot afford to lose *one* hour.'

I heard Willoughby say in a low voice to Miss Marianne, 'There are some people who cannot bear a party of pleasure. Brandon is one of them. He was afraid of catching cold, I dare say, and invented this trick for getting out of it. I would lay fifty guineas the letter was of his own writing.'

'I have no doubt of it,' came her mocking reply.

I was annoyed, because his influence on her was not a good one, but I let them think what they would, for I had to go.

'There is no persuading you to change your mind, Brandon, I know of old, when once you are determined on anything,' said Sir John. 'But, however, I hope you will think better of it. Consider, here are the two Misses Carey come over from Newton, the three Misses Dashwood walked up from the cottage, and Mr Willoughby got up two hours before his usual time, on purpose to go to Whitwell.'

'I am sorry to disappoint you all, but I am afraid it is unavoidable.'

'Well then, when will you come back again?'

I was about to reply when I was spared

the necessity by Mary's intervention, and I was grateful for her good breeding, which made my going easier.

'I hope we shall see you at Barton as soon as you can conveniently leave town,' she said, 'and we must put off the party to Whitwell till you return.'

I silently thanked her for her kindness, but said that, as I did not know when I would have the power to return, I could not engage for it.

'Oh! he must and shall come back,' cried Sir John, with ill-timed jocularity. 'If he is not here by the end of the week, I shall go after him.'

'Ay, so do, Sir John,' cried Mrs Jennings, 'and then perhaps you may find out what his business is.'

'I do not want to pry into other men's concerns. I suppose it is something he is ashamed of,' he said with a wink.

To my relief, my horse was announced.

'You do not go to town on horseback, do you?' asked Sir John in surprise.

'No, only to Honiton. I shall then go post.'

'Well, as you are resolved to go, I wish you a good journey.'

I took my leave, saying to Miss Dashwood, 'Is there no chance of my seeing you and your sisters in town this winter?'

'I am afraid, none at all,' she replied.

'Then I must bid you farewell for a longer time than I should wish to do.'

I bowed to Miss Marianne and left the room. As the door closed behind me, I heard Mrs Jennings saying to Miss Dashwood in a low voice, 'I can guess what his business is, however. It is about Miss Williams, I am sure. She is his natural daughter.'

I was not surprised to hear her say so, for she had intimated her belief to me in the past, but I wished she would have kept quiet, all the same, the more so because she was wrong in her conjecture.

But I had no more time to waste on thoughts of Mrs Jennings. My horse was ready, and I was soon away.

Thursday 27 October

As soon as I arrived in London, I went immediately to the address Eliza had given me in her letter. I was relieved to see that, although nothing grand, it was at least respectable. A maidservant let me in, and when I asked for Eliza, a woman came bustling from the back of the house. She was clean and homely, and said to me, 'Did I hear you say you'd come for Eliza? Mrs Williams?'

I started at the use of *Mrs,* and I wondered if she was, after all, married, but then I realized that she would not have used her own surname if that had been the case.

However, her landlady thought she was married, and I did not wish to disabuse her of the notion.

'Yes, I have.'

'At last! I've been expecting someone to come for weeks past.' She turned to the maid. 'I'll take care of this,' she said.

'Yes, Mrs Hill.'

The maid departed.

' "Write to them," I said to her,' continued Mrs Hill, leading me into the house. "Your family'll help you. You shouldn't be on your own, not in a state like this." But, "I don't like to trouble them," she said. "Where's the trouble?" I said, but you know how women are in her condition. You've come with news of Mr Williams, I hope? Have you found him.'

'I regret to say that I have not.'

She shook her head and clucked her tongue.

'It's a bad business. I said to my sister, "What's the world coming to when fine young gentlemen abandon their wives?" and she said, "He could be dead," and I said, "I'm sure I hope he is, for at least that

200

would explain it, only he seemed too young to die." And then she said, "Maybe he's got the smallpox," but as I said to her, "I hope it's not the smallpox. Just think of my sheets," so then she said he probably dropped off his horse, as gentlemen have a habit of doing.'

By this time we had reached a set of rooms at the back of the house and she knocked on the door.

'Mrs Williams. Mrs Williams, my dear. Here's your cousin come to help you.' She turned to me. 'I'll fetch you some tea,' she said to me, as she opened the door. 'I'm sure you could do with some, and her, too, poor mite.'

I thanked her and entered the room. It was shabbily furnished and the paper was peeling off the walls at the corners, but it was clean, and to my relief, there on the sofa was Eliza.

She sprang up on seeing me, her face a mixture of misery, shame, joy and despair. Her flowing gown rested on her front and I saw that her time was near. She put her hand to her back to support herself and I moved forward quickly, helping her to sit down again, but not before she had thrown her arms round my neck and wept great hot tears.

'There, now, there is nothing to cry about,' I said. 'Everything will be all right. You may depend on me. I am here.'

She wiped her eyes with her hand, and the sight of it set my heart aching, for, despite her condition, she was still such a child.

'I did not know if you would come,' she sniffed.

'You should have trusted me; you should have written to me sooner. I have been so worried about you, not knowing where you were, whether you were safe or happy, nor even knowing if you were alive or dead.'

She hung her head.

'I wanted to write to you, but somehow there was always something to prevent it,' she said in a small voice.

'You had better tell me everything, from the beginning,' I said, sitting down on a chair by her side, for I thought it would be a relief to her to tell me all. 'You met him in Bath?' I prompted her, when she did not begin.

'Yes,' she said. 'He was there visiting friends.'

'Does he have a name?' I asked her.

'He does, but I cannot tell you.'

'You mean you will not. Why is it such a secret? He has seduced you, Eliza. He deserves to be brought to account for his crime.'

She shook her head. I tried to coax her but she was resolute, and I pressed her no further, hoping she would tell me of her own free will before much more time had passed.

'Your friend knew him?' I asked her.

'Yes, Susan knew everything. We met him in the circulating library one morning, when we were exchanging our books.' Her voice took on strength, and her face gained some animation. 'He was lively and friendly, and we saw no harm in talking to him, for he was a gentleman, and we were in a public place with lots of people around us. Indeed, he seemed to know most of them. He had many friends, and it was clear that he was well thought of and well respected. He talked to us about the books we were borrowing, and he recommended some we should try. They were perfectly respectable, and we thanked him for his recommendations. He made us a bow and he said he hoped we would enjoy them. As we went home, Susan said he had been much taken with me. I thought so, too, but as it had been a chance encounter, I did not think I would see him again.'

'But you did?'

She nodded.

'Yes, we seemed to be always coming across him.'

'When you were out without a chaperon?' I asked her.

'We did not go out alone. Susan's father was infirm, but he always sent her maid with us.'

'And did she stay with you?'

'No, not all the time,' she admitted.

'But Susan was always with you?'

'Yes, for the most part.'

I looked at her enquiringly.

'Once, I met him without Susan, for we were late leaving the house and so Susan went on to the milliner's with her maid, where she had some business, whilst I went ahead to the library. I met him on the way and he carried my books for me. How he made me laugh!' she said, her face brightening as she spoke of him. 'He was always so good-humoured. And after that, I seemed to be always seeing him. He offered to escort us home one day and we accepted his offer, but then, as we were walking past the coachmakers, he said he had to collect his curricle. He said he would take us home in style, but as there was only one spare seat and as Susan had some shopping to do, it was arranged that he should take me home and that Susan would join me there later.'

'And her maid went with you?'

'No, her maid went with Susan.'

'And did she not object to your going in the curricle alone?'

'No. She said I was a lucky girl to have such a treat.'

I gave a sigh. 'I see.'

'And then he offered to take me driving the following day, and Susan and I met him at the corner of the street. She was a great friend to me. She knew I was falling in love with him, and so she helped us to see each other. I had told her all about my mother, you see, and how my mother had been prevented from marrying the man she loved, and how it had ruined her life. And so Susan said nothing to anyone, for she was not going to behave like Mama's maid and betray me.'

'And did you never think that it was wrong?' I asked her.

'How could it be wrong to fall in love?' she asked me innocently.

'And could you not have told me about him?' I said gently.

'He said we would surprise you, and how romantic it would be to elope.'

I shook my head, and she looked perplexed.

'I thought that you, at least, would understand, for you were going to elope with Mama.'

'That was different,' I said. 'Your mama and I had known each other for many years. We knew each other in all our moods, and we knew that we could trust one another. We intended to marry in church, and we only planned to elope because my father wanted to force your mother into marrying someone else. But no one was trying to force you into a distasteful marriage, my dear.'

The door opened and the landlady entered with a tray of tea. I eyed the cups dubiously, but it was obvious that Eliza was used to drinking from cracked cups, for she set them on the table without a thought and proceeded to pour the tea.

'He's dead, is he?' asked Mrs Hill, hovering by the door. 'I knew how it would be.'

Eliza's eyes filled with tears.

'Indeed, he is not,' I said.

'Ah, well, that's a blessing,' she said. 'It's an injury, I suppose. I was talking to my brother. "There's a lot of people falls down stairs and breaks their neck," he said to me. Poor dear,' she added, looking at Eliza.

'Thank you, we must hope for the best,' I said, not wanting to give her any details, and then waited until she left the room.

Eliza handed me a cup of tea. I took it and drank it, more to encourage her than because I wanted it, and she seemed better for the drink.

'You said you eloped, but in your letter you said you were not married?' I asked her.

Her eyes filled with tears.

'No. But he said we would be. He told me we would be married as soon as we reached town. It would be easier in town, he said, because no one would know us there and so no one could object on account of my age. And then we would go to Delaford and see you.' She smiled. 'I was looking forward to it so much. I wanted you to meet him, for I was sure you would like him. And it pleased me above all things to know that I would be a respectable wife and that you would be able to acknowledge me as your friend and that you need not be ashamed of me.'

I was startled.

'I have never been ashamed of you!'

'Susan's maid said that people whose parents were not married are always a source of shame to those around them.'

'Susan's maid would have been better attending to her own concerns,' I said angrily. 'But go on. What happened when you reached town?'

Her face fell.

'He found there was something wrong with the licence. I do not know what it was, something trivial, but it meant he would have to get another one. But then there was some difficulty about it, so he decided it would be better if he contacted a church in the neighbourhood and asked them to read the banns. So then we had to wait another three weeks for the banns to be read.'

I began to see how it had happened. She had been lured to London with the promise of marriage, and then lured to stay by circumstances; which, I did not doubt, had been manufactured, for her seducer must have known that no clergyman in England would officiate at a marriage with a sixteen-year-old bride unless her parents or guardians approved of the match.

'And after the three weeks were over?' I asked.

'The clergyman who was to perform the ceremony was ill,' she said.

She turned her handkerchief over in her hands, and I knew she suspected that it was a lie, but that she did not want to face it.

'So you had to wait until he was better?' I asked her gently.

'Yes.'

'And did you speak to the clergyman yourself?' I asked, though I knew it was a vain hope.

'No. I did not need to,' she said. 'He told me that everything was arranged and I believed him. He is a good man, he loves me. I know he does.'

'If he was a good man, he would not have deserted you,' I said gently.

'He didn't desert me. He had to go away for a while because his benefactress was ill, and then he was going to find a house for us to live in when we were married. He promised me he would come back soon, but it has been two months and I am dreadfully worried,' she said, looking at me with sick apprehension. 'I think something must have happened to him.'

'It is possible,' I said, more to soothe her pride than for any other reason. 'If you give me his name, I will make enquiries and find out what has become of him.'

She did not want to do so, for I could tell that she was afraid of what I would say to him when I found him, but at last, reluctantly, she gave in.

'His name is Willoughby,' she said.

I stared at her, aghast. Willoughby! She could not have given me any name that would have shocked me more.

But then, as I thought over the matter, I realized it must be another Willoughby. The man I knew might be shallow and frivolous but he was at least a gentleman; he could surely not be so base as to leave a sixteen-year-old girl alone in London whilst she was carrying his child, and then go to Barton and make love to another young woman without a care in the world. No, it was impossible.

'What is his Christian name?' I asked.

'John,' she said. 'Here, I have a sketch of him.'

She raised herself on her elbow and opened a small book which lay beside her. She turned the pages until she came to the sketch of a young man. It was poorly executed, but the likeness was unmistakable.

I shook my head in dismay.

'Do you know him?' she asked.

'I am sorry to say that I do.'

I did not want to hurt her, but I knew that she had to be told. As gently as I could, I told her that I had spent the last few weeks in company with him, that he had been happy and carefree, and that he had never once mentioned her, nor thought about her, for he had been courting another.

'No! It cannot be true!' she said, falling back on the sofa.

'It gives me great pain to say it, Eliza, but I am afraid it is so,' I said.

'I do not believe it!' she said, rallying.

'Then you must ask Sir John Middleton,' I said. 'You have paper on your table. Write to him and ask him if he knows a man named Willoughby.'

'I never suspected . . .' she said, ashen. She looked at the paper and then said, 'No, I will not write. I know you to be honest. If you say it is so, then it must be so. But Willoughby. To have abandoned me, promising to return, and then to leave and never to think of me again? Do I mean so little to him, and his child, too?' she asked, as fresh tears began to fall.

'Hush,' I said. 'You are with friends now.'

I knew that friendship could do little to alleviate her suffering, but what it could do would not be wanting.

'He is not the man I thought he was,' she said, drying her tears. 'And I? What am I? I am not the person I thought I was, either, for I thought I was a dearly loved woman who eloped with her fiancé, but instead I am a dupe. And yet I love him still. Oh! I have been so wrong. I cannot bear it.'

She covered her face with her hands, and I put her head on my shoulder whilst she wept until she could weep no more.

'Never fear, you are not alone,' I told her. 'As soon as your lying-in period is over, I will take you to the country. There you can grow strong and happy again.'

'Strong, perhaps, but I do not believe I will ever be happy again,' she said sorrowfully.

I made allowances for her circumstances and her condition, and soothed her and talked of pleasanter things. But she did not listen to me. Her mind was still in the past, with Willoughby.

Friday 28 October

I have found a nurse for Eliza, and hired a maid and a manservant to look after her, and installed her in more elegant lodgings, but now the only thing I can do for her is to sit with her and cheer her until her child is born, for her time is very near. She does not complain, though I can see that she is in discomfort, and she has begun to show an interest in her life after her child is born, for I tempt her with thoughts of her own establishment in the country, where she and her child can be together.

Wednesday 2 November

My feelings are all confusion, for Eliza has had her child, a girl, as like her mother as it is possible for a newborn baby to be. I am thankful for her safe delivery, and full of tenderness when I look at the child, but I am conscious of feelings of guilt as well, for I should have protected her from such a fate.

However, there will be no debtor's prison for her, no consumption, no early death. I will make it my business to see that she is well cared for. I am convinced that she is young enough to regain her spirits and that, in time, she will be happy again.

Friday 4 November
Having seen Eliza through her ordeal, my thoughts turned to her seducer, and I went in search of Willoughby. I was about to board the stage and travel back to Barton when a chance remark from an acquaintance told me that he was in town.

'Saw him at my club last night,' said Gates.

'Thank you, you have spared me a journey, and an embarrassing scene at the end of it,' I said, for I had not been looking forward to confronting Willoughby at Barton, where it would worry my friends and neighbours. 'Is he staying at the club?'

'No, he is in lodgings.'

'Do you happen to have his direction?'

He gave me the address and I went there straight away. Willoughby was out, but I said

I would wait and the landlady let me in. I sat and waited an hour for him. He entered in high good humour, looking as handsome as ever, and with not a care in the world.

'What, Brandon? I never thought to find you here. I thought you were attending to urgent business,' he said impudently. 'Well, what is it then? You must have some reason for coming here, and I cannot suppose it is for the pleasure of my company. You never struck me as a man who courted pleasure! Indeed, the last time I saw you, you were doing everything in your power to avoid it.'

I took my glove and slapped his face. He looked startled, and his hand went to his cheek, and then he laughed.

'What! Are you calling me out! I cannot believe it. For laughing at you? No, that is impossible. For what then? I have done nothing — unless you wish to call me out for taking Miss Marianne for a drive when you were called away?'

'I am not here about Miss Marianne, though, God knows, if I were her brother, I would be tempted to give you a thrashing,' I said. 'I am here about Eliza Williams.'

'Eliza Williams?' he asked incredulously, and then something wary entered his eye and the smile left his face. 'I know no one of that name.'

'Then let me refresh your memory. She is the young girl you met in Bath, and then seduced and abandoned,' I said.

'Oh, hardly that. She took no seducing —' He stopped as he realized that he had admitted to knowing her, but then he shrugged and went on, 'And as for abandoning her, I did no such thing.'

'You left her alone in a strange city where she had no friends,' I said, restraining the impulse to knock him down. 'The very circumstances that should have aroused your compassion instead aroused your cruelty. She was an orphan, with no one to protect her, and so you used her as you pleased.'

He shrugged, and said, 'And if I did, what business is it of yours? You cannot mean to champion every waif and stray you discover. Not even your chivalry would stretch to that.'

'She is my ward,' I said.

He went pale.

'Your ward?' he asked, and he put his hand out behind him and supported himself on the back of a chair.

'Indeed. My ward. I am here to tell you that you must marry her. You cannot give her back her heart, but you can at least give her the protection of your name,' I said shortly.

'Marry her? Come, now, Brandon, you cannot expect me to marry her. She is not at all the sort of girl I would wish to marry, and besides, she has not a penny to her name. A man does not marry his mistress, Brandon, you know that,' he said, gaining courage again and smirking at me insolently.

'She is not your mistress. She is a young girl of good family who has been cruelly deceived. I have been lenient with you in offering you a chance to marry her, but I confess that I am pleased you have refused, for I would not have liked to see her tied to a man of so little worth. If you will give me the name of your seconds, we will meet at a time and place of your choosing and settle this matter.'

'Now look here, Brandon, you are a man of the world. Let us settle this as men of the world.'

'That is what I am here to do.'

'On the field of honour? Oh, come now, Brandon, you are making too much of it. I am sure she will be happy as long as she has an income. I am not rich, but I can give her something, I am sure. And then, when Mrs Smith dies and I inherit my fortune, I can give her something more. I will set her up in her own establishment, with a maid and everything comfortable.'

'If you will not repair the damage you have done to her by marrying her, then you will name your seconds. Which is it to be?'

He protested, but as he was adamant that he would not marry her, there was only one course of action open to me.

Leaving him, I sought out some of my friends from my regiment. As luck would have it, Green and Wareham were in town. I made my way to their lodgings and I found them in their shirtsleeves, cleaning their pistols.

'Brandon! Come in, man, come in,' said Green, as he opened the door.

I went in, and found that Wareham, too, was at home.

'Good to see you again, Brandon,' he said, looking up from cleaning his gun.

'And you.'

After the customary greetings, I said, 'Gentlemen, I am not here on a social visit. I am in need of your help.'

They looked at me curiously and Green said, 'That sounds serious.'

'It is,' I said, taking off my hat and gloves. 'I need you to act as my seconds.'

They were immediately alert, and wanted to know all the details. As soon as I had satisfied them as to what had happened, they agreed at once to act for me.

'The dog!' said Green.

'He should have been in the army. It would have taught him a sense of duty,' said Wareham.

'I would not have wanted a man like that in my regiment,' I said, to which they both agreed.

'You have challenged him already?' asked Green.

'Yes. I have just come from his lodgings.'

'You know we will have to give him a chance to marry her?' said Green. 'There is a code of conduct in these things and we must stick to it, if we want to consider ourselves gentlemen.'

'Of course. I have already given him a chance and he told me he would not marry a penniless girl.'

Green's face showed his disgust.

'Nevertheless, we have to give him another chance,' said Wareham.

'As my seconds, I would expect you to do no less.'

'What weapon do you think he will choose?' asked Green with interest.

'A pistol, I suspect. He probably fences, but I doubt if he has any experience with a sword.'

'And will you agree to his choice?'

'I will.'

'Whatever it is?'

'Whatever it is.'

'He will be able to choose the ground,' said Green.

'Let him,' I said. 'It makes no difference to me where I fight him.'

'Then we will go and see him now, and return as soon as possible,' said Wareham, reaching for his coat.

They left me to kick my heels whilst they sought out Willoughby and returned just over an hour later.

'Well?' I demanded.

'He still refuses to marry her. He says he would rather die at once than die a slow death being married to a woman with nothing to recommend her but a beauty which has now surely gone.'

'It is a pity he did not think of that before he seduced her,' I remarked. 'And what weapon has he chosen?'

'Pistols. The place to be Hounslow Heath, the time tomorrow at dawn.'

'That suits me well.'

'Where are you lodging?'

'In St James's Street.'

'Then we will meet there in the morning and travel to the heath together.'

Saturday 5 November

I slept soundly and I was roused by my valet well before dawn. The morning was cold and I dressed with alacrity, eating a hearty breakfast before Green and Wareham called for me. I put on my coat, grateful for the warmth of its capes. Then, donning my hat and gloves, I went out into the mist-shrouded morning.

Lighted flambeaus pierced the gloom, their flames flickering fitfully as they strove to push back the dark, revealing the grey streets beyond.

I heard the muffled cry of the night watchman, 'All's well.'

'All's well for some,' said Green, as I climbed into the carriage.

'For us,' I said. 'I am ready to finish this business.'

'Ay,' said Wareham. 'Let us be done with it.'

The carriage pulled away. The horses' hoofs sounded strangely muted, and the turning of the wheels was no more than a grating whisper as the carriage bumped over the cobbles.

'This damnable fog,' said Green, peering out of the window. 'I hope it clears by the time we reach the heath, or you will not be able to see each other, let alone fire.'

We were in luck. When we stepped out onto the heath, we could see for twenty paces, enough for our business.

There was no sign of Willoughby's carriage.

Ten minutes later Willoughby arrived, attended by two men who looked nervous, as well they might. They were dandies, not soldiers, and had probably never been seconds in their lives.

'I will give him another chance to change his mind,' said Green.

He went over to Willoughby, they had words, and Green returned, saying, 'The duel is to go ahead. It is for you to choose the distance, Brandon.'

That done, the seconds met in the middle and loaded the pistols in each other's presence to ensure fair play, then Green and Wareham returned to hand me my weapon.

'Willoughby's man is to count the paces. After the count of ten, you may turn and fire at will. Is this agreeable to you?'

'It is.'

'Then let us get it over with.'

I removed my coat. Across the heath, Willoughby removed his. The fog was lifting minute by minute, and I could see him clearly. We came together and stood back to back. His man counted the paces. One . . .

two . . . three . . . four . . . five . . . I thought
of Eliza abandoned and left all alone . . .
six . . . seven . . . eight . . . nine . . .

'Ten!'

I turned.

He turned, too, his arm already raised. He
rushed his shot, firing without taking proper
aim, and the bullet went wide, so wide I did
not even feel it pass. He blanched, and
dropped his arm. I saw his knees begin to
buckle. I lifted my arm. And then he turned
and I thought that he would run. But the
horrified look on the faces of his seconds
curtailed his cowardice, and he turned back
towards me, white-faced and trembling,
then turned sideways to present as small a
target as possible.

For Eliza, I thought.

I took aim.

But as I did so, I saw not Willoughby and
not Eliza, but Marianne. I imagined her face
as she heard that Willoughby was dead; I
imagined her grief, and I was horrified, for,
if she was still enamoured of him, she would
not grieve easily or quietly, but would suffer
with all the depth of her being. If I killed
him, I would cause her great pain, and with
her nature, it was a pain she would not be
certain of overcoming. And so I raised my
arm and fired into the air.

Willoughby fell to his knees, and had to be assisted to his feet by his seconds.

I walked over to him and looked at him in disgust.

'You are not worth shooting,' I said.

Then Green brought me my coat, and we climbed into the carriage. It pulled away, jolting over the heath before turning on to the road.

We went back to Green's and Wareham's lodgings. By the time we reached them, a wind had sprung up, and it had driven most of the fog away, revealing a cold, clean light as a pale sun broke through the clouds.

'You deloped,' said Wareham, as we went inside. 'Why?'

'Because there is another young woman caught in Willoughby's toils,' I said, as I took off my outdoor clothes and threw myself into a chair, 'and I feared that, if I killed him, she would love him for ever.'

'Another one?' said Wareham. 'How many women does the fellow have?'

'A face like that brings them fluttering like moths to a flame,' said Green, as he sat down on the sofa, flinging his arm along the back of it.

'Ay, I wish I had his handsome features,' said Wareham, laughing, as he caught sight of his crooked nose and scarred cheek in the glass. 'It would make a change. I would dearly love to have all the women dangling after me. I would parade myself through the ballroom and pretend not to notice them following me, then I would turn around, astonished, and smile, just so' — he simpered — 'and bow' — he bowed low — 'and consider which lucky lady to take onto the floor. And then consider which lucky lady to take into my bed!'

'Whereas I *do* have his handsome features,' said Green.

'True, but in all the wrong places!' said Wareham.

'Brandon is the handsome one amongst us,' said Green.

'Which is like saying the clean one amongst chimney sweeps!' said Wareham.

'Perhaps he is handsome enough to win the lady for whom he spared Willoughby's life,' said Green.

'I cannot think what you mean,' I said.

'No?'

'No.'

They roared with laughter, and Green leapt on me and wrestled me to the ground.

'Admit it!' he said as he held me down.

I threw him off, and in another minute the positions were reversed.

'Never!' I said.

'Never?' said Wareham, adding his strength to Green's.

They had me!

'Oh, no, you don't get up until you admit it,' said Green, as I struggled.

'Very well,' I said, pretending I was beaten. 'She is someone I met at Barton.'

They let me up and I dusted myself off before launching myself at Green, and then Wareham, catching them off guard and knocking them down one after the other.

We wrestled for some time until at last we were out of breath, and Green said, 'Well, what is her name?'

'A gentleman never bandies a lady's name.'

'Camilla,' guessed Green.

'Arabella,' said Wareham.

'Griselda!' said Green.

'If you must know, it is Marianne,' I said, sitting up, for I knew that I could trust them and that her name would go no further; and, moreover, I was longing to speak of her.

'Marianne,' said Green thoughtfully.

'Be still my beating heart!' said Wareham, clutching his chest.

'And is it serious?' said Green.

The mood changed and they both looked at me expectantly.

'Yes, I think it is,' I said.

Green let out a whoop! and Wareham clapped me on the back.

'At last! You have been unhappy for long enough,' he said.

'And look set to be unhappy for some time to come,' I said. 'The lady has no interest in me. The last time I saw her, she was besotted with Willoughby.'

'She will not be so besotted when she discovers his true character,' said Green. 'You have only to tell her about Eliza and she will be cured of her affliction. No woman could love him after that.'

I sat down and rested my elbows on my knees.

'It is not so easy,' I said.

'Why not? If you like her, and you can show him to be a scoundrel —'

'That is just why I cannot tell her. It cannot come from me or it would look like jealousy.'

'Is that really the reason?' asked Green, as he continued to look at me. 'Or is it because you think that she would hate you for destroying her dreams?'

'Both,' I admitted.

'Then what are you going to do?' asked Wareham.

'I am not sure. His presence in town is

perhaps a sign that he has already tired of her, in which case she might already be aware of his true character, and she might even now be rejoicing in the fact that she has escaped him. And if not, I am hoping that she will soon realize his heart is not deep enough for her.'

'And then you can court her,' said Green.

'Yes, I can.'

To court Marianne, I thought, and I smiled. What could life offer me that was better than that? Unless it was to win her.

Wareham was growing restless, for he was a man of action, not words, and he jumped up as soon as I had finished, saying, 'Well, that is settled then. Just remember to invite us to the wedding! And now we must have something to eat! There is nothing like a duel to sharpen the appetite. You will stay for a second breakfast, Brandon?'

'No,' I said, rising, too. 'I want to go and see Eliza, and then I am going to Delaford, to look at the cottages on my estate and decide which one of them would make the most suitable home for her.'

They bade me farewell and I went to Eliza's lodgings, stopping at the shops on my way to buy her a new comb to cheer her. I chose one with a mother-of-pearl inlay, and I was rewarded by her delight in it.

'It is so pretty,' she said.

'And how are you feeling today?'

'Much better, and longing to be up again,' she said.

'It will not be long now.'

I told her I was going to Delaford to choose a cottage for her.

'Oh, thank you,' she said. 'I am so weary of the town. I am longing to be in the country again. Even in the winter it is better than being here, where there are nothing but grey streets outside the window. Have the leaves fallen yet at Barton?'

'They have just started to fall.'

'I want to walk in the copse and kick the leaves and see them swirl up in the air and hear the dry crackle as they swish to the ground,' she said with a sigh.

'It will be soon, Eliza.'

I praised the baby, who was sleeping in the crib, before I left, and then set out for Delaford.

Tuesday 15 November

I have found a suitable cottage for Eliza, one I am persuaded she will like. It is a pretty building with a small garden, and it has views down the valley. I have given instructions for one or two improvements to be carried out, and as soon as she is well enough to travel, I mean to take her there.

I returned to town and told Eliza about her cottage. She was cheered by the news, and she is looking forward to the move.

I have some business to attend to, but then I will accompany her to Delaford, and afterwards I will return to Barton, where I hope to find that Miss Marianne has recovered from her infatuation with Willoughby, and that I can court her.

I want to arouse her interest in the wider world and to stimulate her intelligence, which must be wasting away with only Sir John and his family, good though they are, for company; I want to discuss with her books she has never thought of, poems she has never discovered; I want to show her places she has never been.

I want to open up the world for her, as her sensibility has opened it up once again for me.

Monday 21 November
I was walking down Bond Street this morning when I saw a familiar face, that of Mrs Jennings's daughter, Charlotte; Charlotte Palmer as she is now, for of course she has married. After introducing me to her hus-

229

band, a grave-looking young man of some five or six and twenty, with an air of fashion and sense, she told me that her mother, sister and brother-in-law were well, and that their children were thriving. And then she confounded me by saying:

'There is a new family come to Barton Cottage, I hear, by the name of Dashwood. Mama sends me word they are very pretty, and that one of them is going to be married to Mr Willoughby, of Combe Magna.'

My spirits sank, and all my ideas of showing Marianne a wider world evaporated like the morning mist.

She was in love with him. She was going to marry him.

There was no hope for me.

Should I have told her? Should I have made her aware of his true character? Should I have prevented her engagement?

I was so lost in my thoughts that I scarcely heard the rest of Mrs Palmer's speech, though she talked for some time, saying how glad she was to hear of the engagement; how everyone in Devonshire thought Mr Willoughby extremely agreeable; and how nobody was more liked than Mr Willoughby wherever he went.

She paused, and I roused myself, for it was necessary for me to say something, though I scarcely know what I said.

'There will be another wedding in Barton before long, I dare say,' she continued, and I forced myself to concentrate on her conversation. 'Mama says that the Dashwoods have had a young man to stay, a Mr Edward Ferrars, and that he is sweet on Miss Dashwood.'

I remembered Miss Margaret saying that her sister had left someone behind, and that his name began with an F. It seemed likely that the elusive gentleman was Edward Ferrars, and if he was worthy of her, then I was happy for her.

But I could not concentrate for long, and I was glad when the Palmers left me.

Should I have spoken? Should I have said something?

I asked myself the questions again and again.

But it was fruitless to speculate.

Marianne was engaged to Willoughby. My chance to speak had gone.

She was lost to me.

Wednesday 7 December

Eliza is recovering her strength rapidly, and although I have not yet finished my business in London, tomorrow I mean to take her to Delaford. Her spirits are changeable, and I am persuaded that, once she is in the country, they will settle into a cheerful pattern.

Thursday 8 December
We travelled slowly, to make the journey easier for Eliza and the baby, and we both enjoyed the leisurely pace. The weather was fine and bright, with brilliant skies, and the countryside was beautiful in its bareness, with the traceries of small twigs showing up against the sky.

Saturday 10 December
We arrived at Delaford this afternoon, and we were glad to get out of the carriage. Eliza looked at her new home with happiness and walked round the garden, which was brightened by some colourful foliage, before going inside.

She was delighted with the house, and with the nursery, which I had had newly papered, and with her bedroom, which had a large window looking down the valley.

'I will have to see about finding you a companion, but you have Susan and John to look after you for the moment, and I will be here as often as I can. You will want to rest now, I dare say, but I will call for you in the morning and we can go for a walk, if you are feeling well enough, and then we can go to the mansion house and you can choose some books from the library or whatever you wish.'

She thanked me with a smile and I left her arranging her new home.

And now it only remains for me to see her cheerfully settled and then I can return to London, to see to my unfinished business there.

1797

Tuesday 3 January

London is cold and damp. The sky is grey and the streets are dirty. I have diversion here but my spirits are low. I dined with Leyton this evening, but not even his cheerful company could lift my spirits. To have the hope of a life held out to me and then to have it dashed . . . I am sick of the winter, and sick of England. I think I will travel as soon as the spring arrives.

Thursday 5 January

I saw Mrs Palmer this morning in Bond Street. I had no desire to talk to her and to hear about the arrangements for Marianne's wedding, and so I went into a shop, but something must have delayed her, too, because when I came out again she was just passing the door and she greeted me heartily. I tried to hurry away but it was impossible, and, to my surprise, this turned out to be a good thing, for I discovered that all was not well between Marianne and Willoughby; indeed, Marianne had not seen him for months.

'Has Willoughby left Barton, then?' I asked Mrs Palmer in surprise, for, although I had met him in town, I had assumed that he would soon be returning to the country.

'Oh, yes, he left there in November when Mrs Smith sent him to town on business; and he had to oblige her, or she might have cut him out of her will.'

'But he must have dealt with her business long ago. And yet he has not returned to Barton?' I asked.

'No, not for so much as a day.'

'That is strange, when he is engaged to Miss Marianne. You did say that they were engaged?' I enquired.

'Oh, yes, it is spoken of everywhere. Everyone says how lucky she is, for Willoughby has a handsome face and a handsome fortune; or will have, when Mrs Smith dies, and that cannot be long, you know.'

I began to wonder if the engagement was real or if it was just a rumour, and hope stirred within me.

'Has their engagement been announced?' I asked.

'No, to be sure, there has been no

announcement,' Mrs Palmer admitted, 'but with Mrs Smith so ill, it was not to be expected. They were waiting for her to recover, or, more likely, die, before they announced it. Mama was certain of it. Poor Marianne! She is monstrous unhappy without him. She is quite cast down by his absence. She cannot eat and cannot sleep, for she has great sensibility, you know. Now if it had happened to Miss Dashwood, I dare say she would have sighed and then got on with her needlework, but Miss Marianne roams around the countryside thinking of him, and plays all his favourite songs, and encourages every melancholy feeling. It has quite broken Mama's heart to see her. So Mama, knowing he was in town and wanting to be of use to the two young lovers, invited Miss Marianne to stay with her when she comes to London, and of course she invited Miss Dashwood, too; so now Miss Marianne will be able to see Willoughby again, for Mama will be here very soon. And if an engagement is not announced before the month is out, then I will be very much surprised.'

I wondered if it was true or if Mrs Palmer was embellishing the story. Was Marianne really downcast? And if so, was it because of Willoughby? Was she coming to town to see him, or simply to enjoy the shops and entertainments that London had to offer? And was she really engaged, or was it just a mistake on the part of Mrs Jennings?

'My sister is coming to town, too, with her family,' said Mrs Palmer. 'How I long to see them all again! Dear Mary and Sir John and the children. We shall all be together again. Will it not be delightful?' she said to her husband.

'It will be abominable,' he said.

'Mr Palmer is so droll!' she said with a laugh. 'He is always out of humour!'

I found myself looking forward to seeing Sir John again, and Miss Dashwood, but my feelings on thinking of seeing Marianne again were more difficult to determine.

I still do not understand them, though I have thought about them all day.

I have a great desire to see her, to hear her voice, and to be with her, but I fear that the anticipation might prove more enjoyable than the event, because if she is still in love with Willoughby, then my meeting with her can bring me nothing but unhappiness.

Saturday 7 January
The time is passing very slowly. I have never known it to go so slow. Marianne will be arriving in town on Monday, and on Tuesday

I mean to call.

I slept badly and rose before dawn, riding down Rotten Row in order to pass the time until I could call on Mrs Jennings. I returned for breakfast, and then, having made myself presentable, I set out.

The morning was cold and a few snowflakes twirled around me as they fell from the overcast sky before dissolving on the pavement, and I was glad to get indoors, where I shed my caped coat, gloves and hat before going into the drawing room. Miss Dashwood was sitting by the fire, sketching, but my eyes were drawn to Marianne, who almost flew into my arms, her eyes bright and her smile one of rapture.

I knew a moment of intense joy as I thought, She is not in love with him! And she is happy to see me!

But then she checked, and her look of relief gave way to a look of anguish, and she ran past me, out of the room.

I was so full of concern that I scarcely heard Miss Dashwood welcoming me, but, recollecting myself, I replied to her, and then said, 'Is your sister ill?'

'I am afraid so,' she said, in some distress. 'She . . . has a headache. She is in low spirits

238

and over fatigued.'

From her awkward manner I guessed that something was wrong, and it did not take me long to realize the truth: that Marianne had heard a carriage and had seen a man entering the room; that she had flown towards him; and then she had realized that he was not the man she wanted to see.

My spirits sank. I could no longer be in any doubt. She was still in love with Willoughby.

I felt myself growing grim as I thought of him. He had not visited her for months at Barton; he had not called on her in London. He had abandoned her, as he had abandoned Eliza. And, as with Eliza, he had not told her that his ardour had cooled. Instead, he had left her to watch and wait for him, in the expectation that he would return.

Miss Dashwood offered me a seat and I took it, then she asked me if I had been in London since leaving Barton, but I believe both our thoughts were elsewhere. Mine were on Marianne. Should I tell her what I knew? Would some knowledge of his true character help her, or would it hurt her more? Or perhaps I should tell her sister and ask for her advice?

Before I could decide, Mrs Jennings came in, and her noisy cheerfulness filled the room. Making an effort, I paid attention to her as she said, 'Oh! I am monstrous glad to see you. I am sorry I could not welcome you before, but you know one has always a world of little odd things to do after one has been away for any time, and then I have had Cartwright to settle with. Lord, I have been as busy as a bee ever since dinner! But pray, Colonel, how came you to conjure out that I should be in town today?'

'I had the pleasure of hearing it at Mr Palmer's, where I have been dining,' I said, my thoughts still on Marianne.

'Oh! you did. Well, and how do they all do at their house? How does Charlotte do? I warrant you she is a fine size by this time.'

We continued to talk of her family until she said, 'Well, Colonel, I have brought two young ladies with me, you see — that is, you see but one of them now, but there is another somewhere. Your friend Miss Marianne, too, which you will not be sorry to hear. I do not know what you and Mr Willoughby will do between you about her. Ay, it is a fine thing to be young and handsome. Well! I was young once, but I never was very handsome — worse luck for me. However, I got a very good husband, and I don't know what the greatest beauty can do more. Ah! poor man! he has been dead these eight years and better. But, Colonel, where have you been to since we parted? And how does your business go on? Come, come, let's have no secrets among friends.'

I replied to all her enquiries, but without satisfying her in any of them, for I was not about to divulge the reason for my sudden journey to London and so expose Eliza to gossip.

Luckily, she preferred to talk instead of listen, and continued, 'We shall soon have an addition to our society. My daughter Mary and Sir John are coming to town, and two of my relations, the Misses Steele, will soon be here as well, for they are to stay with their cousins in Holborn. What fun we shall have when they all arrive!'

Miss Dashwood began to make the tea, and Marianne appeared again, but she said not two words to me. Now that I had leisure to look at her, I found that I could scarcely bear to do so, for her face was pale and drawn, and I believe the sight of her would have wrung a harder heart than mine. She was thinner than the last time I had seen her, too. Her dress hung from her shoulders and her sleeves gaped around her wrists.

I drank my tea.

Then, unable to bear it any longer, for I

wanted to take her hand and comfort her, and that, of course, I could not do, I took my leave.

'You must come and visit us often,' said Mrs Jennings, as I was going out of the door. 'Do not wait for an invitation. We will be pleased to see you in Berkeley Street whenever you have time to call.'

I thanked her for her invitation and went back to my lodgings.

Monday 16 January

I dined with Mrs Jennings this evening, and whilst I listened to her talking about her eagerness to see Mary, Sir John and the Misses Steele, I watched Marianne. Her spirits were as changeable as the sky on an April day, ranging from cheerfulness to silence. When cheerful, she sang to herself under her breath, and her face was lit with a brilliant light that made me want to do nothing but watch it. But then the light dimmed, and she plucked at her skirt and paced about the room.

What did it mean?

Did she know that Willoughby had played her false? But no, because then she would not be cheerful. But had he renewed his attentions? No, because then she would not be cast down.

Try as I might, I could not discover the meaning of it, until Mrs Jennings, seeing my eyes following Marianne, said to me, 'Ah! You see how it is! Willoughby was here this morning, when we were out. He left his card and Miss Marianne found it on the table when we returned. She was vexed with herself for having left the house, and now she can settle to nothing in anticipation of seeing him tomorrow.'

So! He had left his card. Then he had not dropped the acquaintance. But what did he mean by it? If he was in love with her, why was he not with her? And if he was not in love with her, then why had he called?

And if his behaviour was perplexing to me, how much more perplexing must it be to Marianne?

As I watched her, I wished I could bring her some ease. But there was only one man who could do that, and that man was Willoughby.

Wednesday 18 January
I received a note from Sir John, telling me that he and his family were in town and inviting me to dine with them tomorrow, and I was glad to have something to take my thoughts from Marianne, for, where she is concerned, I feel helpless, and that is not

a feeling I am used to. Nor is it a feeling I like.

Thursday 19 January

Sir John got up a dance after dinner this evening — a fact which displeased Mary, for she did not want it known that she had given such a small dance with only two violins and a sideboard collation — and I was hoping that it would put some life into Miss Marianne, but the music did little to rouse her, and although she danced, she did so without any spirit. After a while she sat out, saying that she had a headache. Her face looked grey, and what worried me more was that she did not look outwards, at the dancers, but inwards, at her own thoughts.

I hated to see her so cast down. It cut me to the quick. I was about to go over to her and see if I could cheer her, or at least distract her thoughts, when Sir John joined me, saying, 'Ay, Miss Marianne's in love all right! I cannot think what Willoughby is about! He should be here by now. I saw him this morning in the street and told him he must come along this evening. Once he arrives, she will be happy enough.'

I looked at her again and thought that she was pale because she was wondering why he did not come, but then I discovered that she did not even know that he had been invited.

I thought, If she looks so ill now, when she believes he is not a guest, how will she look when she learns that he was invited but did not come?

But no one enlightened her, for which I thank God, for I do not think she could have borne it.

And I — I can no longer bear it. Should I say something or should I remain silent? So much depends on whether she is engaged or not. If she is, I cannot speak, for she will not believe me. If not . . .

Is there any hope for me? Is there a chance that I might yet win her?

Or must I resign myself to living without her?

I cannot sleep for thinking about it.

Tomorrow I must ask her sister and find out once and for all.

Friday 20 January

I rose early and was at Berkeley Street as soon as it was seemly.

I went in, and as soon as I did so, I saw the servant carrying a letter to Willoughby, addressed in Marianne's hand.

I felt a cold wave wash over me. If they were openly corresponding, then there could be no doubt: they must be engaged.

Miss Dashwood greeted me kindly, but I could not concentrate on civilities, and I blurted out my thoughts, asking her when I was to congratulate her on having a brother and saying that news of her sister's engagement was generally known.

'It cannot be generally known,' she returned in surprise, 'for her own family does not know it.'

I was startled.

'I beg your pardon,' I said. 'I am afraid my enquiry has been impertinent, but I had not supposed any secrecy intended, as they openly correspond, and their marriage is universally talked of. Is everything finally settled? Is it impossible to — ?' And then I lost the last vestiges of my control and begged her, 'Tell me if it is all absolutely resolved on; that any attempt — that in short, concealment, if concealment be possible, is all that remains.'

For I knew that if Marianne was indeed engaged, then I must endeavour to hide my own feelings and wish her happy.

Miss Dashwood hesitated before replying.

'I have never been informed by themselves of the terms on which they stand with each other, but of their mutual affection I have no doubt,' she said.

Their *mutual* affection. Nothing could have been plainer. I felt myself grow cold.

There was nothing left except for me to gather what remained of my dignity and to say, 'To your sister I wish all imaginable happiness; to Willoughby that he may endeavour to deserve her.'

And then, unable to bear Miss Dashwood's look of sympathy, I took my leave.

Their *mutual* affection.

The words rang in my ears.

It was worse than an engagement. An engagement might be ended, however unlikely that might be. But *mutual affection . . .* I could not fight against that.

I had only one thing to fight against now, and that was despair.

Tuesday 24 January

I was disinclined for company this evening, but I could not sit at home and brood. I leafed through my invitations and set out for the Pargeters' party, knowing that it would be well attended and that it would lift my spirits to be in company.

I saw some of my acquaintance there as I waited on the stairs to be received, which made the waiting tolerable. But on entering the drawing room, I received a shock, for there was Willoughby, and he was talking to a very fashionable young woman. From the way their heads were held close together, and the way he smiled at her, it was evident that she was no casual acquaintance, but that he was courting her.

But how could this be, when he was in love with Marianne?

'Miss Grey is a lucky young woman, is she not?' asked Mrs Pargeter, seeing the direction of my gaze. 'Mr Willoughby is popular wherever he goes, and she has done well to catch him. They are well suited, fashionable people both, and with handsome fortunes, for though he has only a small income at present, he has expectations, and she is a considerable heiress with fifty thousand pounds. They make an attractive couple.'

'A couple?' I asked, with a peculiar feeling which was a mixture of elation and despair.

'Yes, the marriage is to take place within a few weeks, and then they are to go to Combe Magna, his place in Somersetshire, where they intend to settle.'

I could not believe it, although why I could not, I did not know, for I had had every proof that he was not a gentleman. And yet this . . . It was almost worse than what he had done to Eliza, for it was not thoughtless selfishness, it was wanton cruelty. He knew that Marianne was in town, for he had left his card and he must have received her letters. If he was really betrothed to Miss Grey, then why had he not written to Marianne and explained? It would have cost him nothing, demanded no sacrifice, as marriage to Eliza would have done. It would have taken him a few minutes, no more, and yet he had not even bothered to spend so small an amount of time to write to her and put her out of her misery.

He did not see me, for which I was grateful, for I could not have brought myself to acknowledge him. I was so sickened by his behaviour that I wanted to leave, but there was a crush of people coming up the stairs and it was impossible for me to force my way down them. I retired to the card room, therefore, to fume in silent rage, for it was evident that he had deserted Marianne as callously as he had deserted Eliza, with more cruelty, but — thank God! — to less ruinous effect.

After a few hands of cards I thought the crush would have abated and that I would be able to make my way down the stairs, and so I left the card-table and walked back into the saloon. As I entered it, my eye was drawn to a young woman just entering the room through the opposite door, and I saw that it was Marianne. She was looking very beautiful. Her eyes were bright and there was a spot of colour in each cheek which intensified her loveliness. Her dress was simple, but she needed no elaborate gown to set off her graceful figure. Her manner was animated and her gaze darted hither and hither, and I realized with dismay that she was looking for Willoughby.

At that moment she saw him, and her countenance glowed with delight. She began to move towards him, but her sister held her back, evidently fearing a scene, and guided her into a chair, where she sat in an agony of impatience which affected every feature as she waited for him to notice her.

At last he turned round and Marianne started up. Pronouncing his name in a tone of affection, she held out her hand to him. He approached, but slowly, and he addressed himself rather to Miss Dashwood than Marianne, talking to her as though they were nothing more than casual acquaintances, instead of intimate friends.

Marianne looked aghast.

'Good God! Willoughby, what is the meaning of this?' I heard her cry. 'Have you not received my letters?' And, as he stood with his hands resolutely behind his back, 'Will you not shake hands with me?'

I saw him take her hand, but only because he could not avoid it, and heard him say, 'I did myself the honour of calling in Berkeley Street last Tuesday, and very much regretted that I was not fortunate enough to find yourselves and Mrs Jennings at home. My card was not lost, I hope?'

The insolence! It was beyond anything. To speak to her in such a fashion, after the way he had behaved towards her at Barton!

She searched his eyes, as if unable to believe what was happening.

'But have you not received my notes?' she cried. 'Here is some mistake, I am sure — some dreadful mistake. What can be the meaning of it? Tell me, Willoughby — for heaven's sake, tell me, what is the matter?'

He made no reply; his complexion changed and all his embarrassment returned; but, on catching the eye of Miss Grey, he recovered himself again, and said, 'Yes, I had the pleasure of receiving the information of your arrival in town, which you were so good as to send me.'

Then he turned hastily away with a slight bow and rejoined Miss Grey.

Marianne was white and stood as one stunned.

I thought, She is going to faint.

I stepped forward, but her sister was there

before me and the carriage was sent for, and before very long she had left the house.

I did not linger. I was in no mood for entertainment after what I had just seen, and I was soon back at my club, where my heart was full of love and tenderness for Marianne and where I cursed the name of Willoughby.

Wednesday 25 January

I rose early, too restless to stay in bed, and went riding in the park. Having worked off the worst of my energy I went to Mrs Jennings's house. I discovered that Marianne was resting, but I spoke to her sister and I soon found that they had learnt from Willoughby that he was engaged. He had written to Marianne pretending that he had never felt anything for her and saying that she must have imagined his regard. He had concluded by saying that he was engaged to Miss Grey and that they would soon be married.

'That is abominable,' I said. 'Worse than I expected. And all this time he has let her suffer, knowing that his passion had cooled and that he had no intentions towards her.'

'It is despicable, is it not?' she said. 'I would not have believed him capable of such a thing.'

'He is capable of anything! And how is she?'

'Her sufferings have been very severe: I only hope that they may be proportionably short. It has been, it is a most cruel affliction. Till yesterday, I believe, she never doubted his regard; and even now, perhaps — but *I* am almost convinced that he never was really attached to her. He has been very deceitful!'

'He has, indeed! But your sister does not consider it quite as you do?'

'You know her disposition, and may believe how eagerly she would still justify him if she could.'

I wondered if I should tell her what I knew of Willoughby, but I did not know if it would bring her comfort or only distress her more, and in the end I left without speaking, to curse Willoughby and to love Marianne all the more.

Thursday 26 January

I was thinking over my dilemma this morning as I walked down Bond Street when I saw Mrs Jennings.

'Well, Colonel! And what do you think of this business between Miss Marianne and Willoughby? I never was more deceived in my life. Poor thing! She looks very bad. No wonder. I can scarce believe it, but it is true. He is to be married very soon — a good-for-nothing fellow! I have no patience with him. Mrs Taylor told me of it, and she was told it by a particular friend of Miss Grey herself, else I am sure I should not have believed it; and I was almost ready to sink as it was. Well, said I, all I can say is that if it is true, he has used a young lady of my acquaintance abominably ill, and I wish with all my soul his wife may plague his heart out. And so I shall always say. I have no notion of men's going on in this way: and if ever I meet him again, I will give him such a dressing down as he has not had this many a day. But there is one comfort, he is not the only young man in the world worth having; and with her pretty face she will never want admirers. There is a chance for you now, Colonel.'

Before I had a chance to reply, she went on, with scarcely a pause for breath.

'Poor girl! She cried her heart out this morning, for a letter came from her mother and it was full of his perfections. Her mother, you see, believes them to be engaged. Ah, me! Miss Dashwood has a sad task before her, for she has to write to her mother and let her know how matters stand.

Go to them, Colonel. You will do them good.'

My mind was made up. I would tell Marianne the truth. On arriving at the house I saw that Miss Dashwood, too, looked thinner than formerly; Willoughby's perfidy was taking a toll on her as well as her sister.

'I hope you do not mind me calling at such a time, but I met Mrs Jennings and she thought I would be welcome,' I said. 'I was the more easily encouraged to come because I thought that I might find you alone, which I was very desirous of doing. My object — my wish — my sole wish in desiring it — I hope, I believe it is — is to be a means of giving comfort — no, I must not say comfort — not present comfort — but conviction, lasting conviction to your sister's mind. My regard for her, for yourself, for your mother — will you allow me to prove it, by relating some circumstances, which nothing but a *very* sincere regard — nothing but an earnest desire of being useful — though where so many hours have been spent in convincing myself that I am right, is there not some reason to fear I may be wrong?'

I stopped, for I was finding it more difficult than I had anticipated.

'I understand you,' she said. 'You have

something to tell me of Mr Willoughby that will open his character farther. Your telling it will be the greatest act of friendship that can be shown to Marianne. *My* gratitude will be ensured immediately by any information tending to that end, and *hers* must be gained by it in time. Pray, pray let me hear it.'

'You shall; and, to be brief, when I quitted Barton last October — but this will give you no idea — I must go farther back. You will find me a very awkward narrator, Miss Dashwood; I hardly know where to begin. A short account of myself, I believe, will be necessary, and it *shall* be a short one. On such a subject,' I said with a sigh, 'I can have little temptation to be diffuse.'

I stopped a moment to gather my thoughts, and then I gave her an account of the whole: my love for Eliza, her marriage to my brother, her fall, her divorce, her child, and then her daughter's disappearance.

'I had no news of her for months, but she wrote to me last October,' I said. 'The letter was forwarded to me from Delaford, and I received it on the very morning of our intended party to Whitwell. Little did Mr Willoughby imagine, I suppose, that I was called away to the relief of one whom he had made poor and miserable; but *had* he known it, what would it have availed? Would he have been less gay or less happy in the smiles of your sister?'

'This is beyond everything!' exclaimed Miss Dashwood in horror, when I had told her the whole.

'His character is now before you — expensive, dissipated, and worse than both. When I came to you last week and found you alone, I came determined to know the truth, though irresolute what to do when it *was* known. My behaviour must have seemed strange to you then, but now you will comprehend it. To suffer you all to be so deceived; to see your sister — but what could I do? I had no hope of interfering with success, and sometimes I thought your sister's influence might yet reclaim him. But now, I only hope that she may turn with gratitude towards her own condition when she compares it with that of my poor Eliza.'

'I am very grateful to you, Colonel, for having spoken. I have been more pained by her endeavours to acquit him than by all the rest, for it irritates her mind more than the most perfect conviction of his unworthiness can do. Now, though at first she will suffer much, I am sure she will soon become easier,' she said with gratitude.

'Thank you, you relieve my mind,' I said.

'Is Eliza still in town?' she asked me kindly, showing a genuine interest in my dear Eliza's fate.

'No; as soon as she recovered from her lying-in, I removed her and her child into the country, and there she remains.'

Recollecting then that I was probably keeping Miss Dashwood from her sister, I left her, hoping that she could now give some solace to Marianne.

Friday 27 January
I called on Mrs Jennings today and was warmly received.

'Ah, Colonel, you have done her good,' were Mrs Jennings's first words to me. 'You have your chance, now. She is yours for a few kind words.'

I had thought about it over and over again, and although I wanted nothing more than to win her, I did not want to do so when she was weak and unable to resist. I wanted her love, not just her acquiescence, and she was in no condition to give it.

'Oh, I know how it will be!' she went on. 'A summer wedding, and the two of you made happy.'

'Please, I beg you, do not talk of it,' I said, for I did not want her to distress Marianne.

'We will all be talking of it soon!' she said.

Fortunately, she was on her way out and so she could not talk about it any more.

I was announced, and when I went in, I saw Marianne sitting by the fire. I expected her to look disappointed at my arrival as she usually did, but instead she rose and came towards me with an expression of such sweet feeling that I was almost unmanned.

'How good of you to call,' she said, with a voice full of compassionate respect. 'I never knew, never suspected, that you had had such a tragedy in your life. I always thought you a dry and soulless man. How easily we are deceived! And Eliza . . . how is she?'

'She is well, thank you,' I said, thinking how good she was to trouble herself with Eliza when she herself was suffering.

'I am glad of it,' she said sincerely.

She made no further allusion to Eliza, but she asked me if I was enjoying my stay in London, and talked to me for a quarter of an hour. In all that time, she spoke to me as though I was her fellow sufferer in grief, and I felt a pang at her heartfelt generosity, for I had had many years to get over my tragedy, whilst she had had only a day to accustom herself to hers.

Saturday 28 January

I called on Mrs Jennings again this morning and found her from home, but Miss Dashwood was there, whilst Marianne was lying down with a headache.

'I am worried for her,' said Miss Dashwood, 'for although her mind is settled, it is settled in gloomy dejection.'

'If she should wish to go home before your visit to Mrs Jennings draws to an end, I will be very happy to escort her, and you, of course,' I said. 'I am entirely at your disposal.'

'You are very kind, but we have decided to stay. My mother thinks it for the best, for here in London there are things to distract my sister, whereas at home there is no society or occupation, and every corner will remind her of Willoughby. I hope that, in a few days, she might be able to visit the shops, or go for a walk in the park, and the bustle of the scene will help to distract her thoughts. Then, too, our brother John will be in town before the middle of February, and my mother wishes us to see him.'

'I think you are wise. Diversion must eventually lift her spirits. I only wish there was more I could do to help.'

'You have already done a great deal. She no longer tries to excuse Willoughby, and this has given some rest to her thoughts. Then, too, in comparing her situation to Eliza's, she realizes she is fortunate, which is a further source of — I will not say happiness, for she feels very deeply for your ward — but gratitude.'

Sir John and his wife called at that moment with the Palmers, and they joined in our conversation. Sir John was loud in his indignation.

'I had always thought so well of the fellow, for I do not believe there is a bolder rider in England! It is an unaccountable business, but I may tell you, Miss Dashwood, I wish him at the devil with all my heart. I will not speak another word to him, meet him where I might, for all the world! No, not if it were to be by the side of Barton covert, and we were kept waiting for two hours together. Such a scoundrel of a fellow! Such a deceitful dog! Why, it was only the last time we met that I offered him one of Folly's puppies! And this is the end of it!'

Mrs Palmer, too, was angry.

'I am determined to drop his acquaintance immediately, and I am very thankful that I had never been acquainted with him at all. I wish with all my heart Combe Magna was not so near Cleveland; but it does not signify, for it is a great deal too far off to visit; indeed, I hate him so much that I am resolved never to mention his name again, and I am determined to tell everyone I see what a good-for-nothing he is. And to think, he is having his portrait painted and buying a new carriage and a new suit of clothes, whilst your sister is cast down in misery because of him.'

I could tell that such talk, though kindly meant, was distressing to Miss Dashwood, and so I turned the conversation on to less sensitive topics.

The visitors rose at last to take their leave, and I went with them. On the street outside the house, we met Mrs Jennings, just returning from her outing.

'So, Colonel, have you been proposing to Miss Marianne?' she asked.

I endeavoured to smile at her sally, but I fear it was more of a grimace.

'No.'

'Ah, me, I thought you would be married by Midsummer, but if you do not look sharp, it will not be until Michaelmas!'

Friday 3 February
And so Willoughby is married, and to neither of the young women whom he ought, by rights, to have wed.

They have had a narrow escape. And he, I hope, will think riches a sufficient recompense for the sweetness of the young women he has lost.

Saturday 4 February

I called on Mrs Jennings again today, hoping to learn from Miss Dashwood how her sister had taken the news of Willoughby's wedding, and I found on arrival that there had been an addition to the party, for some young relatives of Mrs Jennings had just arrived. I was pleased, for I hoped that they might be able to divert Miss Marianne.

'You must let me introduce you, Colonel. Miss Steele and her sister, Miss Lucy Steele. We met in Exeter, and lord! Wouldn't you know it, we found out we were distant cousins. So Lucy and Nancy came to stay with us at Barton after you left, and it did my heart good to see all the young people together, Nancy, Lucy, Elinor and Marianne. Well, my dears,' said Mrs Jennings to her two young cousins, 'and how did you travel?'

'Not in the stage, I assure you,' replied Miss Steele, with quick exultation. 'We came post all the way, and had a very smart beau to attend us. Dr Davies was coming to town, and so we thought we'd join him in a post-chaise; and he behaved very genteelly, and paid ten or twelve shillings more than we did.'

I gave an inward sigh. There was no chance of the Misses Steele diverting Miss Marianne, for they were decidedly vulgar and she could have no pleasure in their company.

'Oh, oh!' cried Mrs Jennings. 'Very pretty, indeed! And the Doctor is a single man, I warrant you.'

'There now,' said Miss Steele, affectedly simpering, 'everybody laughs at me so about the Doctor, and I cannot think why. My cousins say they are sure I have made a conquest, but for my part I declare I never think about him from one hour's end to another. "Lord! here comes your beau, Nancy," my cousin said t'other day, when she saw him crossing the street to the house. "My beau, indeed!" said I, "I cannot think who you mean. The Doctor is no beau of mine." '

As she spoke, I found myself thinking that, although the Misses Steele were decidedly vulgar, they might do Marianne some good after all: Mrs Jennings must have someone to tease about love affairs and marriage, and in Miss Steele she had found someone who enjoyed the teasing as much as she did, so that Marianne would be spared her attentions.

'Ay, ay, that is very pretty talking — but it won't do — the Doctor is the man, I see,' went on Mrs Jennings, enjoying herself heartily.

'No, indeed! and I beg you will contradict it, if you ever hear it talked of,' said Miss Steele, in high good humour.

Mrs Jennings directly gave her the gratifying assurance that she certainly would *not,* and Miss Steele was made completely happy.

I did not stay long; only long enough to ask Miss Dashwood, in a quiet moment when the Misses Steele were talking to Mrs Jennings, how her sister had taken the news of Willoughby's marriage.

'With resolute composure. She made no observation on it and shed no tears, at least at first; but after a short time she could not contain them. However, I hope they will do her good. Now that Willoughby has gone from town there will be no chance of her meeting him, and I hope to persuade her to drive out with me tomorrow. And, once our brother, John, arrives in town, she will go and visit him, too.'

'If I can be of any assistance, you only have to say.'

'Thank you. Your kindness and good sense have been a great support to me over the last few days,' she said. 'Indeed, I do not know what I would have done without them.'

'My carriage and my time are at your disposal. A note will bring me to you at any time.'

I stood up to take my leave. As I did so, I heard Mrs Jennings saying to Miss Steele, 'Miss Marianne had better look out, or her sister will have him yet!'

They giggled, and I felt annoyed, though on behalf of Miss Dashwood rather than myself. She coloured, but then we exchanged glances, for we each held the Misses Steele in the same estimation, and we both knew that Mrs Jennings could not help her nature.

I returned home, sorry that I had not seen Marianne, but full of hope that, now Willoughby was married, she would be able to forget him.

Wednesday 8 February
I dined with Sir John and his wife, and found that they had already met Marianne's half brother, Mr John Dashwood, who was newly arrived in town.

'Doesn't seem to know much about

horses,' said Sir John.

'Mrs John Dashwood is a woman of elegance and style,' said Mary. 'I believe she will be a great addition to our circle. She is particularly happy at the moment because her brother, Mr Edward Ferrars, is about to contract a brilliant alliance . . .'

Edward Ferrars. The name was familiar to me, though I could not recall where I had heard it.

'. . . with the Honourable Miss Morton, the daughter of the late Lord Morton. She is a very accomplished young woman, for she paints delightfully, and I have it on good authority that her last landscape was exquisite.'

'Oh, ay, it is a splendid match, for she has thirty thousand pounds,' said Sir John. 'A man might buy many a pointer for thirty thousand pounds! Though Mrs Dashwood did not say if he hunted. If he does not, I might ask him to stay with us at Barton.'

At the mention of Barton, I recalled that that was where I had heard the name of Mr Edward Ferrars, and that his name had been linked with Miss Dashwood. I hoped that she, too, was not to be disappointed in love.

'Ferrars is staying with his sister at the moment. We should see something of him by and by,' said Sir John.

I found myself interested in making his acquaintance and seeing what manner of man he was.

'And who do you think we have invited to stay with us?' went on Sir John.

'I cannot imagine,' I replied.

'The Misses Steele! Delightful girls, eh, Mary?'

'Indeed, charming girls,' said Mary.

I was astonished to find anyone could think them charming, but the reason soon became clear: the Misses Steele had made themselves useful at Barton, where they had doted on the children and flattered Mary, and thus had become indispensable.

Tuesday 14 February

I dined with the John Dashwoods tonight, and as soon as I walked into the drawing room, I saw Marianne! It was an unexpected pleasure, for I had not expected to see her there. She smiled when she saw me, and greeted me kindly, but she was otherwise pale and listless. A moment's reflection, however, showed me that, so soon after Willoughby's marriage, it was only to be expected.

I accepted her invitation to sit beside her, and I talked to her of music because I thought it would amuse her. I cannot say that I was altogether successful, but at least I gave a new turn to her thoughts, which, in that company, was a good in itself.

Mr John Dashwood made a favourable impression on me to begin with because he had a look of the Misses Dashwood about the eyes, but it soon became apparent that there the resemblance ended, for he had none of their goodness or intelligence.

His wife was very elegant, but in nature she was limited and selfish.

His mother-in-law, Mrs Ferrars, was a proud woman with an ill-natured aspect. For some reason she seemed to have taken a dislike to Miss Dashwood, and from time to time she favoured her with a sour look. Quite why she did not like Miss Dashwood I could not imagine; unless it was that Miss Dashwood, by her breeding, intelligence and common sense, showed Mrs Ferrars to be deficient in all three.

The Misses Steele added their own brand of silliness to the party, and Sir John, Mary and Mrs Jennings made up the rest.

Dinner was announced, and we went into the dining room, where I found myself disgusted by the opulence on display, for, in the midst of so much plenty, Dashwood had spared nothing for his sisters; they were not in London at his invitation but through the kindness of Mrs Jennings, and they were sitting at his table in old dresses.

I tried to tempt Marianne to eat, but she did nothing more than toy with the food on her plate, and she sat still and silent until the ladies withdrew. The gentlemen soon followed, and I was about to go and sit next to Marianne when her brother decided to show me some screens that Miss Dashwood had painted.

'These are done by my eldest sister,' he said, 'and you, as a man of taste, will, I dare say, be pleased with them. I do not know whether you ever happened to see any of her performances before, but she is in general reckoned to draw extremely well.'

He might as well have said, 'Will you not admire my sister, Elinor, Brandon? For she is exceedingly accomplished, and furthermore, she would make you an excellent wife.'

I disliked his attitude, but I praised the screens nevertheless, for they were very well done, and I am very fond of Miss Dashwood.

Mrs Ferrars, piqued by my praise, requested to look at them, but when she had examined them, she dismissed them with a 'Hum, very pretty,' and proceeded to say how well Miss Morton painted; Miss Morton being the wife she had chosen for her eldest son, Edward.

I turned away from her in disgust, but a moment later I was pleased that she had spoken, for Marianne was roused from her thoughts by the slight to her sister, and springing up, she took the screens into her own hands.

'This is admiration of a very particular kind!' she said. 'What is Miss Morton to us? Who knows or who cares for her? It is Elinor of whom we think and speak.' She looked at the screens and admired them herself as they ought to be admired, saying, 'Look at the workmanship! The taste and the artistry! See how the colours complement each other. This is fine workmanship indeed.'

I loved her for her affectionate heart, and I was overjoyed to see a spark in her eye and some colour in her cheek.

But Mrs Ferrars was not to be outdone, and Marianne, in her weakened state, was no match for her. Having done all in her power to defend her sister, she moved over to her chair, and when Mrs Ferrars renewed her attack, she put one arm round her sister's neck and one cheek close to hers, saying in a low but eager voice, 'Dear, dear

Elinor, don't mind them. Don't let them make *you* unhappy.'

I was overcome with sympathy for her tender heart. I stood up, oblivious of the company, and went over to her, for her spirits were quite overcome; and in another moment she had hidden her face on her sister's shoulder and burst into tears.

'Ah! poor dear,' murmured Mrs Jennings, handing her some smelling salts, whilst Sir John changed his seat to one close by Lucy Steele, and gave her, in a whisper, a brief account of the whole affair.

In a few minutes, however, Marianne was recovered enough to put an end to the bustle, and I returned to my seat, only to find myself addressed by John Dashwood.

'Poor Marianne!' he said. 'She is very nervous; she has not Elinor's constitution, and one must allow that there is something very trying to a young woman who *has been* a beauty in the loss of her personal attractions. You would not think it perhaps, but Marianne *was* remarkably handsome a few months ago — quite as handsome as Elinor. Now you see it is all gone.'

I was tempted to say, 'Marianne is the most beautiful woman of my acquaintance; and if you had any sense, you would see that I am in love with her, instead of trying to persuade me to offer for her sister,' but the evening had had enough dramas, and so I kept my peace.

He invited me to dinner again, and though I had no desire to spend another evening in his company, I knew I would find Marianne at his house, and so I accepted.

To look at her and listen to her, and to be with her: this is my sole delight.

And, if she will allow it, to comfort her and to love her will be the purpose of my life.

Saturday 18 February

I was looking forward to dining with Mr Dashwood this evening, but to my disappointment, his sisters were not there: Marianne had a headache, and her sister had stayed behind to look after her.

His wife's brothers were there, however, and two more dissimilar men it would be difficult to meet. Mr Robert Ferrars was a coxcomb who waxed lyrical about his new toothpick-case, before telling me that his brother was extremely gauche on account of having been educated by private tutors instead of going to school.

'If Mama had only sent him to Westminster as well as myself, instead of sending him to Mr Pratt's, he, too, could have been a man of fashion,' he remarked.

Mr Edward Ferrars, far from being gauche, was a man of good sense and breeding. He was somewhat shy, it is true, but at least he did not breathe a syllable about toothpick-cases, nor did he lower himself by belittling his brother. Of Miss Morton he made no mention, and I suspect that the idea of a marriage is in his mother's mind and not his own.

I liked him. He was not the sort of young man it would be possible to know in half an hour, or even half a month, but he had an intelligent mind, and I was sorry when our seating at dinner separated us, for, apart from Sir John, he was the only man there to whom I cared to speak.

Thursday 23 February
Mrs Palmer has had her baby, a son and heir! Mrs Jennings is delighted, and Palmer, though he says little, is evidently pleased; a fact which escapes Mrs Jennings, who cannot understand why he will say that all infants are alike, instead of saying that his son is the finest child in the world.

Saturday 25 February
I was impatient to see Miss Marianne again, but feeling I could not call too early at Mrs

Jennings's house, I called on Sir John instead. To my delight, I found the Misses Dashwood there!

'I'm a lucky man, Brandon, to have two such pretty young ladies staying with me,' he said heartily, his good humour making them smile. 'We hope we will have you for some time to come: Mrs Jennings is besotted with her new grandchild and is out of the house all day, and so we have stolen her guests! Her absence is our gain, eh, Brandon?'

I murmured a reply, I know not what, for my eyes were on Marianne. I was delighted to see that she was looking brighter, and that her cheeks were not so hollow. Sir John's company, rather than Mrs Jennings's, was doing her good.

'I am pleased to see you, Colonel,' she said, coming forward with a smile.

The warmth of her greeting and the touch of her hand made my heart glow.

'And I am pleased to see you looking so much better,' I said.

Sir John being distracted by the children, I sat down with Marianne by the window.

'Ah, yes, I was not very well the last time you saw me, was I? But I have recovered, and it is in no small part thanks to you. I honour you for taking my sister's part the other evening. You were generous in your praise, and I could have listened to you for half an hour as you talked of her screens, for everything you said was true. You thought, perhaps, that I was too warm in my support of her —'

'Not at all,' I said. 'Quite the contrary, I esteemed you for your love and loyalty.'

'Ah, yes, I might have expected as much, for you are a man who understands both of those emotions. It does me good to know that there are men such as yourself in the world, else I might be in danger of losing faith. For myself it is nothing; I will never love again; but for my sister, I want only the best: a loving husband, one who is honest and loyal and good; one who will esteem and value her, and make her happy.'

I wondered for a moment if she meant me, but there was a faraway look in her eye that convinced me that she was thinking of someone else, and my heart beat again.

'You, too, perhaps —' I ventured.

'No. That can never be,' she said with finality.

I did not press her, for I knew it was too soon, but in time, I hoped, she would be ready to move forward.

I looked around for a new subject. It was not hard to find, for the Misses Steele were also there, sitting at the far end of the room, flattering Mary and spoiling the children.

'What delightful boys!' said Miss Lucy, as William and his brother tugged at her hair. 'I quite dote on them! You are so fortunate to have two such spirited boys. If there is one thing I like in a boy it is spirit.'

'That is very intelligent of you,' said Mary. 'A boy without spirit is something I cannot abide.'

'No, indeed!' said Miss Lucy, as William tugged at her sash and ripped it. 'Quite the worst thing in the world!'

'They will not be here for much longer,' said Marianne, following my gaze. 'They will soon be going to my brother's house.'

I was even more surprised, for he had only just met them.

'I see what you are thinking,' she said. 'You are thinking it odd that we, who are family, are not invited, when the Misses Steele, who are nothing, are.'

'I was not presuming to think —' I said, for politeness's sake.

'Come, let there be no such deceptions between us. We both value the truth. You were thinking it odd, were you not?'

'Very well, yes, I was.'

'But you see, it is simple to explain. Elinor and I do not flatter our sister-in-law, nor do we spoil the children. The Misses Steele do both.'

'You will, perhaps, be happier here than at your brother's house,' I said. 'You will at least be spared the impertinences of the Misses Steele.'

But her spirits, which were not yet strong, had made all the effort they were capable of making for the time being, and she replied, 'As to that, it is a matter of perfect indifference to me where I am,' then relapsed into silence.

I tried to lift her out of it, but she had gone where I could not follow, and I could not pierce her sad thoughts.

I did not despair, however, for time will lessen her pain and I am persuaded she has weathered the worst. Young as she is, she will soon begin to take an interest in life again.

I believe that London has done all it can for her. She has diversion here, it is true, but she is hemmed in by a code of conduct that is stifling for her. She will be better once she returns to the country, where her spirit can be free.

Monday 27 February
'Do the Misses Dashwood ride?' I asked Sir John this morning.

'Ay, they are good horsewomen by all accounts. Willoughby was all for giving Miss Marianne a fine piece of horseflesh, Queen Mab, but her mother had nowhere to keep it and she had to refuse.'

'And you have nothing for them to ride,' I mused.

'Mary is no horsewoman,' he said by way of explanation.

'I am going to Tattersall's next week. If I see anything suitable, I will buy it, I think.'

'What, thinking of inviting them to Delaford, are you?' he asked.

'I will have to return Mrs Dashwood's hospitality,' I said.

'Ay, you're inviting them for their mother's sake!' said Sir John, laughing heartily.

I had to bear his teasing, but it was worth it to have discovered that Marianne was a horsewoman, and to learn that I could bring her some happiness.

I am persuaded that she will like Delaford. To be in a place that has no unhappy memories for her will do her good. And once there, she can ride to her heart's content. The fresh air, the exercise, and the freedom from restraint will all help to restore her spirits.

I am longing to see her happy again.

Thursday 9 March

I ran across Sir John at Tattersall's this morning as I was examining a grey mare, a neat stepper with a good temperament. He gave me his opinion on the mare, and proceeded to look at road horses for himself.

As he inspected one of the horse's mouths, he said, 'Have you heard the news? Edward Ferrars is engaged to Miss Lucy Steele.'

'What?' I asked, my hand stilling on the mare's mane in astonishment.

I could not believe it! A man of Ferrars's stamp, with all his superiority, to marry a vulgar creature like Lucy Steele?

'Ay, I thought it would surprise you! "Lord," said Mrs Jennings, "to think they kept it secret all this time!" Twelve months they've been engaged.'

'Twelve months!' I exclaimed.

'True, upon my word,' he said, laughing at my surprise. 'No one knew anything about it except her sister Nancy! Met at Longstaple. His tutor was Miss Lucy's uncle! They took a fancy to one another and got engaged, but never said anything about it because they knew Mrs Ferrars wouldn't like it. She wanted Edward to go into parliament, or make a noise in some other public fashion, not sink into obscurity; and as for marrying his tutor's niece, why, she had chosen an heiress for him to marry!'

I remembered her praising Miss Morton and I thought, Little did she know, when she was admiring Miss Morton's painting, that her son was already engaged!

'His mother told him of her plans for him, I suppose, and he said that he could not marry Miss Morton, and that is what brought matters to a head,' I said.

'No such thing. Miss Lucy's sister popped the whole thing out! A good creature, but without a grain of sense. Thought Miss Lucy was so well liked by Mrs John Dashwood that neither she nor Mrs Ferrars would object. Went to her as she sat at her carpet-work and let the whole thing out! You can imagine what a blow it was to Mrs Dashwood's pride and vanity. Fell into violent hysterics immediately; her husband heard her; and then they turned on poor Miss Lucy. *Then* Mrs Dashwood fell into hysterics again, and the doctor was sent for. And that is how I learnt of it —'

He paused as the mare was taken away and another one brought for me to inspect, and then continued.

'— for after seeing Mrs Dashwood — who is not ill, by the by, but just temporarily overcome — the doctor went on to see Mrs Palmer, who was in a fright about the baby catching a cold or something or other, and there he met Mrs Jennings, who had the whole story out of him.'

'And you had it from Mrs Jennings?'

'I came across her just now, on her way home.'

I was amazed at the whole story, but I hoped they would be very happy and I said so to Sir John.

'Ay, all this fuss about money and greatness, what does it matter, as long as two people love each other, eh, Brandon? There is no reason on earth why Mr Edward and Lucy should not marry, for Mrs Ferrars is very rich by all accounts and may afford to do very well by her son; and though Lucy has next to nothing herself, she will know how to manage on very little, I am sure.'

He left me examining the mare, a bay with good paces, and went off to look at road horses.

I saw three more mares and chose one with a good temperament but plenty of spirit.

I mean to take her to Delaford myself tomorrow, so that she will be used to her new home by the time Marianne arrives.

Friday 10 March
I fell in with John Dashwood on my way to

the stables this morning, and as soon as he saw me, he said, 'Ah! Brandon, you have heard all about it, I suppose.'

I had no desire to talk to him, for his behaviour to his sisters had given me a disgust of him that nothing could overcome, but I could not escape him, for he walked along beside me, talking all the while.

'Never has anyone been so deceived,' he said. 'My poor Fanny! She has borne it all with the fortitude of an angel! She says she will never think well of anybody again.'

She was the most ill-used of women, according to Dashwood, and so was his mother-in-law, Mrs Ferrars; but everything he said made me like them less and made me like Edward Ferrars the more, for he had stuck to his engagement, though his mother had threatened to disinherit him on the one hand, and had bribed him with the promise of riches if he married Miss Morton on the other.

'I cannot understand it,' said Dashwood as we crossed the road. 'He will be penniless if he marries Miss Lucy, for his mother will never see him again; and she has made it clear that if he enters into any profession with a view of better support, she will do everything in her power to prevent his advancing in it.'

I wondered if he was speaking in jest, but he was quite serious; then I wondered if he could be sane, for he evidently thought that Mrs Ferrars had been sensible to act in such a manner.

'He left her house yesterday, but where he is gone, or whether he is still in town, I do not know; for *we* of course can make no inquiry. It is a melancholy consideration. Born to the prospect of such affluence! I cannot conceive a situation more deplorable. We must all feel for him, and the more so because it is totally out of our power to assist him.'

'As it was out of your power to assist your sisters,' I remarked, but he did not understand my sarcasm.

'Quite. I knew you would understand. The price of everything these days —' he said, shaking his head. 'And there is one thing more preparing against him, which must be worse than all — his mother has determined, with a very natural kind of spirit, to settle *that* estate upon Robert immediately, which might have been Edward's. I left her this morning with her lawyer, talking over the business. Can anything be more galling to the spirit of a man than to see his younger brother in possession of an estate which might have been his own? Poor Edward! I feel for him sincerely.'

'But not sincerely enough to help him,' I remarked as we arrived at the stables.

He did not understand me, and when he opened his mouth to continue, I said that I was leaving for the country shortly and that I would bid him good day.

'Oh, yes, you must be going to visit your estate, a fine estate, by all accounts. My sister, Miss Dashwood —'

'Good day, Mr Dashwood,' I said firmly and went inside.

The carriage was soon ready, and with Cinnamon tethered to the back of it, I set out for Delaford.

Saturday 11 March

Cinnamon is now in the Delaford stables, and I am looking forward to seeing Marianne ride her.

Eliza and the baby are thriving. I think Willoughby's recent behaviour has done Eliza good, for she has ceased to speak of him in affectionate terms, and she has begun to see him differently.

She would not think badly of him when he hurt her because her own feelings were too closely involved. But when he deserted Marianne, she felt compassion for her fellow sufferer, and when he then went on to marry Miss Grey, for the sake of her fortune, she could begin to see him in his true colours, as a mercenary, shallow man, who thought of no one's feelings but his own.

I left her playing with the baby and returned to the house.

There was a messenger there, waiting for me, and on asking him his business, I discovered that Dewson, the rector, was dead; a sad blow, for I had always held him in affection, but at almost ninety years of age he had had a good life and I gave thanks for it.

Sunday 12 March
Today's service was taken by Mr Walker, the curate, and I found myself wondering whether I should offer him the living, but then I remembered that Edward Ferrars said he was intending to go into the church, and I thought, Here is a way for me to help him.

I am only sorry that the living is so poor and that the parsonage so small, but both are capable of improvement, and it will at least give him an income and somewhere to live.

Tuesday 14 March
I was hoping to offer Ferrars the living this

morning, but on reaching town I realized that I did not know where he lived. I made enquiries but I could not discover Ferrars's address, for his sister went into hysterics when I called on her and I did not know where else to apply. And then I remembered that Mrs Dashwood had spoken of inviting him to Barton Cottage, and I thought that the Misses Dashwood might be able to help me.

I went, therefore, to Mrs Jennings's house, where I found Marianne playing the piano. I did not like to disturb her, for although the air was a sad one, it seemed to be giving some relief to her feelings.

Instead, I spoke to Mrs Jennings, who welcomed me with. 'Ah! Colonel, I do not know what you and I shall do without the Misses Dashwood, for they are to go to Cleveland with the Palmers for Easter. They will not come back to me afterwards, for they are quite resolved upon going home from there. How forlorn we shall be when I come back! Lord! we shall sit and gape at one another as dull as two cats.'

I was pleased rather than otherwise, for I felt that London had done all it could for Marianne, and that it must now be up to her home and her mother to complete her cure; after which I hoped that she and her family would accept an invitation to stay with me at Delaford.

Mrs Jennings turned her attention to some matters of her own, and I was free to speak to Miss Dashwood. I followed her over to the window, where she had gone in order to see the print she was making more clearly.

'I have heard of the injustice your friend Mr Ferrars has suffered from his family,' I said. 'Will you be so good as to tell him that the living of Delaford is his if he think it worth his acceptance, for unfortunately it is a poor one.'

She was astonished, and seemed at first stunned, but she soon recovered and thanked me warmly, saying that she was sure he would be grateful for it, and saying also that she was sure I would be pleased with him, for he was a man of great worth, with good principles and disposition.

'I wonder, would you tell him about it? I know him so little I would not know how to speak to him. I would not wish him to feel under any obligation to me,' I said.

'I will undertake it with pleasure, if you are sure it is really your wish to give such an agreeable commission to another,' she said.

'It is. Perhaps you know where he is to be found?'

'I believe he is still in town; fortunately I heard his address from Miss Steele.'

'I only wish the living was better and the parsonage was larger,' I said.

'The smallness of the house, I cannot imagine any inconvenience to them, for it will be in proportion to their family and income.'

I was surprised to hear her speak of a family.

'I fear I have given you an exaggerated idea of the worth of the living,' I said. 'This little rectory can do no more than make Mr Ferrars comfortable as a bachelor; it cannot enable him to marry.'

'That will be for him to decide,' she said.

'Of course,' I replied, though I still thought, privately, that it would be impossible.

I took my leave soon afterwards and returned to my lodgings in St James's Street. I had not been there for very long when Ferrars was announced.

'Brandon,' he said, on entering the room, 'I have just come from Miss Dashwood, and I must give you my thanks, my sincere thanks, for thinking of me and standing my friend.'

He did not seem particularly pleased, despite his words, and I wondered if it was because the living was such a poor one, but then his manner was explained when he said that he would not be able to take it up at once as it would be several months before he could be ordained.

'As to that, there is no hurry. I will make arrangements to cover the period in between, and I hope to see you at Delaford Parsonage by Michaelmas.'

He thanked me again, and I said, 'I hope you and Miss Lucy will be very happy.'

His manner was diffident, but he thanked me for my good wishes, and then went on his way.

Friday 17 March

'So, Brandon, you have given Ferrars the living of Delaford, eh?' said Sir John, when I called in on the Palmers this morning. 'Capital, capital! He seems like a fine fellow. Audacious, too! Marrying Miss Lucy! Ay, she's a sly puss! Never said a word about it, not though she stayed with us for months. Can't say I wonder at it. Afraid of his mother, and right to be afraid, too. Cast him off without a penny! Can't think why. Nothing wrong with Miss Lucy. No fortune, of course, but Ferrars had enough for two. Ah, well! It's worked out well for us. Now we get to see both of you when we come to

Delaford.'

'We are going to Cleveland shortly, for the Easter holidays,' said Palmer. 'Charlotte has had enough of town and wants to go home with the baby. Will you join us?'

'Nothing would give me greater pleasure,' I said, for it meant I would be with Marianne, and I was looking forward to seeing her recover her health and vigour.

'The ladies will be taking two days on the road. It will be easier for Charlotte and the child that way. But we need not travel so slowly. I have some business to finish in town, and I propose to start out the day after my wife but arrive not many hours later.'

I said that this suited me, and it was agreed.

Monday 3 April

I seem to have spent the last few days being thanked for my small kindness, for this morning, when I called on Mrs Jennings to tell her that I would be going to Cleveland, I found Marianne alone, and as I hesitated by the door, she sprang up and took my hands.

'Oh, I am glad to see you. I have been wanting to thank you for helping Edward ever since Elinor told me of it. You have been a true friend to him when those who should have been his friends, his own family, deserted him. But you are a man who knows the meaning of loyalty, as I am only too well aware. Will you not sit down? Mrs Jennings is visiting Charlotte, but she will be back directly.'

She waved a hand towards the sofa and I was pleased to see that her wrist was not so thin as formerly.

'And so Edward is to live at Delaford,' she said, as I sat down.

'He is.'

A variety of emotions flitted across her face and then she said, with a sigh, 'How difficult everything is! A few months ago, I would not have thought . . .' Her eyes left mine and wandered unseeingly around the room. Then they came to rest on a picture her sister had been painting. 'But perhaps there is still some hope, if not for me, then . . .' Her eyes found mine again. 'The living is not enough for him to marry on, I believe you said?'

I could not follow her thoughts, but I replied to her question, saying, 'No, I do not see how it can sustain a family.'

'How could it? With only two hundred a year, they will not be able to marry.'

'I do not believe so, though Sir John seems

to think they will manage. I dined with him at the Palmers last night. Mr Palmer was good enough to invite me to Cleveland.'

'Ah, Cleveland,' she said, her face falling.

'You do not want to go? I thought you would be glad to leave town, with its unhappy memories.'

'And so I am. And yet I was happy here, too. I cannot forget that when I arrived, I was full of hope. I sat by that window, I played that pianoforte, when I waited for him to call.'

'But in the country you will be able to enjoy the wide-open spaces, taking country walks —'

'Do not tempt me with country walks, for it was on one such walk that I met *him*,' she said in agitation.

'The variety of scene will lift your spirits, I hope,' I said.

'It is too near . . .'

I understood her, for Cleveland was in the same county as Willoughby's seat.

'You thought to go into Somersetshire in happier circumstances.'

'How well you understand me,' she remarked, looking at me with gratitude. 'You are the only one who does. Elinor tells me that we will not be near him there, but she does not understand that being in the same county will be torment to me. It is good of you to listen to me. I cannot burden Elinor any further, she has her own troubles, and Mrs Jennings is not someone I can confide in. But to have you here as my friend eases my mind more than I can say.'

'I am only too happy to do anything I can to help you,' I said sincerely.

'I am glad you are coming with us to Cleveland.'

The simple sentence meant more to me than she could possibly know.

'I . . .' I cleared my throat. 'I am looking forward to it, too. You will be staying at Cleveland for a week, I understand?'

'Yes. And then I can go home, to Barton, and to Mama.'

At that moment, Mrs Jennings entered the room and I told her that I was to join her in the country. She was pleased, and we all parted in the certainty of seeing each other again before very long.

Thursday 6 April
Palmer and I left London this morning and stopped at Reading. Tomorrow we will reach Cleveland.

Despite her protestations to the contrary, I hope that the change of scene will do Marianne good.

We arrived at Cleveland just as the light was beginning to fade, but as we turned into the drive, I could see that it was a spacious, modern-built house, situated on a sloping lawn. There was no park, but the pleasure-grounds seemed tolerably extensive, with an open shrubbery and closer wood walk. The drive wound round a plantation, past lawns dotted over with timber — a mixture of fir, mountain-ash and acacia, interspersed with tall Lombardy poplars — and took us to the front door.

We were soon inside. It was a tranquil scene. Mrs Jennings was sitting with her carpet-work, Marianne was playing the pianoforte, and Miss Dashwood was reading.

'Oh, Mr Palmer, we thought you would never get here!' said Charlotte. 'We have held dinner back on purpose. You will like to dress first.'

'The day a man needs to dress in his own home after spending all day in the saddle is not one I want to see. We will have it at once,' he replied tersely.

'Mr Palmer is always so droll!' said Charlotte, nevertheless giving the order, so that before very long we were in the dining room.

'How was your journey?' asked Miss

Dashwood.

'Very good,' I said.

'It was barely tolerable,' snorted Palmer. 'Potholes all the way.'

'We thought you might have found it difficult going in the rain,' said Elinor.

'We had no rain,' I said.

'No? It has been raining all morning here.'

'But it has not prevented us having a high time,' said Charlotte. 'What do you think we have been doing, Mr Palmer? We have been showing baby to Mrs Harding.'

'Ay, a finer child never drew breath, so Mrs Harding said, and she should know, for she has been housekeeper here for twenty years,' said Mrs Jennings.

'One child is much like another,' said Palmer provokingly.

'Why, Mr Palmer, how can you say so?' exclaimed his wife and her mother.

'There is every difference in the world between children, and if yours is not the most intelligent child I have come across in many a long day, then my name is not Jennings,' finished that lady.

He only snorted, but when they are not by, he praises the infant fondly enough.

I was glad of a hot meal, and afterwards my eyes were drawn to Marianne as she sat at the pianoforte.

I saw Mrs Jennings watching me and I became aware that I was staring, and so I said to Miss Dashwood, 'I have in mind some improvements which I mean to make to the parsonage at Delaford when I return. The house is capable of extending at the rear, and a new room might be built above the kitchen. The two front rooms could then be knocked into one, and, with some new decorations, I believe it may be habitable by the time Mr Ferrars has been ordained.'

She listened to my plans whilst carrying on with her needlework, and I tried to keep my eyes away from Marianne until it was time to retire.

Saturday 8 April
Rain kept us indoors today. Palmer and I whiled away the morning with billiards, for he has a fine billiard room, and this afternoon we joined the ladies. Mrs Jennings was sitting over her carpet-work and Charlotte was playing with her baby. Miss Dashwood was engaged in needlework and Marianne sat with a book.

'She always finds her way to the library, wherever we stay,' said Miss Dashwood.

When Marianne put aside her book, I engaged her in conversation and told her of my library at Delaford.

'I hope you and your family will visit me there. You will be able to see your friends in the parsonage, and you may have free rein of my library. There are many books I am sure you would enjoy. Have you read Cowper?'

'Oh, yes,' she said enthusiastically. 'But I have not been able to find all of his work.'

'Then you have a treat awaiting you. And there are some plays I believe you will also enjoy.'

'Your library is well stocked?'

'With older volumes, yes, for my grandfather was very proud of the library, but with newer volumes, no. My father was not fond of books, and although I have been adding to it ever since I inherited, and have purchased some modern tomes, I still have some way to go before I can claim it is a fine library.'

'Our library at Norland was also neglected,' she said. 'I used to dream of buying every new volume of poetry and filling the shelves with all my favourite works. Indeed, I thought that if I were to come into a fortune, I would like nothing better than to send for all the newest works from London.'

'Then perhaps you will help me choose some books when you come and stay at

Delaford with your mother and sisters.'

'I would like that. And Edward, perhaps, might be able to use the library, too.'

'Of course,' I said, but mention of Edward seemed to have upset her, and she fell silent.

Sensing her mood, I agreed to Palmer's suggestion that we should have a game of cards, and Marianne sought solace once more in her music.

Monday 10 April
The weather was again wet, and when I returned from the billiard room, I was alarmed to find that Marianne, who had gone outside after dinner, had not returned.

'She should not be outside in such weather,' I said to her sister, for the rain was pouring down outside the windows.

'She often likes to walk in the evenings. I do not believe she can bear to be indoors.'

I sat and talked to her, but my eyes were always looking through the window for Marianne. I pictured her running through the woods, trying to ease her spirits by fresh air and exercise, and I wished the sun could have shone for her. A smiling April would have done much to heal her heart, I was sure.

She returned at last, wet and bedraggled, and looking no happier for her exercise.

'There, now, you shouldn't be sitting in those wet shoes and stockings,' said Mrs Jennings when she entered the room.

'I am too tired to change at the moment,' said Marianne as she settled herself into a chair by the fire.

Nothing more was said, but it was some time before she retired to her room to change, and I was not surprised when, this evening, she complained of a sore throat and head.

'You do not look very well,' said Mrs Jennings, with maternal solicitousness. 'You must have a tincture.'

'No, it is nothing, or at least, nothing a good night's sleep will not cure,' said Marianne.

'I will go upstairs with you,' said Miss Dashwood, laying down her needlework.

'There is no need, but I think I must retire.'

She bade us good night, and we were left to pass the evening without her; not a great loss to the others, but a sad blow to me, for her presence is becoming more and more necessary to me. When I see her, when I hear her, I am happy; and when she is not there, I feel as though a part of me is missing.

I was pleased to see Marianne appear at breakfast this morning, and I asked her how she did. She replied that she was well, but though she tried to convince herself that she was indeed the same as always, it soon became apparent that she was not. She sat over the fire, shivering, for most of the day, and when she was not by the fire, she was lying on the sofa, too listless to read.

I was astonished at Miss Dashwood's composure, for, although she tended her sister during the day, she seemed to think that a good night's sleep would mend matters, whereas to my eyes her sister was really ill.

However, I could say nothing beyond a general wish for her improved health, but I could not sleep when I retired to my own room and spent most of the night in pacing the floor.

Had I been too sanguine in believing her to be recovering from Willoughby? In a low mood, I thought that I had, for she had not recovered from him at all. And my hopes that she could love me were equally ill-founded. I had been too optimistic. I had thought that she would recover from Willoughby, fall in love with me and that we would be married.

What a fool I had been.

Marianne joined us for breakfast this morning, but it soon became obvious that she
could not sit up, and she retired, voluntar-
ily, to bed.

'Poor girl, she is very bad,' said Mrs
Jennings, with a shake of her head. 'Miss
Dashwood, I advise you to send for Charlotte's apothecary. He will be able to give
her something to make her feel better.'

'Yes, indeed, Mama, we must send for him
at once,' said Charlotte.

'You are very kind,' said Miss Dashwood,
and her ready compliance showed me that
she, too, thought the case to be serious.

The apothecary came, examined his patient, and though encouraging Miss Dashwood to expect that a very few days would
restore her sister to health, yet by pronouncing her disorder to have a putrid tendency,
and by speaking of an infection, gave instant
alarm to Charlotte on the baby's account.

Mrs Jennings looked grave, and advised
Charlotte to remove at once with the baby.

Palmer at first ridiculed their fears, but
their anxiety was at last too great for him to
withstand and within an hour of the apothecary's arrival, Charlotte set off, with her

little boy and his nurse, for the house of a near relation of Palmer's, who lived a few miles from Bath.

She urged Mrs Jennings to accompany her, but Mrs Jennings, with a true motherly heart, declared that she could not leave Cleveland whilst Marianne was ill, for, as Marianne's mother was not with her, she must take her place.

I blessed her for her kindness, and I regretted that I could do nothing except be there, in case the ladies should have need of me.

I took out my frustrations on the billiard table, and did not retire until the early hours of the morning.

Thursday 13 April
If Marianne had not fallen ill, she would have been on her way home by now, for she and her sister were due to leave Cleveland today, but she is still too ill to think of travelling.

I am beside myself with worry. She should be getting better, but she seems to be getting worse. If only I could go into the sick room! Then I could see how she fared. Her sister tells me that she is tolerable, but I fear the worst. I imagine her pale and drawn, with dark rings under her eyes, and no matter how much I tell myself that I must not indulge in such fancies, I cannot help it.

Not wanting to be a burden to Mrs Jennings, I offered to leave the house, even though my heart cried out against it, but she, good soul, would not hear of it. She said that I must remain, or who would play piquet with her in the evening when Miss Dashwood was with her sister?

Her words came from the goodness of her heart, for she knew of my feelings for Marianne, and I thanked her silently for allowing, nay, encouraging me to remain.

Palmer encouraged me, too, for he had decided to follow his wife, but he did not like to leave the ladies alone, without anyone to assist or advise them should they need it.

And so it was settled that I should stay.

Friday 14 April

The apothecary called again this morning. He was still hopeful of a speedy recovery, but I could see no sign of it. Miss Dashwood and Mrs Jennings were kept busy all day nursing the patient, and when I asked Mrs Jennings how she went on, she told me that Marianne was no better.

I did not retire until late, in case I was needed, but even so, once I reached my bed-chamber, I could not sleep. I could only pace the floor and think of Marianne.

Saturday 15 April

'I knew how it would be,' said Mrs Jennings, as we sat together this evening. 'Right from the beginning, I knew how it would be. She was ill, poor girl, but would not acknowledge it, and so she made herself worse before she gave in to nature and took to her bed. It is because she has been lowered by a broken heart. Ay, Colonel, I have seen it before, a young girl fading away after her lover proves false. Willoughby! If I had him here, what would I not say to him, behaving in such a way to my poor young friend. I hope he will be sorry when she dies of it.'

I tried to reason myself out of believing that death would follow, particularly as the apothecary did not seem despondent, but when I had retired and I was alone, I could not help giving in to gloomy thoughts and fearing I would see Marianne no more.

Sunday 16 April

The dawn dispelled my gloom, and I told myself that this was nothing but a common cold; neglected, it is true, but otherwise susceptible to a warm bed and tender care. In a few days, Marianne would be sitting up; in a few days more, she would leave her room; and before the week was out, she would be well again.

The apothecary confirmed my views when he came again this morning, saying that his patient was materially better. Her pulse was much stronger, and every symptom was more favourable than on the previous visit.

Reassured, I went to church for the Easter service.

When I returned, I found that Marianne was still improving.

Miss Dashwood, confirmed in every pleasant hope, was all cheerfulness.

'I am relieved that I made light of the matter to my mother when I wrote to her to explain our delayed return,' she said to me, as we sat together whilst Mrs Jennings took her turn in the sick room. 'I would not have liked to worry her for nothing. As it is, I believe I will be able to write again tomorrow and fix a day for our return.'

But the day did not close as auspiciously as it began. Towards the evening, Marianne became ill again, and when Mrs Jennings relinquished her place to Miss Dashwood, she looked grave.

'I do not like the look of her. She is growing more heavy, restless, and uncomfortable than before,' she said, as she entered the drawing room.

Miss Dashwood rose.

'It is probably nothing more than the fatigue of having sat up to have her bed made,' she said. 'I will give her the cordials the apothecary supplied, and they will let her sleep.'

She left the room, and Mrs Jennings and I settled down to a hand of piquet.

'Poor girl, I do not like the look of her,' she said, shaking her head. 'Mark my word, Colonel, she will get worse before she gets better.'

Her words proved prophetic. As I went upstairs when Mrs Jennings retired for the night, I heard a cry coming from the sick room: 'Is Mama coming?'

I paused on the stairs, anxious at the feverish sound of her voice.

'But she must not go round by London,' cried Marianne, in the same hurried manner, 'I shall never see her if she goes by London.'

A bell rang, and a maid hurried past me.

Recalled to myself, I went downstairs again, where I paced the length of the room, wishing there was something I could do to help. Another moment and Miss Dashwood entered.

'I am anxious, nay, worried, very worried,'

she said, wringing her hands. 'My sister is most unwell. If only my mother were here!'

At last! There was a way in which I could help.

'I will fetch her. I will go instantly, and bring her to you at once,' I said.

'I cannot impose on you . . .' she began, with a show of reluctance.

'It is no imposition, I assure you. I am only too glad to be able to help.'

'Oh, thank you! Thank you,' she said. 'I do confess it would relieve my mind greatly if she were here.'

'I will have a message sent to the apothecary at once, and I will be off as soon as the horses can be readied.'

The horses arrived just before twelve o'clock, and I set out for Barton to collect Mrs Dashwood and bring her to her daughter.

Monday 17 April

I arrived at Barton Cottage at about ten o'clock this morning, having stopped for nothing except to change horses, and braced myself for the ordeal to come. I knocked at the door. The maid answered it, and Mrs Dashwood appeared behind her, already dressed in her cloak.

Her hand flew to her chest as she saw me.

'Marianne . . .' she said in horror.

'Is alive, but very ill. Miss Dashwood has asked me to bring you to her.'

'I am ready. I was about to set out, for I was alarmed by Elinor's letter, no matter how much she tried to reassure me, and I wanted to be with Marianne. The Careys will be here at any minute to take care of Margaret, for I cannot take her into a house of infection, and as soon as they arrive, we will be on our way. But you are tired. You must have something to eat and drink.'

I shook my head, but she insisted, and as we had to wait for the Careys, I at last gave way. I ate some cold meat and bread, washed down with a glass of wine, and I felt better for it. The Careys arrived just as I was finishing my hasty meal.

'Don't you fret,' said Mrs Carey to Mrs Dashwood. 'I'll take care of Miss Margaret. You go to Miss Marianne, my dear.'

'Bless you,' said Mrs Dashwood.

I escorted her out to the carriage, and we set off.

'My poor Marianne, I should never have let her go to London alone,' she said. 'I should have gone with her, but I had no idea! I believed in Willoughby. He was well known and well liked in the neighbourhood. I never suspected . . . I thought she would have such fun in London, but instead she found nothing but misery and mortification. And now this! Is she very ill?'

I could not deceive her, but I said that the apothecary was hopeful.

'And Elinor? What does she think?'

'That her sister will be more comfortable when you are at Cleveland.'

'Then pray God we will soon be there. It is terrible, terrible. Oh, my poor Marianne! I should never have encouraged her attachment to Willoughby, but he seemed perfect in every way: young, handsome, well connected, lively; matching her in spirits and enthusiasms; sharing her taste in music, poetry, and everything else they discussed. They seemed made for each other. And yet he deceived her, abandoned her and married another. I should have made enquiries as soon as I saw her preference; I should have ascertained what kind of man he was, instead of relying on the assurances of Sir John which, though kindly meant, were based on nothing more than the fact that Willoughby was a fine sportsman and a good dancer. I should have asked her if they were engaged, instead of feeling I could not speak of it. I thought too much of her privacy and not enough of her health. Oh, what folly!'

'You cannot blame yourself,' I told her.

'But I do, Colonel, I do!' she said in anguish. 'And now she is ill . . .'

I tried to comfort her.

'It is no good,' she said, 'I can see by your face that she is very ill. Tell me truthfully, do you think she will die?'

'Oh God, I hope not!' I cried, unable to contain my feelings any longer.

She regarded me in surprise, and then a look of understanding crossed her face.

'You care for her as much as I do.'

I could not deny it.

'I love her,' I said wretchedly.

She took my hand.

'I am so pleased,' she said, with a tearful smile.

Her kindness cut through the last of my restraint.

'It is hopeless,' I said. 'Even if she recovers, it is hopeless. She can never love me.'

'You are wrong, Colonel. She can, and I believe in time she will. She is an intelligent girl, for all her sensibility, and she cannot help but see, when her hurt has subsided, that Willoughby was nothing but a tawdry tale bound in gilt and leather, whereas you, dear Colonel, have in you the poetry of Shakespeare, though your cover is not so fine. If she lives . . .' Her voice broke, but then she recovered herself. '. . . If she lives, it will be my greatest happiness to do anything within my power to promote the match.'

'You are too good,' I said, overcome. 'But I hope for nothing for myself. If I can but see her well, I will be happy.'

'Amen,' said her mother.

We both of us wished the journey over and at last . . . at last . . . we approached Cleveland.

'Good Mrs Jennings! To stay with Marianne. But Elinor, my Elinor. . . .'

The carriage stopped, and without waiting for anyone to open the door for her, without waiting even for the steps, she sprang out and ran to the door.

I was beside her; I lifted the knocker; it dropped with a hollow sound; and the door was opened by the butler. Miss Dashwood was behind him and received her mother, who was nearly fainting from fear.

'It is all right, Mama, it is all right! The fever has broken. She is sleeping peacefully.'

Marianne, well! I thanked God.

I stood back so that mother and daughter could comfort each other and then, seeing that Mrs Dashwood was trying to walk into the drawing room, but that she was still weak with shock, I supported her on one side whilst her daughter supported her on the other, and between us we helped her into the room.

She began to cry with joy, and embraced her daughter again and again, turning to press my hand from time to time, with a look which spoke her gratitude and her certainty of my sharing it.

As soon as she had recovered herself, she left the room with her daughter, and the two of them went upstairs to see Marianne, whilst I sank into a chair. All the anxiety of the last few days flowed over me, and I sat still and silent until the weakness had passed, and then I gave thanks, over and over, for her life being spared.

Tuesday 18 April

I woke at three o'clock this morning, sitting in the chair in the drawing room. I was stiff and uncomfortable, but my discomfort was soon banished when I remembered that Marianne was out of danger.

I went into the hall and, passing the maid coming downstairs with a bowl of water, asked if Marianne was still sleeping.

'Yes, sir, sleeping like a baby,' said the maid happily.

I returned to my room where, stripping off my clothes, I fell into bed.

I awoke early, feeling much refreshed, and was soon downstairs. The news from the sick room was still good, and I made a hearty breakfast, then went out for a ride. The world was new-dressed in the freshest of greens, the leaves unfurling from the trees, and the pine cones budding on the branches. I rode on, breathing deeply, filling my lungs with the air that was rich with the smell of spring, and as I did so, I found hope stirring in my breast. Hope!

I tried to fight it down, but it would not be denied. Marianne was on the way to recovery. The world, which had been dull and hard and grey, was full of joy and optimism, from the brilliant blue of the sky to the diamonds of dew that caught the sunlight and reflected it in rainbow hues.

I rode until I had rid myself of all my energy and then returned to the house.

I went inside and found Mrs Dashwood sitting down to breakfast. Her cheerful look showed me that her daughter continued to mend.

'Ah, Colonel, I am so pleased to see you. Is it not splendid news? Marianne has passed a quiet night. Her colour is good and her pulse strong. We will have her well again before long.'

I could not hide my delight.

'To have a true friend such as you, Colonel, has been a great relief to me, and to Elinor. She has spoken of your steadfast friendship, and she is as grateful for it as I am. And she is just as pleased about your attachment to Marianne.'

'I should not have spoken to you as I did last night,' I said, for I had not asked her permission to court Marianne.

'Come, now, you are made out of flesh and blood, Colonel, and not stone. Could you help speaking in such circumstances? And I am very glad you did. Only give it time, and I am sure you will have your heart's desire. Marianne's heart is not to be wasted on such a man as Willoughby. Your own merits will soon secure it.'

'I allowed myself to hope for it once, but after seeing her so ill, I believe her affection is too deeply rooted for any change, at least not for a great length of time; and even supposing her heart again free, I do not think that, with such a difference of age and disposition, I could ever attach her,' I said.

'You are quite mistaken. Your age is an advantage, for you have overcome the vacillations of youth, and your disposition is exactly the very one to make her happy. Your gentleness and your genuine attention to other people is more in keeping with her real disposition than the artificial liveliness, often ill-timed, of Willoughby. I am very sure myself that had Willoughby turned out to be as amiable as he seemed, Marianne would not have been as happy with him as she will be with you.'

I could not help but be cheered by her words, for I knew that it meant I had her permission to court her daughter and win her, if I could.

Saturday 22 April

Marianne was well enough to move into Mrs Palmer's dressing room today, and Miss Dashwood said, 'My sister would like to see you, Colonel.'

'Me?' I asked, surprised.

'Yes,' she said with a smile.

I followed her to the dressing room, where I was relieved to see that Marianne was sitting up, but horrified to see her so thin and pale. There were dark rings under her eyes, and a lack of animation in her eye.

'Ah, good Colonel, it pains you to see me like this,' she said, seeing my expression.

'It does,' I confessed, going down on one knee beside her sofa, so that I could be on a level with her.

'But if not for you, it would be far worse. You brought my mother to me, and for that

I can never thank you enough.'

'No thanks are needed,' I assured her.

'But I wish to thank you anyway,' she said warmly, and with more animation. 'I have been very much deceived in one friend this year, but I have been humbled by the devotion of another.'

Devotion. Yes, she had chosen her word well, for I was devoted to her.

'Anything I can do for you, you have only to name it,' I said.

She gave a weak smile.

'There is nothing more I need, only to be here, with my friends.'

'And to get strong,' put in her mother.

'Yes, indeed, to get strong.'

She sank back, and I stood up, for I did not want to tire her. I left the room, and as I went downstairs, I did not recognize myself in the mirror, for I looked so different. I wondered what the difference was, and then I saw that I was smiling.

Monday 24 April

'Mrs Jennings, I cannot tell you how grateful I am to you for all you have done for my daughter,' said Mrs Dashwood at breakfast this morning. 'To stay with her and care for her, when your own daughter has just had a child, was friendship indeed.'

317

'I couldn't do any less, not when she was my guest,' said Mrs Jennings good-naturedly. 'I'm just glad it all turned out so well.'

'Marianne is so much recovered that I think it is safe to move her, so we must trespass on your hospitality no longer.'

'My dear Mrs Dashwood, it is no trespass, I do assure you. You must stay here as long as you like,' she said.

'That is very kind of you, but I think it is time for us to go home.'

'You must accept the use of my carriage,' I said. 'It will make Miss Marianne more comfortable on the way.'

'Colonel, you have done so much for me and my family, you have earned the right to call my daughters Elinor and Marianne.'

I thanked her.

'I accept your offer of the carriage. You must reclaim it by visiting us in a few weeks' time, when Marianne has fully recovered.'

I was delighted to accept the invitation.

Wednesday 26 April

The morning was all bustle as preparations were made for the Dashwoods' removal. Maids ran to and fro with rugs and stone hot-water bottles for Marianne, to keep her warm on the journey; footmen carried boxes and bags downstairs, and coachmen loaded them on to the carriage.

When all was ready, they took their leave, with Marianne taking a particularly long and affectionate leave of Mrs Jennings, for I believe she felt she had neglected her hostess's kindness in the past, and then I handed her into the carriage.

'Thank you for all you have done for me,' she said to me in heartfelt tones.

I pressed her hand, and then said, 'Have you everything you need?'

'Yes, thank you, everything.'

Her mother and sister joined her in the carriage, and then it pulled away.

I left soon afterwards, having thanked Mrs Jennings for her hospitality, and returned to Delaford.

Friday 28 April
The weather was wet, but I scarcely had time to notice it as I went over the accounts and paid attention to business which I have been lately neglecting. I was glad to be busy, and I talked over the planting of new timber with Havers, as well as the building of a new wall at the bottom of the long field and the extension of the home farm.

Saturday 29 April

I spent the morning on estate business, and this afternoon I went to the stables to see Cinnamon. She was looking sleek and healthy.

From there, I walked over to the cottage to see Eliza. I found her playing with the baby in the mild spring sunshine. She sprang up, delighted to see me, and came towards me dandling Elizabeth in her arms.

'She looks just like you,' I said, as I took the baby. 'She has your eyes and your smile.'

She chucked her daughter under the chin, and we talked of the baby until she began to cry. I handed her back to Eliza and then went on to the parsonage. I looked around it, inside and out, and made a note of the repairs that needed carrying out, and then returned to the mansion house, where I pored over the accounts until bedtime.

Tuesday 2 May

I took Tom Carpenter over to the parsonage today and I pointed out everything that I wanted him to attend to. He told me that he could have the work finished in a month.

'But the roof needs fixing,' he said, as he felt the wall. He took his hand away and it was damp. 'I'll send Will over to look at it this afternoon.'

From the parsonage I returned to the mansion house. I passed Robert Lambton on the way, and I stopped to talk to him, for he had been on his way to see me. He wanted to take over the derelict barn at Four Lanes End, and I was pleased to learn that his farm was prospering enough for him to need it.

'Ay, I am doing very well,' he said.

As he spoke, his eyes strayed over my shoulder, and, turning my head, I saw what had caught his eye. It was Eliza, who was in the garden of her cottage again, playing with the baby. I had forgotten how beautiful she was, for I had grown accustomed to her face, but Robert had not forgotten, and as he watched her, it was clear he was attracted to her. He knew her history, for in such a small village nothing could be kept secret, but still he watched her, and I found myself thinking that if a good man such as Robert Lambton should fall in love with her, then what a happy outcome of all the past year's trials it would be.

Thursday 4 May
I walked down to the parsonage this morning, and I saw that the works were proceeding as quickly as could be expected. Then I went to see Eliza. Knowing that Robert

would be at Four Lanes End, I suggested a walk and I bent our steps in that direction. Sure enough, there he was, overseeing the work on the barn.

I introduced him to Eliza and he greeted her with respect. After some minutes talking to him about the barn, we went on our way, and his eyes followed us.

I returned to the mansion house at last and ate my dinner in solitary splendour.

I miss Marianne.

Friday 5 May
The wet weather reminded me that the path by the river needed raising so that it will not flood next year, and I gave instructions for the matter to be attended to.

Monday 15 May
I received a letter from Mrs Dashwood this morning. Marianne is growing in strength daily and is now well enough to be allowed outside when the weather is fine. She ended her letter by inviting me to stay, and I wrote back at once to accept.

Tuesday 16 May
I dressed slowly this morning, for I was apprehensive about going to Barton, and as I travelled to Devonshire, I wondered if

Marianne would ever see me as a husband, or if she would never see me as anything more than a friend.

Wednesday 17 May

I reached Barton in good time, and I knocked on the door and was shown in. Marianne was sitting by the window, and I was heartened to see how well she looked. She had lost her pallor and her skin was as brown as it was when first I saw her last year. Her figure, which had been gaunt after her illness, had regained its fullness, and she was blooming.

She sprang to her feet when she saw me and came forward to welcome me with a smile.

'We did not look for you so soon. You are very welcome.'

Then Mrs Dashwood came forward and welcomed me.

'We have missed you. We have *all* missed you, have we not, Marianne?' she said.

'Yes, indeed, Mama,' said Marianne, looking at me warmly. 'We always miss our friends. Do sit down, Colonel. How was your journey?'

'It was excellent, thank you,' I said, looking at her all the while.

'This is a day for visitors,' said Mrs

Dashwood, as tea was brought in, 'for we have another guest.'

'Oh?' I asked, wondering who it could be.

'Yes. It is someone you will like to see, for it is Edward Ferrars,' said Marianne. 'He is presently out walking with Elinor.'

'We have a great deal to tell you, have we not, Marianne?' said Mrs Dashwood.

'We have,' said Marianne.

'You see, Colonel, Mr Edward Ferrars is soon to be my son-in-law. He and Elinor are engaged.'

'But I thought he was engaged to Miss Lucy?' I asked in surprise.

'And so he was. But the engagement was not to his liking. He had entered into it as a very young man when he was far from home, and when he later realized that she did not have the qualities he needed in a wife, it was too late; they were already engaged. To make matters worse, Edward then met Elinor and discovered that she was exactly the sort of superior young woman he ought to be marrying.'

'And I gave him the living of Delaford, thinking I was helping him,' I said, with a shake of my head.

'It was very kind of you. You were a true friend to him,' said Marianne. 'You were not to know that he did not look forward to the marriage.'

'He thought the case was hopeless, for he would not go back on his word to Lucy. But then the engagement became known and he was cast off by his mother, who made the estate over to his brother, Robert,' said Mrs Dashwood.

'At which Lucy, although protesting that she did not mind being poor, went to see Robert, pretending that she needed his advice,' said Marianne. 'Lucy is very pretty, and Robert is very stupid, so that it did not take her long to win his affections, and she married him quickly, before he could change his mind. Leaving Edward free.'

'Free to marry Elinor,' I said. A smile spread across my face. 'But this is wonderful news.'

I saw Marianne looking at me, startled.

'It *is* wonderful news?' I asked, wondering if there was any part of the story I did not yet know.

'Oh, yes, quite wonderful,' said Marianne. 'It was not your comment that startled me, it was your smile.'

'Marianne!' said her mother.

'I have never seen the Colonel smile before,' she said, unabashed, as she continued to watch my face, and I was pleased to see that, although her recent experiences had tempered her outspokenness, they had not rid her of it altogether. 'You look different when you smile.'

'Then we must make sure the Colonel has plenty to smile about in the coming months,' said Mrs Dashwood, with a kind look towards me.

At that moment Ferrars and Elinor returned from their walk, and I sprang to my feet.

'You see,' said Margaret, who followed them into the room, fresh from playing in the garden. 'I told you that Elinor's beau's name began with an F!'

We all laughed.

'Allow me to congratulate you,' I said. 'Elinor, I am more pleased than I can say.' I turned to Ferrars and shook him by the hand. 'You are a lucky man.'

'I know,' he said with a smile. 'I must thank you again, properly this time, for the living. It was a very great kindness to give it to me when I had no claim on it, save that of mutual friends. When you first made the gift, I am afraid I was ungrateful, for I feared that it would hasten a marriage that was distasteful to me, and yet which seemed unavoidable. Yet now I can thank you from the bottom of my heart.'

'And I must thank you, too,' said Elinor.

'You have been a true friend to all my family.'

'I only wish I could do more.'

'As to that, I hope that I might now be able to help myself,' said Ferrars. 'I aim to go to town in a few days' time and see if it is possible to be reconciled with my mother. Now that Robert has married to displease her, she may look kindly on me once more.'

We were interrupted at that point by Sir John, who had brought the mail. He was surprised to see me but made me welcome, and invited me to stay at the Park, an offer I accepted as Mrs Dashwood's house was full.

He was soon apprised of Elinor's betrothal, and he offered his heartiest congratulations. Then, after sitting with us for a time, he went to give his wife the news.

'Is there anything from Mrs Jennings?' asked Mrs Dashwood as Elinor sorted through the letters. 'I can never thank her enough for looking after Marianne, and she promised to write to me and let me know how Charlotte and the baby are getting on.'

'Yes,' said Elinor.

'Read it to me, would you, Elinor dear?' she said.

Elinor began to read, and the letter, which a few days before would, I am sure, have caused pain, caused only mirth.

'What do you think? Lucy has deserted
her beau, Edward Ferrars, and has run off
with his brother! Poor Mr Edward! I cannot
get him out of my head, but you must send
for him to Barton, and Miss Marianne must
try to comfort him.'

'I think I will leave the task of comforting
him to my sister!' said Marianne.

'And here is another letter,' said Elinor. 'It
is from John.'

'Ah! Let us hear what your brother has to
say,' said Mrs Dashwood.

The letter began with salutations, but
soon began to talk of Robert Ferrars's marriage.

'Mrs Ferrars is the most unfortunate of
women,' *read Elinor.* 'Robert's offence was
unpardonable, but Miss Lucy's was infi-
nitely worse. I have made up my mind not
to mention either of them to Mrs Ferrars
ever again, and I beg you will do the same;
and, even if she might hereafter be induced to forgive Robert, his wife will never
be acknowledged as her daughter, nor be
permitted to appear in her presence. The
secrecy with which everything has been

carried on between them only made the crime worse, because had any suspicion of it occurred to the others, proper measures would have been taken to prevent the marriage. I am sure you will join with me, Elinor, in thinking that it would have been better for Lucy to marry Edward, rather than to spread misery farther in the family.'

At this, we all laughed again.
'But finish the letter,' said Mrs Dashwood.

'Mrs Ferrars has never yet mentioned Edward's name, which does not surprise us; but, to our great astonishment, not a line has been received from him on the occasion. Perhaps, however, he is kept silent by his fear of offending, and I shall therefore give him a hint, by a line to Oxford, that his sister and I both think a letter of proper submission from him, addressed perhaps to his sister Fanny, and by her shown to her mother, might not be taken amiss, for we all know the tenderness of Mrs Ferrars's heart and that she wishes for nothing so much as to be on good terms with her children.'

'A letter of proper submission!' Edward said. 'Would they have me beg my mother's pardon for Robert's ingratitude to *her* and breach of honour to *me?*'

'You may certainly ask to be forgiven,' said Elinor, 'because you have offended. And when she has forgiven you, perhaps a little humility may be convenient while acknowledging a second engagement, almost as imprudent in *her* eyes as the first.'

He had nothing to say against it, but, feeling that it would be easier to make concessions by word of mouth rather than on paper, it was resolved that, instead of writing to his sister, he should go to London, and personally ask for her help.

'And if they really *do* interest themselves in bringing about a reconciliation,' said Marianne, 'I shall think that even John and his wife are not entirely without merit.'

'What do you say to the idea of calling in at Delaford on your way to London?' I said. 'You can see the parsonage, and we can decide on some improvements. Then I can set the work in hand.'

He agreed to the proposal and then suggested to Elinor that they should resume their rambles around the countryside. Mrs Dashwood having some housekeeping to attend to, and Margaret running out into the garden once again to play, Marianne and I were left alone.

'And so, Colonel, I find I cannot cling to my belief that second attachments are unpardonable: Edward's love for Elinor is a second attachment, and if I were to follow my former philosophy, then he would be condemned to a life of misery with Lucy, instead of a life of happiness with Elinor,' she said thoughtfully. 'And yet, perhaps in some cases it might not be possible to make a second attachment, if the first was felt too deeply,' she went on, shaking her head. Then she raised her eyes and looked into mine. 'You loved deeply once. Do you believe it is possible, after such an attachment, to be happy again?'

'For a long time I thought not, but now, yes, I do think it is possible,' I said.

'I hope you are right,' she said with a sigh, 'otherwise I am destined for a lonely life.'

I said gently, 'I do not believe that that will be your fate.'

Saturday 20 May
Ferrars and I arrived at Delaford this afternoon. He complimented me on the mansion house, and then we walked down the road to the parsonage.

'This is better than I expected, much better,' he said. 'From what you had told me, I was expecting some dilapidated cottage, but it is a house of good proportions and not inconsiderable dimensions.'

'It can be added to,' I said. 'It would be easy to build on at the back and build another room above. The gardens, also, are capable of improvement.'

He cast his eye over the whole, and then we went in.

'It needs new papers,' I said, 'and carpets on the floor.'

'I am sure Elinor will want to choose those. I will leave it all to her,' he said. 'I am a lucky man, Brandon. A few weeks ago I despaired of happiness, but fate has delivered it into my hands. Now all it needs is for my mother to relent, and I will have more happiness than any man has a right to expect. I hope the same good fortune might befall you.'

He looked at me knowingly, and I could not help smiling, and he said that he hoped we would be very happy.

'Nothing is certain,' I said.

'What in life is certain? But that does not mean you cannot hope. Hope is every man's friend.'

We went out into the garden.

'I can imagine Elinor here, cutting flowers for the house,' he said.

'The wall can be moved to make the

garden bigger,' I said. 'If you take it out as far as the orchard, it will be a pretty size.'

We went on discussing improvements, and by the time we had done, we both began to feel that the parsonage could be turned into something like a gentleman's residence without too much trouble or expense.

Tuesday 23 May

Ferrars left for London today. I wished him luck, and I felt he would need it, for a mother who could cast aside her son for so slight a reason was not a mother who could be relied upon to reinstate him in her affections.

Friday 26 May

I spent the morning catching up on estate business, and this afternoon I went to see Eliza. I arrived at the cottage in time to see Robert Lambton leaving it. He asked me if he might come and see me tomorrow morning, and I said yes. It was obvious from his manner that he did not want to talk to me about the farm, and from Eliza's smiles I am expecting a happy interview.

Saturday 27 May

Robert Lambton came to see me this morning. He was embarrassed, and hummed and hawed, and he obviously did not know how to begin.

He started at last, however, and, haltingly, told me that he had fallen in love with Eliza and asked for her hand in marriage.

'And what does she say?' I asked him.

'I was so bold as to ask her, and she said yes,' he said.

'Then it only remains for me to give you my blessing . . .' I said. I was sorry I could not give her a dowry, for although I owned a great deal of land, I had very little in the way of money, the estate not being a wealthy one. And then I realized that it was in my power to give them something after all, and I added '. . . and Four Lanes farm.'

He looked at me in amazement.

'And Four Lanes farm?' he asked, stunned.

'I will have the papers drawn up tomorrow. You will be a landowner, Robert.'

'I never expected . . .' he began.

'I know, and that is why I am so happy to give it to you. You are the very man I would have chosen for Eliza. She has had a great deal of unhappiness in her life, but now she has found happiness with you. I am more grateful to you than I can say.'

He thanked me from his heart and went to tell Eliza the good news.

She came to call on me this evening and told me they would be married in the autumn. She asked me if I would give her away, and I told her I would be proud to do so. She has matured a great deal over the last few months and improved in character and spirits, so that I have no doubt that she and Robert will be happy.

Tuesday 30 May
I had hoped to hear something from Ferrars, telling me of his luck in London, but there was still no letter this morning. If I have not heard anything by tomorrow, I think I will go to Barton and make enquiries there. It is as good an excuse as any for seeing Marianne again!

She likes me, I know.

It now remains to be seen if she can ever love me.

Thursday 1 June
Sir John was happy to see me, as always, and laughed at me for my frequent visits. I replied by saying that he must come and visit me soon at Delaford, and he readily agreed. Then I walked down to Barton Cottage.

Margaret was playing in front of the house, whilst Marianne was cutting flowers.

She welcomed me with a smile.

'I have heard nothing from Mr Ferrars, and I could wait no longer, so I thought I would come and see if you had any news. Has Mrs Ferrars relented towards her son?' I asked.

'She has,' she said, cutting a final bloom. 'But poor Edward has had to endure a great many lectures in order to bring it about. But will you not come inside? Margaret, run and fetch Elinor and Mama. They have just set out for a walk,' she explained to me.

'I would not wish to disturb them —'

'They can walk at any time. They would much rather see you, I am sure,' she said.

I followed her into the cottage.

'And has Mrs Ferrars restored him to the position of an elder son?' I asked.

'No, that would be too much to hope for. She has promised him ten thousand pounds, which is the sum she gave to Fanny on her marriage, but other than that she is content for him to take holy orders for the sake of two hundred and fifty pounds a year. And this, when his brother has a thousand a year! But it is enough. Now that Elinor has Edward, she needs nothing more to be happy.'

Mrs Dashwood and her daughters returned at that point, and the subject was much discussed.

'Edward meant to tell you himself. He intended to call at Delaford on his way here,' said Elinor.

'I should have waited for him, but I was eager to discover the news.'

'And I admire you for it,' said Marianne warmly. 'Where our friends are concerned, how can we abide any delay which will prevent us from learning of their happiness?'

'Edward is expected here in a few days' time,' said Elinor. 'You must stay and see him.'

'Thank you, I will. And then you must all come to Delaford. You will be able to see the parsonage, and,' turning to Elinor, 'tell me what improvements you would like me to make.'

'You are very kind, Colonel. I can think of nothing I would like better,' she said.

I waved her thanks aside, and Mrs Dashwood said that she and her family would be glad to accept my invitation.

And so I am to have them at Delaford! Marianne is to see my home for the first time. And, perhaps, if fortune favours me, it will be her home soon, too.

Friday 2 June
Sir John called at the cottage this morning

337

to invite the Dashwoods to dinner. Mrs Jennings was with him.

'What a time we've all been having!' she said. 'Was there ever such news! Lucy engaged to Mr Edward Ferrars and then marrying his brother instead! And you, my dear,' to Elinor, 'you are to marry Edward, and never a thing did I suspect! How you must have laughed at me.'

'I assure you —'

'You young people with your assurances. I never was more taken in, though I should have known. "His name begins with an F," Miss Margaret said. And I never thought, when I met Mr Ferrars, that he was an F! And you, Miss Marianne, looking blooming, when I thought Willoughby had killed you. Ah, was there ever such a scoundrel, leading you on when all the time he was engaged to someone else.'

'He did sincerely love Marianne,' said Elinor, with a glance at her sister. 'He came to see her when she was ill, and he confided his feelings to me.'

I had never suspected it, but in a few words she said that Willoughby had arrived at Cleveland when I had gone to fetch Mrs Dashwood, and that he had protested his affection for Marianne, saying that he had always loved her but that he had been forced into marriage with Miss Grey by poverty as Mrs Smith, hearing of his behaviour towards Eliza, had disinherited him.

Mrs Jennings was horrified, though whether she was more horrified to discover that Willoughby had seduced an innocent or that she had not been apprised of the gossip, it would have been difficult to say. But now that Marianne was no longer in danger she was willing to forgive him.

'Ah, well, I dare say it was not his fault,' she said.

'No indeed. Nothing is ever Willoughby's fault,' said Marianne, with surprising asperity. 'I have heard all his excuses, for he was good enough to make them to Elinor when I lay ill and in danger because of his behaviour, and they are compelling indeed. It was not his fault that he seduced an orphan; instead it was her fault for not being a saint. It was not his fault for leaving her without giving her his address; for, if she had had any common sense, she could have discovered it for herself.

'It was not his fault for refusing to marry her when his relation, Mrs Smith, discovered his conduct and told him he must, for how could he be expected to marry a young woman who could bring him nothing except the child he had given her, and of whom he had already tired? Only a woman of Mrs Smith's purity, and with her ignorance of the world, could have expected such a ridiculous thing.

'And it was not his fault that he made love to me whilst Eliza was alone and discarded in London; nor that he abandoned me when Mrs Smith disinherited him and ran off to London, where he married the first heiress who would have him.'

'My dear . . .' began Mrs Dashwood in surprise.

'No, Mama, I must speak. I have given the matter a great deal of thought, and though to begin with I was soothed by his race to my bedside, I soon saw that it was all of a piece with his earlier behaviour. If a man were judged by words, then Willoughby would be a great man indeed. But his actions, what of them? When he came to my bedside, he was already married to another woman, and he was betraying her trust by visiting me, as he had earlier betrayed mine by leaving me. And yet did he see this betrayal? No. He saw only what he always saw, that he had been cruelly used by everyone about him, and that he himself was innocent. The orphan who had not resisted his determined seduction; the benefactress who expected him, oh! how unreasonably! to marry the mother of his child; the wife who did not love him; and the wild young girl in Devonshire who threw herself at his head, driving around the countryside with him unchaperoned and giving him a lock of her hair; all these conspired against him. There could be no blame attached to him, for if they had behaved in such reprehensible ways, then what could they expect?'

'Marianne, you do not know that he has said any such thing about you!' said her sister. 'He loved you, I am sure of it.'

'Or so he said to you, but what did he say to his wife, and to his London friends? How did he explain my behaviour at the party? As the distress of a young girl he had encouraged and then abandoned, or as the wild behaviour of an unprincipled girl whose family were careless of her honour? A man who can blacken the character of one woman behind her back can do the same to another.

'I was deceived in him because I saw what I wanted to see. I used no judgement, no discretion . . . I was so young; I, who thought myself grown up. Willoughby was my idea of perfection, and yet, for all his handsome face, he was nothing but a libertine, concerned with his own pleasure and careless of anything else.'

'Well!' said Mrs Jennings.

'Ay, he was a rogue, for all he had a pretty little bitch of a pointer,' said Sir John. 'I wonder if he might sell her?'

'Never did I think I would see the day when she would speak so of Mr Willoughby,' said Mrs Jennings, ignoring Sir John. 'However, it is just as well, for he is not a young man I would like to see attached to one of my family. And now, I have been thinking: Sir John, we must invite Miss Steele to stay, for she is all alone now her sister has married, and as the doctor hasn't come up to scratch, we must find her another beau.'

He was delighted with the idea and said they must invite her at once.

'Have you really recovered from Willoughby?' I asked Marianne as, Sir John and Mrs Jennings departing, we set out for a walk, falling some way behind the others.

'I am. I feel I can see him now with perfect clarity, and I am ashamed that I almost died because of him. I have matured, I hope, since then, and discovered that unbridled sensibility is not the good I once thought it to be, for it clouds wisdom, judgement and common sense. I allowed myself to fall in love with Willoughby without truly knowing him. And once he left me, I gave way to my sensibility again, making myself ill, so that I almost died. And for whom did I almost die? A man who did not deserve my love.

'I mean to become more rational in the future; indeed, I have already sketched out a programme of self-improvement. I mean to rise at six and spend my time between music and reading. Our own library is too well known to me to be resorted to for anything beyond mere amusement, but there are many works well worth reading at the Park and you have been kind enough to say that I may borrow some books from your library. By reading only six hours a day, I shall gain in the course of a twelve-month a great deal of instruction which I now feel myself to want.'

'It does not all have to be study,' I said to her. 'You must have some amusement as well.'

'I never want to slip back into my old ways, and this is how I mean to avoid it.'

'You never will. You have experience to temper you, and friends to help you. Keep some of your sensibility, Marianne. Your warm and open nature brings a great deal of pleasure to your friends. You look surprised. But it is not given to everyone to enjoy life as you do. Your vitality lights up the morning as the sun lights up the sky.

Where would we be without it?'

'Willoughby said many pretty things to me but none, I think, as pretty as that,' she said, looking at me warmly. 'He recited poetry and so his compliments were other men's words in his mouth. They could have been said by anyone, to anyone. But your words are about me and me alone. And they are from the heart.'

I was about to speak, but at that moment the others turned back and hailed us, saying, 'We have walked far enough for one day. Margaret is tired.'

'I am not!' said Margaret, though she was dragging her feet.

'Very well then, *I* am tired,' said Elinor.

We fell in with them and returned to the house. I stayed for tea, and then made my way back to the Park.

'You look cheerful, Brandon,' said Sir John.

'I feel cheerful.'

'Wooing going well, eh?'

'You should marry her tomorrow, Colonel. What's to stop you?' said Mrs Jennings.

'Nay, never rush your jumps, eh, Brandon?' said Sir John.

I bore their raillery easily, because for the first time I feel I am certain of success.

Monday 5 June
I set out for home today.

Wednesday 7 June
Edward Ferrars arrived at Delaford this afternoon. He will be staying with me often over the next few months so that he can oversee work on the parsonage.

'Have you and Elinor set a date for your wedding yet?' I asked.

'Not yet. We want to wait until I have been ordained, by which time work on the parsonage should be complete. With luck we will be married by Michaelmas. I was wondering, Brandon, if you would stand up with me? I had always thought I would ask my brother, but as things now stand between us, I cannot bring myself to ask him. He rejoiced in my downfall, and he is not a man I wish to have at my wedding.'

'I would be honoured,' I said.

Thursday 8 June
The house is almost ready for my other visitors. Mrs Trent has worked wonders. Rugs have been beaten, curtains washed, mirrors polished and furniture dusted, so that everything shines in a way it has not shone since my mother was alive. The garden, too, has had some much-needed attention, with

grass cropped, trees pruned and flowers trimmed.

The recent fine weather has resulted in a profusion of blooms, and everywhere there is scent and colour.

I have sent out invitations to a ball, and I am looking forward to seeing Marianne's reaction to my home.

Friday 9 June
I went out riding with Ferrars this morning, knowing the Dashwoods would not be arriving until this afternoon or even this evening, but after a cold collation I could not bring myself to leave the house. Ferrars went down to the parsonage to oversee the workmen, and I remained behind to attend to my accounts.

At last their carriage arrived. I heard the wheels crunching on the gravel and the horses' hoofs, and I ran to the door, then slowed my pace as I went outside.

The carriage rolled to a halt, and I saw Marianne's face at the window, looking out on to what I hoped would one day be her home. Her face was alight with pleasure, and I knew she approved of the drive, the grove and the edifice. I only hoped she would be as well pleased with the inside.

I opened the door and the coachman let

down the step, then I handed Mrs Dash-wood and her daughters out. I escorted the ladies inside, where they looked about them with interest.

'You have a very fine property here, Colonel,' said Mrs Dashwood. 'The hall has noble proportions. The staircase reminds me of Norland. Does it not remind you of Norland, Marianne?'

'Perhaps, but it is not as big. It is lighter, however; the staircase at Norland was always rather dark.'

'And gloomy,' said Margaret. 'I didn't like the picture of Great-great-grandfather Charles.'

'Margaret!'

'Well, I didn't,' said Margaret. 'He always looked very fierce.'

We went into the drawing room and I saw its beauty anew, with the windows cut down to the floor, revealing the gardens and parkland beyond. I saw Marianne's eyes linger on the fireplace, an ornate piece of marble which I have always admired, and then rove over the console tables, with their vases of fresh flowers, and the damasked sofas, newly covered, and the Aubusson rugs.

'It is a beautiful room,' said Marianne. 'Elegant and refined.'

'Yes, indeed,' said Elinor.

'But more than that, it has heart,' said Marianne.

Tea was brought in, and afterwards we walked down to the parsonage, where Elinor and Edward had an affectionate meeting.

The ladies were delighted with the parsonage.

'It is far bigger than I imagined,' said Elinor, 'and the prospect is pleasing.'

'More than pleasing, it is quite beautiful,' said Marianne, going over to the window. 'Look, you can see right down the valley. With the river winding its way through it, it is a lovely sight. It will be equally beautiful in winter, I believe.'

'It will need new curtains and so forth,' I said to Elinor, 'but I am sure you will enjoy choosing them.'

'Yes, indeed. I think green for the parlour, with gold curtains. Mama, what do you think?'

'I think that would look very well,' said Mrs Dashwood. 'A plain wallpaper or a stripe?'

'A stripe, I think.'

'And perhaps I can beg the portrait of Great-great-grandfather Charles to hang in Margaret's room,' Elinor teased her.

'Will we be staying with you?' asked Margaret eagerly.

'Often, I hope, when the work is complete.'

'And until then, you are welcome to stay with me,' I said. 'Perhaps you would like to see some more of the estate?'

'Oh, yes,' said Margaret. 'Can we see the mulberry tree?'

'Of course, if you want to,' I said, mystified.

'Mrs Jennings has told me all about it. She said that she and Charlotte stuffed themselves when they came here!'

We all laughed, and I remembered Charlotte and her mother, eating the fruit fresh from the tree, with the juices running down their chins.

'I am afraid you will not be able to do the same. They will not be ripe until the autumn,' I told her.

'We will just have to come back again, then, will we not, Mama?' she asked her mother. She turned to her sister. 'Elinor, you must invite us in October. Mrs Jennings says the Delaford mulberries are the best she has ever tasted.'

'And what else did she tell you?' I asked Margaret, as we set off towards the walled garden.

'She told me about the dovecots and the

stewponds and the canal. Can we see the canal?'

'We will go and see it once we have seen the mulberry tree.'

'And the other fruit trees, too?'

'Margaret! The Colonel will think you are nothing but a walking stomach!'

'Well, and perhaps I am. Mrs Jennings says she likes to see a girl with a hearty appetite.'

We came to the door into the walled garden. Once inside, it was hot, for we were sheltered from the breeze. There was the gentle buzzing of bees, and the scent of lavender, and the flutter of colour as butterflies flew from one plant to another, their iridescent wings gleaming in the sunlight.

'Apple trees,' said Margaret, 'and pear trees, and — oh, look, Mama, there is the mulberry tree!' She ran over to it and examined the fruit. 'You will have a good crop,' she said to me. 'I will have to tell Mrs Jennings.'

'You must help me to plan the parsonage garden,' said Elinor to her sister.

Marianne went over to the sundial in the middle of the garden and ran her finger tips over the brass gnomon, letting them run over its filigree before falling to the dial, and tracing the shadow.

'Five o'clock,' she said. 'Is it accurate?' she asked me.

I took out my watch.

'Five past five,' I said.

'Then it is very near.'

She walked round the garden, taking everything in, as Margaret continued to extol the virtues of apples, pears and plums, and Elinor and Edward talked about their plans for their own garden, whilst Mrs Dashwood sat on a seat in the shade.

We decided, as we left the garden, that we would not venture further, for Mrs Dashwood was tired from the journey.

'You are here for a month,' I said. 'There is plenty of time to explore the estate.'

We returned to the house. I changed quickly and then waited in the drawing room for the ladies.

Marianne entered the room in a white muslin gown whose simplicity showed off her beauty. She wore long white gloves and a simple string of pearls at her neck, and I imagined her portrait hanging in the hall.

'You are smiling again,' she said to me teasingly.

'I have plenty to smile about,' I returned.

I gave her my arm, and we went into dinner.

Afterwards Marianne played for us, and

this time it was no melancholy air but a lively sonata, full of energy and spirit.

Saturday 10 June

I gave a small dinner party for some of my neighbours this evening, ostensibly to introduce Edward to some of his future parishioners but also to introduce Marianne to intelligent people who would stimulate her and provide her with the sort of company she needs. After a winter spent with Mrs Jennings, I delighted in seeing Marianne discover the joys of talking to people who could arouse her interest in the world and enlarge her mind.

Her ideas were questioned and she defended them well, or thought about them and adapted them in the light of new information.

I saw her take a step into a larger world, one not bounded by the garden of Barton Cottage, or the downs beyond, or the drawing rooms of London, but one that opened up new vistas of exploration for her to enjoy.

Afterwards we got up a dance, and Marianne danced with me twice, a fact which delighted me as she favoured the other gentlemen with no more than one dance apiece.

Elinor and Edward went down to the parsonage this morning, and we went with them, taking a detour to see the canal. Then Marianne, Margaret, Mrs Dashwood and I returned to the house by way of the stables.

'There is something I want to show you,' I said to Marianne, as we outstripped the others. I took her into the stable yard and we stopped by Cinnamon's stall. The mare nuzzled Marianne, who stripped off her glove and put out a hand to stroke her nose. At the same time I, too, put out my hand to stroke her and our fingers touched. I withdrew my hand at once, and she blushed and took refuge in stroking the mare and fussing over her, but I thought, We will be married soon, and we will be very happy.

'She is for you to ride whilst you are here,' I said.

'For me? Oh, thank you,' she said, abandoning restraint and putting her arms round Cinnamon's neck, telling her how beautiful she was and breathing in deeply to catch her smell.

'How I have missed the stables at Norland,' she said. 'Do you have anything I can give her?'

One of the grooms stepped forward with a carrot, and Marianne fed it to the mare whilst the two of them became acquainted.

'Mama! Mama!' she said, as soon as Mrs Dashwood and Margaret caught up with us. 'Look! The Colonel says I may ride her whilst I am here.'

'Can I go with you?' asked Margaret.

'Of course,' I told her. 'I have a horse that would suit you, too.'

'I need you this morning, Margaret,' said her mother. 'But that must not stop you,' she said to Marianne and myself. 'It is a fine morning for a ride.'

'I am not dressed for it,' said Marianne, looking reluctantly at her gown.

'I am sure the Colonel will not insist on your wearing a habit today,' said Mrs Dashwood.

Marianne turned to me, and for answer I instructed the grooms to saddle the horses. I helped Marianne to mount, and Mrs Dashwood and Margaret waved us out of the stable yard.

Marianne had a graceful seat and rode well, and soon we were cantering across the fields, sharing the exhilaration of the early summer morning, with its smell of wild flowers and its cooling breeze.

'I had forgotten how much I loved riding,' she said, as we came to the road and slowed to a walk. 'We must do it every day.'

'I can think of nothing I would like better,' I told her.

She began to look around her.

'Is this a turnpike road?' she asked me.

'Yes.'

'And it is very near the house.'

'About a quarter of a mile, yes.'

'Then you must always have something to look at. I like seeing the bustle and the activity,' she said. 'It is very quiet at Barton, but here there must be carriages passing all the time, and it will be very convenient for travelling.'

'It is.'

'Have you ever been to the Lake District?' she asked me. 'It is supposed to be very beautiful.'

'No, I have never been, but I hope to go there one day soon.'

'So do I. I have seen so little of the world; indeed, I have seen little of my own country. You, on the other hand, have travelled a great deal,' she said, then she gave a grimace and I looked at her enquiringly.

'I used to laugh at your experiences,' she said apologetically. 'I thought myself so superior, mocking you for your talk of the heat and the mosquitoes, but in fact it was my own experiences that were paltry, and not yours. I had not even been to London

355

at the time! I knew nothing of the world beyond Norland and Barton, and yet I thought I knew so much. But now I want to know more. I want to go to Scotland, and if peace is declared, I want to travel to the Continent. And I think I would like to see India, too. What was it like?'

I told her of the burning heat and the vivid colours; the shimmer of the air in the morning; the pungent spices, and the exotic scents of jasmine and musk.

She listened intently and said, 'There is so much of life I have yet to see. I am humbled to think of it. If I had succumbed to melancholy, I would have missed the chance to see all the wonders that life has to offer, but now I hope that one day I may have a chance to experience them all.'

So engrossed were we in our conversation that it was not until I heard the church clock striking that I realized we needed to turn for home.

We followed Mrs Dashwood and Margaret into the house. Hearing our footsteps, Margaret turned round and said, 'Oh, here is Marianne with her beau.'

'Hush! Margaret,' said Marianne blushing.

But she was smiling as she said it.

We had a celebratory dinner this evening, for Edward has been ordained.

'It won't be long before you move into the parsonage, eh?' said Sir John, who arrived to stay with us yesterday.

'We hope to wait until the work is finished before we marry,' said Elinor.

'Lord! If you wait for the workmen to finish you will be waiting for ever,' said Mrs Jennings. 'There is always some delay. You had better marry at once and have done with it.'

Elinor and Edward exchanged glances, and it was clear to all of us that the same thought had been in both their minds. Before the evening was over, they had decided to marry anyway, saying, 'I am sure we can tolerate the inconvenience.'

'You must get married from Barton,' said Sir John.

'Ay, Sir John, the very thing. We'll hold the wedding breakfast at the great house,' said Mrs Jennings.

'We could not possibly impose on you . . .' began Mrs Dashwood, but she was talked down, and I believe she was happy for Sir John and Mrs Jennings to have their own way.

'Three weeks for the banns to be read,'

said Sir John musingly. 'Then you'll be marrying in September.'

'And I'll be visiting you in the parsonage by Michaelmas, just like I said,' remarked Mrs Jennings.

She was so pleased about it that no one reminded her she had been intending to visit Edward and Lucy, instead of Edward and Elinor!

Monday 11 September

Elinor and Edward were married this morning.

As they set out on their wedding tour, Marianne said, 'You are a good friend to all my family, Colonel. Without you, Elinor's marriage could not have gone ahead, for she and Edward would have had nowhere to live.'

'I hope that, one day, you will see me as something more than a friend,' I said to her.

'A second attachment for both of us,' she said. 'I do not know exactly what happened in your past, only that you had an unhappy love affair . . . do not speak of it if you do not wish . . .'

But I found myself telling her about it, ending with Eliza's death.

'She died in your arms,' said Marianne. 'To think, I judged Willoughby on his handsome face and engaging manners, believing him to be a romantic hero because he carried me home when I sprained my ankle. But beneath his smiles and teasing, he was a wastrel. And yet I dismissed you entirely, though you were ready to elope with your love when your father forced her into a hateful marriage, and you sought her out and protected her when she needed you most, caring nothing for the fact that she had fallen into disgrace. You looked after her daughter, fighting a duel in order to protect her honour, and then brought her here, where she could be happy. You have loved and suffered, and yet it has not made you bitter, for you have the courage to love again. It is you who are the figure out of romance.'

'Marianne,' I said. 'I have no right to hope. You have your life before you . . .' I became suddenly tongue-tied. Now that the moment had come, I was unaccustomedly nervous. 'But if you ever — if I might — if you think — I am putting this badly — but if you should ever want my hand as well as my heart, it is yours.'

'You have given me so much already that I should decline, but I cannot deprive myself of such a gift,' she said, her face turning towards mine until our lips met.

At last we parted, and she blushed.

'Am I to take it that you will?' I said.

'Yes, thank you, Colonel —'

I smiled to hear that word, for the last time, on her lips.

'James,' I said.

'James,' she said. 'I accept.'

Tuesday 12 September

What pleasure it is, to know that our betrothal has given pleasure to all our friends. After accepting their congratulations we walked in the garden.

'I have loved you for so long, I can scarcely believe that, at last, I have the right to call you mine,' I said.

She looked at me in surprise.

'You have loved me for so long? Pray, when did you begin? I thought your feelings were quite new.'

'My dearest Marianne, you are the only one who has not noticed! I have been in love with you for months; since before Christmas. Your open heartedness, your energy, your honesty, your eagerness and your tempestuous nature delighted me and brought me back to life.'

'Then Mrs Jennings's teasings were true?' she asked.

'They were.'

'I thought it was absurd of her to tease you in such a manner. I pitied you for your age, which seemed very advanced, and indeed it was, next to my youth and immaturity. But now, although I am still young in years, I am no longer young in understanding. I have loved and suffered, and I have seen my sister do the same. I have been ill, and my life has been despaired of, and I have seen my mother look old and grey because she feared I would die. I have come back from the brink of death, and I have discovered that the sun still shines without Willoughby, that the wind still blows, and that there is poetry still in life, though I have found it where least I looked for it. I have learned to look beneath the surface of things, and now, I believe, our ages are not so very different; indeed, that the years that lie between us are a good, rather than an evil, for you have a great deal to show me; not just picnics and parties, enjoyable as they are, but matters of deeper import, too. Willoughby was a shallow pool, but I have found a river in which to swim.

'I have been born to an extraordinary fate, have I not?' she said, stopping and turning to face me. 'For I have discovered the falsehood of my own opinions, and now it only remains for me to counteract them by my conduct.'

'Which can never fail to please me,' I said tenderly. 'You have restored me to life, and together we will be happy.'

I kissed her and then we walked on, arm in arm, planning our wedding trip to the Lake District and talking happily of the future.

1798

Sunday 7 October

Marianne and I were married this morning at Delaford church. Leyton stood up with me whilst Edward conducted the ceremony, and Marianne's brother, John, gave her away.

'I am surprised he managed it, for it is the first time he has ever given anything away in his life,' remarked Margaret, who, at fifteen, is becoming decidedly saucy and is a great friend to Mrs Jennings.

'If he'd listened to his wife, he'd have decided he couldn't afford it, and he'd have ended up parting with nothing more than an arm,' said Mrs Jennings, as she enjoyed the wedding breakfast. 'Or, more like, a finger.'

Elinor, with her son in her arms, sat close by, and told them not to speak so loud for John would hear.

'Tush! What if he does?' said Mrs Jennings,

before turning once again to Margaret. 'Now, my dear, you will be sixteen soon. You must come and stay with me in Berkeley Street. You will break a great many hearts, I am sure: London is full of fine beaux!'

ABOUT THE AUTHOR

Amanda Grange lives in Cheshire, England. She has published many novels, including *Lord Deverill's Secret, Mr. Knightley's Diary, Captain Wentworth's Diary, Edmund Bertram's Diary,* and *Harstairs House.* Visit her website at www.amandagrange.com.